Motherland

From the Chicken House

I heard a group of young friends talking about this book in a US library meeting. They all had to pick one favourite title – and this was the one that had moved them most. When I read it, it was easy to see why. It's about not knowing where you belong, but feeling deeply loyal to your family, friends and yourself, and having no one to explain how to make sense of it all. So you do the job yourself. I'm proud to publish MOTHERLAND for the first time in the UK.

Barry Cunningham
Publisher

Motherland

A Novel

VINEETA VIJAYARAGHAVAN

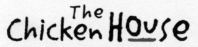

2 Palmer Street, Frome, Somerset BA11 1DS

To Divya and Kavita

First published in the USA by Soho Press, Inc.
Text © Vineeta Vijayaraghavan 2001

First published in Great Britain in 2003
by The Chicken House
2 Palmer Street
Frome, Somerset BA11 1DF
United Kingdom
www.doublecluck.com

Cover illustration by The Pope Twins
Cover design by Ian Butterworth
Typeset by Dorchester Typesetting Group Ltd
Printed and bound in Great Britain

1 3 5 7 9 10 8 6 4 2

British Library Cataloguing in Publication data available.

ISBN Hb 1 -903434-93-9
ISBN Pb 1 -904442-15-3

With deep gratitude, I thank

My mother, who is NOT the mother in this book,
for a love that knows no bounds.
My father, for his infinite patience and generosity.
Sandra, for nurturing this novel from its earliest glimmers.
Emma Sweeney and Melanie Fleishman for
`their enthusiastic and expert guidance.
Carolyn Rendell, Amanda Schaffer, Ali Kincaid, David Kurnick,
Phoebe Hyde, Beth McFadden, and Hiran Cantu for
reading drafts and offering priceless criticism and support.
Dhanyammai, Rajanammavan, Divya, Valliamma, Vallachin,
Nisha and Biju for my home at the other end of the world.

CHAPTER ONE

Migration

I WAS SHIPPED off to India that summer because of the death of a deer. There were deer crossing signs all along the Cross-Westchester Expressway, but this one came out of nowhere. The car was totalled, and when the police came they told us not to feel bad about the deer – it was an aged old thing, and it had died quickly. They helped us get the car off the highway and called our parents, and waited with us for a towtruck. Then they arrested Steve for driving under the influence.

Steve had only had a few beers at his brother's house earlier that evening; I'd had only half of one beer because they'd just put the six-packs in the refrigerator and they were still too warm for my taste. So I hadn't been the one drinking, and I wasn't the one who killed the deer. I hadn't really done anything wrong, but I was the one being sent away for the summer. My mother wasn't interested in the details. She was only interested in confirming why she shouldn't like Steve, and why I should be separated from what she called, in a piercing voice in the car on the way home from the police station, my 'frat-boy boyfriend'. Steve wasn't in a fraternity, he was still in high school, and he would never join a fraternity when he went to college. I wouldn't have liked Steve if he drank a lot at parties, or at football games, or if he drank because he was happy and having fun. Steve drank because he was sad, and I understood that. Sadness had a home in me, too.

DUST WHITED OUT the view as the plane's wheels skidded beyond the undersize tarmac runway into dirt. When my window cleared, I could see men running straight for us, pushing rickety staircases on rollers like they were moving props for a play. There was no control tower, just a short, squat terminal building next to the airfield. I had a lot of hand luggage, mostly gifts my mother sent with me, electronic appliances that would have been stolen if I had put them in my suitcases: a CD Walkman, a battery-operated egg beater, components for my uncle's satellite dish, high-power camera lenses. And two cartons of Camels I had bought, at my father's instruction, in the duty-free shop in Frankfurt during the stopover yesterday morning. I had never bought cigarettes legally before. I had felt conspicuous standing in front of the cashier, but, unblinking, she took my dollars and gave me a handful of Deutschmarks as change.

I gathered together my packages, hoping that my uncle might board the plane to help me carry everything. Last time we had come to India, three years ago, he and my aunt came right on to the aircraft, along with my father's old classmate who ran the airport.

I waited until most of the people had filed past me off the plane, but my uncle was nowhere to be seen. I pretended to be younger, and confused about airports, and a steward grabbed my belongings and escorted me across the airfield towards the terminal. He was short but muscular, and, like everyone else on the government-owned airline, wore a black armband to mourn the former prime minister's death. The heat hovered over the ground in those shimmery waves I'd seen on car commercials. As we walked closer to the terminal, hundreds of people were hanging over the two balconies, one on the second floor and one on the roof, yelling names and greetings. Only villagers who had never seen a plane land before were willing to stand out there in the sun. Since my uncle would not be there, I didn't even bother to look up.

The steward deposited me in the line for passport control for noncitizens, and then he scooted off in the direction of the very short lines for citizens. I half pulled, half kicked my bags forwards through the slow-moving line, until I faced a passport officer across a grubby glass divider.

The officer asked me something I couldn't understand. It must have been in Tamil, but now he tried again, this time in Malayalam, 'How long a stay?' The airport was in the state of Tamil Nadu, but it was on the border of Kerala, so as many Malayalam speakers travelled through it as Tamil speakers.

'Three months,' I answered in English. I could understand Malayalam but I wasn't comfortable speaking it.

He looked at my passport picture and then at me, at my picture again, and then at me.

'I wear contacts now,' I explained, pointing to the big glasses on the little face in the photo.

He asked, 'Where are your parents?'

'They're not here. I came by myself.'

He said, 'You are fifteen and they sent you by yourself?'

He seemed to think my parents had shown poor judgment. 'In America, I always get around by myself,' I said. He shook his head, stamped my passport, and let me through.

My last resort to avoid this India trip had been to appeal separately to my father. I told him how I wanted to get a summer job, in a dentist's office or at the mall, and see my friends, and swim a lot. I told him half of what I earned I would save for college and we could even try a curfew again.

I could almost see my father and me being friends when my mother was out of town on her frequent business trips. She worked for a commercial real-estate firm, and she spent a lot of time in Canada coaxing companies to come down here and build office parks. When she was away, my dad, who ran his own leather goods company, played single parent. I would try to get him to come around to my views on Mother, and he'd listen quietly as I described how she had embarrassed me at the PTA meeting or how she had forgotten to pick me up from swim practice. But then she would come back from her business trip. He would light up when he heard the airport limo purring on the driveway, he'd run out to help her with her luggage, forgetting to wear his coat, or even shoes one time.

So I didn't ask him right away to try to renegotiate this India trip, but waited until the summer got closer. And he actually took my side, he actually said, 'I don't think this is the right way to handle Maya' – this was not said in front of me, but I overheard it like I overheard many things, by hanging around doorways and corners. This was followed by days of tense and terse dinnertable conversations, and seeing my mother carrying pillows and blankets to her home office. It made me a little nervous – it was one thing wanting my father unglued from her but I didn't want them having problems over me.

My father broached it one last time with her while they were weeding the garden, which resulted in another night of pillows and blankets being carried up and down stairs, wardrobe doors slamming. My mother thought spending time with her relatives might teach me to remember where we had come from. My father thought where we had come from wasn't as important as dealing with where we were now. He explained this to me with his shoulders hunched in defeat. Seeing him like that, I started to feel like going to India might be better than staying around to watch everything crumble.

I STACKED MY hand luggage on a cart with screeching unoiled wheels and pushed towards the luggage carousel. The carousel creaked as it started (was there no WD40 in all of India?), and one bag would emerge, make an entire rotation, and disappear into the loading area and then roll out again joined by just one more bag each time. My suitcases were beaten up and dusty, as though they had arrived on the back of a mule rather than in the hold of a jet. I hauled them on to the cart, rearranged everything so the weight was balanced, and put the two cartons of Camels right on top where I could keep one hand on them while steering. I headed for the customs area, where I waited on line behind people from the Dubai flight who were importing laundry machines and VCRs and bars of gold.

The customs people peered at my bags gruffly and squinted over my embarkation card stamped United States of America. It was always easier to get into India than it was getting back into America. In India, my father said, customs officials were only concerned with being well paid for their troubles; in America, they were concerned with preserving the sterilized sanctity of the country. My mother said American customs officials made INS officials look friendly. Invariably, at JFK airport, a customs officer would open all five of our suitcases, pull out a jar of hogplum pickle, and hold it up like it was a science exhibit of sheep organs. He would extract a package of murku and bang it against a table till it crumbled to verify that its wiry shape didn't come from pouring the batter over gold or silver. Lately, with so many more Indian immigrants going back and forth, some officials had adopted a sophisticated weariness. 'Is this tapioca dried or smoked? Because if it's dried, you're leaving it with me.' I wondered if at the end of the day they divided all the loot, and someone went home to Staten Island to eat my grandmother's plaintain chips in front of *Monday Night Football*.

The Indian customs people finally waved me through, and I saw the exit gate just ahead. But four men, dressed in black, all with moustaches, stepped out in front of me. I stopped the cart short to keep from ramming into them.

'Your passport.'

I hesitated. 'But I already went through passport control.'

The man snickered, as one of his colleagues elbowed him and said, 'Do we look like passport control?'

I noticed the sleek black boots, the shiny handguns in their holsters. Two of them had rifles as well as handguns, radios, and walkie-talkies on their belts. They looked like they were in a James Bond movie, an old one.

'We're with intelligence; step over here,' another one of
them said, and steered my luggage cart towards a heavy
steel door on the side. I followed my cart into the room.
They turned on overhead lights and I squinted for a few
minutes in the glare. Half of one wall was covered with
brown flypaper on which hundreds of iridescent winged
beetles had met their end. As the door swung shut, I wondered if the room was soundproof. The four men seated
themselves, their big lumbering bodies cramped together
on one side of a table. I sat across from them, my back perfectly straight, pressed against the unvarnished wooden
chair. One of their legs bumped mine under the table, and
I pulled back, locking my ankles together under my chair.
The sharp fluorescent light made their moustaches look
scraggly and revealed that their seemingly cleanshaven
chins were pocked with stunted bristles.

They took my passport and flipped through the pages.

'The former prime minister Rajiv Gandhi was assassinated three weeks ago in this state. You must be aware of
this?'

I nodded. There had been a flurry of last-minute phone
calls between my mother and her brother here and he had
said that I should still come, that there were no riots or
anything, everything was returning to normal.

'Did anyone in Bombay airport ask you to deliver any
letters or packages?'

I said no.

'Did you see any of these people in Bombay airport?'
The questioner spread a sheaf of photos on the table.
There were three young girls in one photo. Another photo
was of a man in a long white kurta scribbling in a
reporter's notebook and a girl dressed in orange with two
braids as thick as Pippi Longstocking's. Many of the photos showed a girl with black glossy hair framing high

cheekbones and a coy mouth. The last photo they showed me of her was blurry – she was in motion turning away from the camera and shielding her face. On the ground near her, just lying there, was an arm. It was dark enough in the picture that you could believe a body was at the other end of that arm, but if you looked closely, there was only the arm.

I looked away. One of them came around to my side of the table. Leaning over me, his elbows weighing on my shoulders, he held two pictures right in front of my face so that there was nowhere else to look. There was the girl and the arm, and then a photo of a girl lying face up on the ground, next to a single bright white sneaker splotched with red.

They were watching for a reaction, and I tried not to give them the satisfaction of seeing me frightened or repulsed by the blood and the bodies. It's face paint, I repeated to myself. It's face paint, like when I helped my friend Jennifer get dressed as a vampire victim for Halloween.

'Are you sure?' the man behind me said again.

'Young girls are the best criminals,' he said. 'You know why?'

I said no.

'Because you all look innocent.' His emphasis on the word 'look' was insinuating.

The power went out, and we were swathed in darkness. It was better in the dark – my surroundings lost the coldly efficient feel of an interrogation room. One man was appointed to hold the door open so that light flooded in from the hall. I felt braver, an escape route within sight.

'Who is she?' I asked.

'Maybe I wasn't clear enough. We ask the questions,' he said. He looked at me in his smug way, and I looked at the floor, fighting the urge to say, if I knew anything, why would I tell you?

'Let her go,' another one said. He threw my passport on top of my luggage and shoved the cart away from him. I wheeled it out of the room.

I walked through the exit gate. There were people everywhere. People trying to take hold of my luggage cart, people offering rides in their taxis, people selling tea, people selling coconut water, people selling handmade carpets. People asking if I knew whether the Jakarta or London flight had landed, people asking me my name, people asking for money. People staring at my American clothes, people, crippled, sitting on the sidewalk reaching out to touch me, people jostling me to try unsuccessfully to get into the one-way doors I had just passed through. I felt the heat all over again, felt the wetness down my back. Panic struck me for a moment – if my uncle wasn't there I had to find my way back into the terminal, figure out where a call centre was, how to change money, submit an order for the operator to dial the number, try to make myself heard on one of those crackly receivers. And where could I stand and wait for him with all my bags?

'MAYA.' SANJAY UNCLE made his way easily through the crowds, shaking keys held up over his head. He looked so much like my mother, with his high arched eyebrows and uniformly delicate features except for large, slightly comical ears. My mother hid hers by tucking tendrils of hair around them, but my uncle's fast-receding hairline left his entirely exposed. I was glad my ears had come from my father's side. Sanjay uncle kissed me on the cheek, and tried to pick me up and swing me around like he used to. But I was heavier, and so was he; my feet barely lifted up off the ground before he let me down. He laughed, rubbing his shoulders, saying, 'You're not so little any more.' He took charge of the cart, and in Malayalam, told people we want no services, please move, please move.

He shook the keys at the curbside, and his car pulled up next to us. The driver unlocked the boot and started arranging my bags. My uncle clasped my hand and said, 'Your aunt didn't come because she's making sure the servants make a nice dinner for tonight. But come see who's waiting for you in the lounge.' I wondered if it was his daughter Brindha or maybe my other cousin Supriya. They were both younger than me, but last time I was here, we ran around in the hills and swam in the waterfalls, and stayed up late talking and doing each other's hair. We walked to a side entrance, and then my uncle stopped and pushed me ahead. There was a sign that said LADIES LOUNGE – WAITING AREA and then in smaller print below, it repeated, 'ONLY FOR LADIES.' I opened the door, and felt a welcome breeze from the weak, but noisy, air conditioning.

Then I saw my grandmother walk towards me. Ammamma was all in white, as she had been since my grandfather died twenty years ago, though I have seen photos of her wearing a purple-flowered sari at my parents' wedding. She shuffled slowly in my direction, her chappals scraping against the rough stone floor, smiling. She looked older. Her face looked more tired, more sagging, and her glasses were thicker in their black square frames. Her grey hair was knotted in a smooth bun at her neck. I knew from memory that there would be a few extra hairpins stuck in the seam of her blouse, for any necessary replacement or repair.

This was the longest I'd gone without seeing my grandmother. When I was born, I stayed with her for four years until my parents sent for me to come to New York. I used to call her Amma, at first because I couldn't manage to enunciate the whole word Ammamma, and then because I really thought she was my mother. It took a long time in New York to figure out the difference, to understand the hurt look in my mother's eyes. Until three years ago, I'd returned every summer for the whole summer, usually with my parents flying over for two weeks at the beginning or the end. But then there had been summer programmes, our swim club in town, sleep-away camp with my friends. And now I was embarrassed by the neediness I'd shown all those summers, rushing back here to Ammamma. I didn't want them feeling sorry for me the way they had, sensing how motherless I was even though I lived with my mother.

I bent to touch Ammamma's feet in the gesture of respect Mother insisted I use for old people. Ammamma pulled me into a hug, and kept me awkwardly pressed against her in a long embrace. I could smell her distinctive combination of rosewater (which she used in prayer every morning) and Vicks VapoRub. She clutched her Vicks the way asthma patients clutch their inhaler. She had one with her on walks, in the car, in bed. Even in this pre-monsoon heat, she kept a shawl with her, a light wool one from her years in the north.

I walked with her out of the ladies' lounge back to my uncle. I asked her, 'Wasn't it a long trip? Why did you come?'

Sanjay uncle said, 'Maya, don't sound so ungrateful. It's been a very long day for Amma. We told her not to come, but she wanted to greet you.'

'It's nice of you, but you shouldn't have, Ammamma.'

'I just wanted so much to see you.' Ammamma caressed my cheek with her hand. Water trembled in her eyes.

I felt embarrassed by how emotional she was. I remembered how when we were in this very airport three years ago, we all cried saying goodbye, including me. It seemed a long time ago. 'There'll be plenty of time, I'm here all summer, Ammamma.'

'I know, I know, I'm just being silly.' She closed her eyes for a minute, and when she opened them, she'd made the tears go away. 'We'll have a wonderful summer, all of us.'

'Would you like a cola or anything before we start back?' Sanjay uncle asked.

'No, I'm fine. Except I want to go to the ladies' room.'

My uncle and grandmother looked concerned. 'It won't be Western-style here at the airport. Shall I take you into town to Supriya's house or to the Taj hotel?' he said.

'No, no, it'll be fine. I've gone camping, I'll be OK,' I said firmly.

My grandmother said, 'I'll come with you then.'

'No. Really.' But I let her walk with me into the ladies' room, and speak Malayalam to the attendant to purchase some toilet paper for some coins, and then I went into a stall. It was dark and dank, and made me feel nauseated, but I was afraid I was getting my period and I just wanted to be prepared for the long ride home.

'Are you all right?' my grandmother said loudly.

'Yes, fine, I'll be out in a second, Ammamma.'

I came out and looked in the mirror to make sure I was all in order, that there were no lines you could see through my khaki trousers. Ammamma, in her six yards of white starched linen over a starched white petticoat, looked serene standing there, far beyond bleeding at inopportune times. She was waiting for me holding a pitcher of water she had filled from a half-full bucket. I held out my hands and she poured water over them, and then offered me the palloo of her sari to dry my hands. I refused, not wanting to get her sari wet – I wasn't so little any more. She dug in her big black handbag and gave me a handkerchief to use.

WE FOUND OUR driver, Ram, eating and gossiping at the row of toddy stalls next to the car park. He led us to the car, and we started the drive home. My uncle sat in the front with Ram, and I sat in the back with my grandmother.

Ammamma said, 'I brought pillows and a sheet if you want to sleep or lie down.'

When I was small, Ammamma would also bring my nightgown and I would change in the car and sleep all the way home from the airport. She would make my dad scrunch together with my uncle and the driver in the front seat, and then I would lie with my head on her lap and my legs on my mother. I'd been up for two nights in a row, leaving New York in the early evening on Friday, and landing in Frankfurt the next morning. I landed in Bombay on Saturday at midnight, waited out the night in the airport, and flew south from Bombay to Coimbatore at seven this morning.

'That's OK, I can wait to sleep when we get home.'

'Are you sure?' my grandmother said, taking a pillow out of a canvas bag and smoothing a clean towel over it on her lap. 'I brought a feather pillow that's flat the way you like it.'

'The ride is pretty long, three to four hours,' my uncle said. 'Did your mother tell you we moved farther out of the city?'

Mother had said Sanjay uncle had moved high up into the mountains last year when he had transferred to the tea division.

'That's right,' he said, 'I couldn't work for the tea division if I stayed down here near the city.' He said they lived ten minutes from the central tea factory he managed, and that twice a month he travelled around to check on the other tea properties in the region.

'It's even quieter up there than where Sanjay lived last time you came,' Ammamma said. 'He needs to come all the way back down here to go to the bank or to the doctor.'

'I've got used to the drive,' my uncle said. 'At least near the top of the mountain, that last hour or two is much cooler. And today, because it's a weekend, there won't be trucks or buses in our way.'

We were starting to climb the mountain, and there was a cracked wooden sign that said 65. My uncle said the British had carved the road right into the side of the mountain, and it had sixty-five hairpin bends. 'You've probably never been on a road quite like this before.'

'No,' I said. We soon hit our first one, and it was worse than those California highways in Hitchcock movies, where it seemed like the actors had been superglued to their seats so they didn't fall out of the car. We slowly zigzagged our way up the face of a mountain. I felt dizzy looking out the window, seeing the trees growing sideways on the earth, the earth falling away from us as we turned each time. There were no seat belts in the car. I remembered learning from a movie in Driver's Ed that in many Third World countries the steering wheels were still not collapsible, so that in an accident, the driver and the person sitting behind him (me) could be gored.

I tried to ignore the signs counting the bends because it gave no comfort to know when they were coming – there was no way to prepare. I closed my eyes and rested my head against the back of the seat in front of me.

'Are you sure you don't want to lie down?' Ammamma asked.

I didn't think that would make it any better. She took out a lime and made a cut in it with her teeth, releasing its strong soothing fragrance. She handed it to me and I held it under my nose to keep from getting sick. I used to throw up on long drives, so my mother routinely travelled with plastic bags in her bag. The last few years had been much better, except when we came to India where the cars were worse and the roads were worse, and you felt every bump. And that was even without hairpin bends.

'Do you want to stop for some air?' my uncle said some time later, as we neared the sign for the thirty-ninth bend.

My uncle and my grandmother and the driver looked anxious. I could feel something rising in my throat, but I willed it to go away. 'I'll be fine. We should just keep driving, so we get it over with.'

Every time we returned to the States from trips to India, I was in heaven in the taxi home. A big American car, with good brakes, good shock absorbers, leather cushions, and a real road, fully paved and sealed.

My uncle tried a new and fairly transparent tactic to get us off the road without making me admit my carsickness. 'Shall we stop and see the view, Maya? I think we'll catch the sunset right now.'

I went along with it and agreed to stop when we could find a wide enough part of the road. The car soon came to a blissful halt, hugging the mountain side of the road. We walked across to the other side, and my uncle led me on to a rocky ledge that was jutting off the road. I sat down on the rock so I wouldn't lose my balance looking out into the swirling tangle of wilderness.

'It's so nice there is still land that nobody owns,' I said, thinking of the fences and no-trespassing signs and gated communities back home.

My uncle laughed. 'This isn't the frontier, Maya. It may look untamed to you, but all this land is owned, and constantly fought over.'

He said there were some private landowners, and then the tea companies on the top of the mountain who kept trying to exaggerate their boundaries, and then the Indian government owned the rest of it. And all of it was a protected wildlife sanctuary.

Sanjay uncle raised a thumb, then a forefinger, then a middle finger as he enumerated, 'You can't hunt here whether or not it's your land, and you can't drain water from ponds even if they attract malarial mosquitoes, and you can't carry any kind of natural product out of here without paying an excise tax on it at the bottom of the mountain.'

'When the tea companies came, had anyone been up in these mountains before them?' I asked.

'Well, I imagine we dispossessed the tribal people here like everywhere else in India. They had no concept of ownership, they wandered and gathered food, and so the British and Indian tea companies ignored them altogether and measured out everything and created certificates saying who owned what and the tribal people of course had no certificates to show for themselves.'

'That sounds like us and the Native Americans,' I said. Not us, my mother would have said, them, the Americans, the locals. When I did a project on Rosa Parks for Black History Month, she had said, 'You needn't feel guilty for American history – you had no part in it.' I would make sure to tell her when I went back, there was plenty to feel guilty about in India, too.

Sanjay uncle said, 'Yes, well, it's what most people who settled did to people who wandered. It's no different here. Are you ready to get going?'

We walked back to the car. Ram was standing off to the side chewing paan leaves and tobacco and spitting red streaks against the side of the mountain. When he saw my uncle coming, he spat out the last of it, wiped his mouth with his sleeve, and came back to the car. My grandmother was bent over the open trunk. Hearing us, she turned around, and the tiffin boxes in her hands caught the sun and flashed like mirrors. She opened one to show me whipped yogurt with rice and herbs, and another that had idli, steamed cakes made of rice and lentils, and sambar, a lentil soup. The inner compartment within the box had coconut chutney for the idli, wrapped inside a folded-up banana leaf. My grandmother always carted food with her in case I needed it. Like a mother packing for an infant, lugging around tinned carrots and apple sauce and powdered milk, my grandmother continued to try to predict and meet my needs. When we came in the summers, there wasn't time to build immunity to local diseases, so it was easy to get ill. My parents retained some immunity from having lived in India for so long before migrating, but I had lost whatever native hardiness I might have once had. On several trips, I had spent days in bed with a tummy bug, and so we tried to be as careful as possible. I knew the rules by heart. No fruit or vegetables with permeable skin (that meant no grapes, no tomatoes, no berries of any sort), no fish during the monsoon, no shellfish ever, no untreated water, no food purchased at roadside stalls because of the flies and the heat, no unknown restaurants because of potentially unsanitary kitchens. At festivals and wedding feasts, too, there was no point in taking unnecessary risks. I could remember dancing in floorlength silk pavadas at holiday parties and coming out to the car to perch on the back seat and eat my dinner out of Ammamma's tiffin boxes. She cooked spicy and delicate dishes at her house, but when we were out, she brought comfort food, food that wouldn't spoil in the heat and was not messy, food that was not rich but would feel substantial, sustaining.

'I can wait till we get to the house,' my uncle said. 'Reema is arranging for a special meal.'

'I can wait too, then,' I said.

'Eat something, just a little,' my grandmother urged. 'You've had a long flight.'

'Yes, eat something,' my uncle said. 'Even when we get home, we won't eat straight away.'

My grandmother handed the open tiffin boxes to my uncle to hold while she took out a bottle of boiled water for washing our hands. I felt self-conscious eating with my hands at the beginning of each trip, since we didn't eat like that at home. I remembered my maths teacher, Mr Chen, who had brought in Chinese food for the Chinese New Year, teaching us to eat with chopsticks. He had said, at first you think the only objective is to get the food to your mouth by whatever mode available, but then you realize that the mode is an artful end in itself. In India, it was like that, too – watch an Indian bride at her wedding feast, and she will, in all of her gold and silk and brocade and mehndi, eat gracefully with her hands, knowing that it is part of how one takes the measure of her.

Yogurt-rice was easy – the rice sticks together because of the yogurt, and I could roll it into a little ball with the tips of my fingers, so that only the top two-thirds of each finger ever touched the food. Idli-sambar was also easy to handle (one of the reasons it was ideal tiffin box food) – the idli was highly absorbent of the sambar, so I could simply dip and soak, dip and soak. What was much harder was rassam, a clear broth, or payasam, a dessert pudding. At an ordinary meal, these soups and puddings might be served in a cup alongside the plate. But at any kind of feast or religious day, food was served on banana leaves, so it was trickier. First I had to manage to keep the lentil soup in the centre of the leaf. With whatever rice I had left, I made a mound and put the sambar in the centre of it, pretending that I was pouring lava back into the centre of a volcano. But payasam was served at the end of the meal, on an empty leaf, sometimes two or three kinds. There was no way to shore up pudding, no sandbags, no dykes, no sources of support. Here the key was speed and angle, the same things I'd consider for an ice cream cone. Tilting the surface of the banana leaf to slope towards me, I kept stemming the tide before it flowed to the bottom lip of the leaf and on to the table or floor. I made my hand into a little scooper and held the fingers very tightly together and half threw it into my mouth, half slurped it from my hand. From time to time, so that pudding didn't run down my arm, it was acceptable to lick the lower portion of the hand from wrist to little finger. Most times, I refused payasam when it was offered to me. Even if I didn't find it too sweet, it betrayed the limits of my skill.

We washed out the tiffin boxes, stored them in Ammamma's upright jute bag, and closed the boot. 'Shall we?' my uncle said, gesturing the driver onwards. 'Only thirty-eight hairpins to go.'

WE LEFT THE hairpin bends behind, and we were in tea country. The tea hills were as benign as they sounded, slope after graceful slope of verdant green clustered on the top of the mountain. The sun was sinking; it was like a full moon in its tight hard circle of light. No halo, no heat any more. When we were on the last hill before our house, my

uncle flashed his headlights. From the house they would
be able to watch our progress over this sister hill, and then
we would dip into a small valley and come up on our hill.
They would see us coming and know to be ready. No other
cars used this stretch of road. The nearest house was on the
next tea estate along, about five miles, or two hills, away,
in a different direction than the one from which we came.
I had seen maybe five or six cars in total since we came up
the mountain, and not one residence of any sort. My uncle
said houses up here did not announce themselves. Unlike
city houses that crowded around the road and each other
for comfort, the houses here were nestled deep into the
woods and the tea bushes.

We took a little path that veered off the road we had
been on for hours. It looked like we were heading straight
into brush. But we came to a double-gated entrance, and
an old man and a young boy ran down the drive to swing
open the gates for the car to pass. The boy climbed on to
the gate itself, swung in and out on it, and jumped down.
Two more servants clung shyly to the railings on the verandah. We drove under the carport, and there was my cousin
Brindha, a dog captive in her arms, and my aunt Reema.
Then there was the bustle of saying hello, and taking my
bags out of the car, and unpacking household sundries my
uncle had bought in Coimbatore, and setting up a camp
bed in the carport for the driver, who would stay the night
and take a morning bus down to wherever he lived.

Brindha introduced me to her dog, Boli, a yappy white
Pomeranian. She introduced me to the house too, opening
up wardrobe doors, peeking over the edge of the well. It
was an old British house, with British oddities. A fireplace
in every room, for the rainy season, as if the rains were like
English rain and gave chills. When the rains arrived, they
punctuated and relieved the hottest days of the year.

Brindha said the fireplace came in handy in the guest room, where clothes were hung to dry because during the rainy season it was so humid it was hard to get them to dry by themselves. A cotton shirt could take three days to dry and a terry towel five, so they saved the towels for guests and used thorthus (not towels at all but thin cotton-weave sheets) for everyday. The house also had closed eaves, which helped keep the insects out, but put a lot of pressure on the roof when it rained because there was no natural way to drain save for one overburdened gutter. And the glass windowpanes lacked the benefits of the traditional slatted shutters in controlling the shade, directing the breeze, and creating airflow through the house.

Then there was the lawn, which I had never seen in southern India before. Most people had a tidily swept yard, with a few bushes here and there, or if they had a fancy house there would be lots of gardens and trees and bushes and groundcover. Here, there was a big garden on the side of the house, but the front was taken up by an expanse of lawn. Brindha said it looked like a ricefield in the rainy season, swollen and swampy, full of leeches. And in the dry season, it was scorched and grey and brown and no one walked there because there was no shade. The gardener made valiant efforts to keep it looking presentable year-round, and in the two temperate months of the year, he was moderately successful.

There was a gardener who came every day, Brindha told me, and a woman, Vasani, who cleaned house. There was Matthew, the cook, and his son, Sunil, who attended the village school but also worked in the kitchen. They lived out back in a little cottage behind the house. When there were guests from the office, then Matthew brought his wife up the mountain and they acted as waiting staff.

There was Rupa, eighteen, a nanny for Brindha, 'even

though I'm ten,' Brindha said indignantly. For these summer months that Brindha was home from boarding
school, Rupa had been brought to stay at the house.
Brindha only pretended to object. She liked Rupa, and she
had no other playmates here.

The house displayed Indian oddities too, habits clung
to beyond their original motivation. The refrigerator was
in the dining room, the way it was in homes where the
kitchen had a wood-fuelled open fire that could damage
electric appliances. But it had evolved into more of a cabinet than an appliance, and so it sat right next to the drinks
trolley and the china cabinet. And in the kitchen, where
the shiny new mixers and beaters looked unused, there
was a large mortar and pestle and pirate-size daggers lined
up on the floor where Matthew and his boy would sit on
their haunches and grind and cut and chop. Brindha said
some servants were afraid of the appliances, some were
forbidden to use them because they had broken other
ones, but regardless, most still did everything the old way.

The house was organized like a T, with the drawing
room and dining room in the front area. On the left edge
of the T were the two guest bedrooms and on the right
were Brindha's bedroom, Ammamma's room, and my
aunt and uncle's. At the end of that hall was the kitchen,
spilling over into a side yard where there was an outdoor
kitchen that was essentially the front yard of Matthew's little cottage.

Brindha took me to my grandmother's room, where my
bags were lined up against the wall. Ammamma had
just finished her bath and was putting oil in her hair.
Brindha crouched and pounced on the bed and
Ammamma smiled. To me, she said, 'Do you want to put
your things away? I've cleared out some drawers and half a
wardrobe for you.'

I knew I wasn't going to be offered one of the guest rooms. Those were for company guests, or for my parents, but not for me. If you were single, and you were family, whether you were fifteen or thirty or fifty, you piled in with your cousins and siblings and grandparents, as long as everyone was the same sex. When there were lots of relatives over, during holidays or pujas, the men would sleep in the living room or on the porch. Women would sleep horizontally on the two double beds that were usually found pushed together in each room, with other camp beds and bedrolls and mats brought out for the younger girls. My cousins were unbothered sleeping on a thin blanket put over a straw mat on the floor, sometimes with a pillow, sometimes without, like it was no hardship at all; I would twist and turn all night.

In my grandmother's room, there were the expected two double beds pushed together, united under a king-size blue paisley bedcover. She sat on one side of the bed and brushed the oil through her hair, accumulating on her lap a little pile of hair that had fallen out. Ammamma once had very thick black hair, but now I caught frequent glimpses of scalp between the coils of grey hair, and only a rare glimpse of black, when she bowed her head to brush the underside section at the nape of her neck. The bath oil had a strong sweet smell, and there was the smell of the Vicks and the rosewater, and of the incense that was lit every morning and evening in front of the little shrine my grandmother kept in one corner of the room. There on the chest of drawers were the English biscuit tins, adorned with distinguished royal cavalry, that my cousins from London brought on visits. They contained my grandmother's medications, and when the lid to any of them was opened, there would be the musty and tart smell of vitamins and powdery prescriptions and ayurvedic ointments, and dried herb treatments.

It would only be a matter of days before all of that permeated me, my hair, my clothes, my magazines and books.

'Why don't I sleep in Brindha's room and keep her company? We only have a week together before she goes back to boarding school.'

'The nanny sleeps in there with me. But we can let her go early, since this is my last week,' said Brindha.

'Brindha hasn't organized her things yet for school so I'm afraid her wardrobes are a mess. Are you sure you don't want to use all this space?' Ammamma opened the cupboard doors. One whole side was bare and empty, the shelves had been newly lined with pretty paper. The other side was packed tight with my grandmother's things, everything wedged precariously into place: more biscuit tins, blood pressure equipment still stored in its original now tattered box, skeins of wool in garish green and yellow, letters and papers rubberbanded together, a pile of prayer books with the bindings falling off, and then stacked on top of each other in folded squares, drab sari after drab sari. I felt the way I had felt when Bobby, my lab partner in chemistry last year, opened his mouth really wide to show me where he had his tooth extracted, and I saw red gums and a chipped tooth and fat silver fillings and a gaping hole, and I hadn't asked to see any of it.

'I'm sure Brindha and I can manage, Ammamma.'

'I'm good at sharing, remember,' Brindha said to Ammamma. 'I know I'm not tidy all the time, but when I ask for you or Amma to come and sleep in here I make everything nice, don't I?'

She turned to me. 'Not because I'm scared or anything, I just like to have them over for a little slumber party sometimes. The nanny is too tired to stay up late with me.'

'I'll stay up late with you, I promise,' I said.

'What do we do about mosquito nets for Maya?' Brindha asked Ammamma.

'I hope the mosquitoes aren't as bad as last time,' I said. I'd gone home last time with lots of battle scars. Mosquitoes seemed to like foreign goods, my uncle had said. They liked imports better than Made in India, he joked. My cousins and my grandmother and everyone except newborns slept without netting, and somehow they never got more than an occasional bite. I had slept under mosquito nets every night, but was sufficiently tortured during dinner, teatime, early evening walks.

'I'm not sure the mosquitoes will be any kinder to you,' Ammamma said. 'The trouble is, only this room has bed-posts to hang the netting from.'

'I have insect spray with me, I can use that.' Anyway, I didn't want everyone having to bother to put the nets up for me every night and take them down every morning. I didn't want so much fuss this summer; I just wanted to be able to do things for myself.

Brindha and I each started tugging at a suitcase to drag over to her room. Matthew was walking down the hall, and saw us, and called the nanny Rupa to come. He tried to take the suitcase I was struggling with, but I didn't want to let him, so together we half-carried and half-pushed it into Brindha's room. I had forgotten how to act with servants.

Brindha freely relinquished the other suitcase to Rupa, and walked into our room, my sweater draped over her shoulders, my handbag swinging jauntily on one arm. Brindha announced, 'I told her not to feel jealous. She can have you all to herself in just a week.'

'Ammamma's not jealous, don't be silly,' I said.

'Well, not jealous, but lonely, then. Since I have to go back to school, I'm glad you'll be here with her. She doesn't like to go to society things so she's alone a lot unless there are young people around.'

'Society things?'

'You know, that stuff Amma and Achan go to. Teas at the club, and tournaments, and weddings and things. I don't like all that. Do you?'

'Well, sometimes it's fun to get dressed up and meet people.'

'Only cricket matches, those are the only fun ones. Do you like these cricket posters on my wall – I know you don't know the players, but just from these posters, which one's your favourite? I have movie posters too. Amma and Achan don't know I have them, but I can show them to you if you don't tell.'

'Why won't they let you have movie posters?'

Brindha rummaged through a drawer and pulled out a handful of photo clippings. 'Amma says the new Bombay movies are cheap – they don't let me watch them.'

'How do you know the actors if you've never seen the movies?'

'I've seen pictures of them in the magazines and read about them, and some of the girls at school are allowed to watch anything, so they tell us what happens in all the new movies. When I'm at home, Rupa tells me – she loves movies too.'

Rupa had been rearranging Brindha's clothes to make room for me. She looked up when she heard her name mentioned. Brindha took one of the movie star pictures to her, and Rupa smiled and said something in Tamil. Brindha translated for me, 'This one, Rukmini, she just got fired from a movie because she pushed another actress overboard off a cruise ship.' Rupa fingered the pictures lovingly, carefully, as if they were delicate Moghul miniatures, or illuminated manuscripts.

Brindha said something in Tamil to Rupa, and Rupa's hands rose up to cover her face, the movie photos fluttering to the floor. She quickly knelt to gather them up, and

Brindha helped her collect them. Brindha came over to me and whispered, 'I told Rupa we don't need her any more, but she needs this money, she only has her older brothers to look after her and they're always getting into trouble. Amma will wonder why we should keep a nanny on now that you're here, but I'll just say that you didn't want to play my baby games, like Snakes and Ladders, OK?'

I nodded. Brindha went back to Rupa's side, and told her the new plan. Rupa's face lifted, and she put her hands together and bowed in gratitude. Brindha, pleased that Rupa was no longer upset, pressed the movie pictures back into her hands and they chattered more about Rukmini.

I stared at the cricketers on her wall, posed like movie stars themselves, wearing flirty smiles and jeans or leather jackets. Except some of the cricketers were dark, and Indian movie stars were usually light-skinned, especially the women, often with light eyes, hazel or green. The only way I could tell they were not straight out of *Tigerbeat* magazine was because they all had black hair, and they were not pencil-thin like teen idols in America.

A bell rang out from another part of the house, a trilling like the bell on my old bicycle with the pink banana seat.

Brindha said, 'That's Matthew saying dinner is ready. He thinks it's the proper way because that's what Anglos like. Amma keeps trying to get him to stop.'

'I guess I'll unpack later. Is there something for me to change into for now?'

'Amma left some salwar kameezes out on her bed for you to choose from. I'll go and tell Matthew you're coming in a couple of minutes. Don't forget to cut your nails before you come,' Brindha said as she left the room.

Ammamma hadn't said anything earlier, but Brindha was not going to let me get away with anything she couldn't get away with. It was considered unattractive to have long nails on your right hand because food got under them when you were eating. Older women kept their fingernails uniformly short, without nail polish or jewellery. Girls my age often had long nails and nail polish and friendship rings and even little diamonds glued on their nails but only on their left hand – the right one was left completely plain. No one minded the lack of symmetry, but it seemed as weird to me as wearing eyeshadow on one eye and not the other. I filed and trimmed down the nails on both hands.

I went into my aunt and uncle's bedroom and took a couple of salwar sets from the bed. Returning to Brindha's room, I bolted shut the door and took off my clothes. My khakis were crumpled and dusty from the long car trip, and my light cotton sweater had lost its shape because I'd balled it up into a pillow on the international flight. I left everything on the floor near the door so the servants would know to take it for washing. I wouldn't wear those clothes for the rest of the visit. Younger girls wore skirts, but everyone my age wore the pyjama-like salwar kameezes every day. I had brought a few dresses and jeans from home, in case we went to a city or a hotel for a few days where I could wear American clothes, but otherwise, they stayed in the suitcase. I felt like a nun relinquishing my street clothes for a habit. Salwar kameezes were nice enough, some were colourful and pretty, but I didn't look like myself when I looked in the mirror.

I noticed a slight movement in the mirror and turned around. Rupa was crouched in the corner next to the desk facing the wall. I went over to her and tapped her on the shoulder and she stood up, blushing. She had still been in the room, looking at the movie pictures when I'd come in and started undressing, and she hadn't known what to do. She seemed afraid that I was angry, and I shook my head vigorously, to let her know I wasn't. She dropped the movie pictures on the bed, and scurried out of the room.

'Look, Maya, Amma even has VIP curry for you,' Brindha said as I took my chair at the dinner table.

'What's VIP curry?'

Reema auntie laughed. 'It's a mutton curry. I don't serve it all the time but it's one of Brindha's favourite dishes.'

'Amma only serves it when Very Important guests are coming, even though I wish we could have it every day. It has mutton, and eggs, and it's nice and spicy.'

'If you want it again before you leave next week, tell me, Brindha, and I'll bring some good mutton from the city,' Sanjay uncle said.

Mutton and eggs were the last things I felt like eating after travelling for three days on three flights. There was also chicken curry, and green banana curry and cabbage with grated coconut and fried okra. And tamarind chutney and lime pickle and salt mango and peppered poppadum. But nothing tasted quite the way I liked it. This was because Ammamma had been out all day, so the cooking had been left to the cook. Reema auntie had guided his hand, but this was Matthew's cooking, and therefore, Matthew's palate. He had been liberal with the chillis, and the clarified butter and the coconut. Everything was as heavy as North Indian restaurant food. I looked with envy at my grandmother, eating her plate of kanjivellum, rice served in its own water, with cucumber steamed till it softened and then sautéed with mustard seeds. Old people were allowed to be ascetic in their ways without offending anybody. Many grandmothers were like my grandmother, fasting one or two days a week, and at every evening meal, only eating rice and water and maybe one pickle or one vegetable. But all this food had been cooked for me. I tried my best to make my way through it.

'I hope nothing's too hot for you?' my aunt said.

Everything was. I kept adding yogurt to dilute the heat as much as possible. I remembered when Ammamma used to rinse off my food: chicken, vegetables, even pickle – she would run water over it to take away the sting, and then she would put it back on a stainless-steel thali plate held over the open flame to make everything warm again.

'Maybe I can learn to cook some things this summer,' I said.

'You don't want to spend any time in that hot kitchen,' Reema auntie said. 'And you would distract Matthew – he's always looking for excuses to be slow. But I do have to make a cake this week. We're having friends over to say goodbye to Brindha before she goes back to school. You can help me if you want. I was thinking maybe angelfood cake?'

Angelfood cake I could make at home; I'd been making it since I was eight when I got a Barbie oven at Christmas. I wanted to make something difficult, the things my aunt and grandmother knew how to cook that my mother could never seem to duplicate well enough in New York. Mother insisted it was because we couldn't get the same vegetables, although at the Korean grocery store, we could get small aubergine and foot-long string beans that were almost like the Indian kind. For some others there truly wasn't any substitute. But it was really because my mother did what she wanted in the kitchen – she didn't pay much attention to Ammamma's recipes. Now that my dad was doing so much of the cooking, I thought if I could just write down the way it was done here, he wouldn't mind following the instructions. He tried a lot harder to make me happy than Mother did.

'Did you see any Black Cat Commandos at the airport?' Brindha asked.

'No, just the usual policemen standing around,' Sanjay uncle said.

'I think I saw them,' I said. I told them about the men in black and their questions and photographs.

Brindha said excitedly, 'Achan, she's seen the pictures of Dhanu and Subha and everyone.' Even Reema auntie and Sanjay uncle looked excited.

Sanjay uncle asked me to describe the people in the photos and he identified some of them. The dark-skinned girl with slightly protruding teeth and two braids, that was Dhanu, the suicide bomber, who had worn plastic explosives strapped to her body that blew up both her and Rajiv Gandhi and a dozen bystanders. 'The chief masterminds,' as Sanjay uncle put it, of the assassination were suspected to be a man named Sivarasan, and a twenty-two-year-old woman named Subha, who was his second-in-command as well as his 'woman companion' ('his lover,' Reema auntie clarified, as Sanjay uncle blushed). They were being hunted all over the state.

'Subha's the fair one, and Sivarasan is the one with the weird eyes – didn't you notice?' Brindha prodded me. Sivarasan, she said, had one glass eye, because he had lost the other eye on an earlier terrorist mission. I looked at my uncle to see whether she was just making this up to be dramatic.

'It's true,' my uncle confirmed. 'He's called the One-eyed Jack.'

Reema auntie said that the One-eyed Jack was a leader of the Liberation Tamil Tigers, who were fighting for Tamil independence in Sri Lanka. Even though national government politicians like Rajiv Gandhi were against it, many ethnic Tamils in Tamil Nadu state supported the Sri Lankan Tamil cause. The Tigers knew they could come here to hide out and use the hospitals, to buy weapons

and other provisions, and to plot and carry out an assassination. But this time the Indian government swore they
would bring the Tigers to justice.

Brindha said, 'Achan, tell her about the death vows.'

Sanjay uncle explained that the Tamil Tigers were
known to take vows to commit suicide if they faced arrest.
Each of them carried a cyanide capsule expressly for that
purpose.

Reema auntie said, 'There must be a curse on that family. Nehru had a good long life, but to have his daughter
assassinated, and now her son too . . .'

Ammamma spoke for the first time at dinner. 'It's not a
curse, it's a blessing that Indira died rather than see what
happened to Rajiv. No mother wants to outlive her child.'
She gathered some empty dishes and shuffled off towards
the kitchen.

Brindha said, 'You're so lucky, Maya, you've seen more
of the pictures than we have – they'll only show a couple
pictures on the television. Did they show you the fire and
the explosion? Was there blood?'

Reema auntie shook her head, as if she were shaking off
a daydream. She said, 'You mustn't go on talking like this,
Brindha. This is not one of your mystery novels or action
movies. Let's leave it to the police and not sit here conjec-
turing about it.' She got up to tell Matthew to clear the
table.

'And one other thing.' Sanjay uncle touched Reema auntie's wrist to make her pause for a minute. 'Don't talk
about these things on front of the servants or when guests
are in the house. There are a few other out-of-staters like
us, but nearly everybody around here is Tamil. Even
though everyone is denouncing the murder, we can't really know who is a Tiger sympathizer deep down. It is wiser
to assume that anybody could be until this is all over.'

Ammamma had Matthew bring out mango and pome-
granate for dessert – technicolour orange and red. Usually,
there was no dessert, sweet things were eaten at teatime,
not at night. But I loved mango, and she did not want me
to have to wait until tomorrow.

We finished eating. The lights had already dimmed
because the electric company lowered electricity transmit-
ted to each home when the usage was highest to prevent
power failures. My aunt brought an oil lamp to put in the
drawing room so my uncle could read the newspapers.
Brindha took another oil lamp with her to her room where
she and Rupa were trying to empty out a few more drawers for me.

'Can Matthew heat some water for a bath?' I asked.

'It's cool this late at night – you may catch a cold, don't
you think?' my aunt said.

'I won't be cold – you forget what I'm used to,' I said. 'I
have to have a bath after all this travel.'

'But still, the climate change is sudden, and then to go
to sleep with wet hair,' my grandmother said anxiously. 'It
can't be a good idea.'

'Just tell Matthew to put on a lot of hot water, and I'll
make my bath warm enough. Don't worry.'

Ammamma still looked doubtful. 'Make sure you dry
your hair well. And be careful, the floors get slippery. Take
an oil lamp in case the electricity goes.'

Matthew brought a big bucket of boiling water to the
bathroom off the hall from Brindha's room. I didn't want
to ask Matthew because I was too embarrassed, but I called
Rupa to come in the bathroom with me and look for
insects. She had just stretched out on her floor mat to
sleep, but she jumped up straight away, smoothed her petticoat down over her legs, and came to the bathroom. We
shone a torch in the corners, and two lizards quickly

crawled out of sight. There was one large brown-back bee-
tle, and Rupa hit it with a straw broom and when it fell so
its underside was exposed, she crushed it, folded it up in
newspaper and took it away.

I TOOK OFF the salwar trousers and then the kameez top and
then my bra and panties and divided them up among the
hooks on the wall. I was glad my period had hardly started – just a few spots. Hopefully I would sleep easily
tonight and the cramps would only come tomorrow. Mist
was still coming off the bucket of hot water. I turned the
tap on (cold water came through the taps but not hot
water) and ran cold water in a smaller mixing bucket. I
scooped a few jugs of the hot water into the mixing bucket until it was the right temperature. I poured water over
my head, and it bounced off my shoulders and splashed
against the walls, on the floor. I poured more slowly, there
was less splashing, and water sluiced all the way down my
legs. I had brought shampoo/conditioner from my hair
salon, and when I squeezed some out in my hand, it had
that familiar clean apple smell. I preferred separate shampoo and conditioner, sometimes I even shampooed twice
and then conditioned for three to five minutes like they
suggested on the bottle. But in India, I bathed quickly, in
the fewest steps possible. The hot water brought from the
kitchen never stayed hot for long, and there was never
enough light: the black stone floor and the dark cement
walls overwhelmed the dim overhead bulb and the modest porthole-size window. Waterbugs and beetles and mosquitoes – on the last trip, I'd even seen a watersnake in a
bathroom – found this the most alluring part of the
house. I let the shampoo soak into my hair, smoothing the
hair back from my face so it wouldn't get in my eyes.

The Dove soap in my travel soapdish was already soft-

ening like chocolate in the heat. I scrubbed hard everywhere to get the aeroplane air and the tea-hill dust out. If
I scrubbed hard enough, I hoped I would peel away that
layer of Americanness that made me feel clumsy and conspicuous here; I wanted to unearth that other person who
had felt at home here and known how to fit in. Now more
than on earlier trips, I felt how hard and how exhausting it
was to translate, even though we were all speaking English.
There were so many ways of being and expressing myself
that I had to leave behind, and so many I had to relearn.

Then more water, my eyes shut tight, pouring so that the
water and shampoo coursed behind me – a foaming trail
snaking across the floor towards the drain in the corner. A
few more rinses over my back, my chest, and soap bubbles
were also rushing towards the drain, and as the trail of
water got clearer again, I turned the bucket over, and
poured the last of the water on my ankles and feet. I wrung
the water out of my hair as much as I could and then took
the thorthu and pressed it against my face. The thorthu
was instantly soaked – I could feel the weave in the sheet
like thin linen. I rubbed down with the sheet, realizing I
was still slick with soap in parts, but not caring. I put a
fresh salwar kameez on to sleep in – a dark blue one that
was big and loose so it didn't show anything and I didn't
have to wear a bra. Even before I stepped out of the bathroom, I started to feel sticky again under my arms and
around my stomach where the trousers drew tight. My hair
was wet against my back, the only cool part of me, and I
left it like that, so the water could seep down my spine all
night.

Brindha was already sleeping, curled up on one side of
the bed. I put her oil lamp out and then mine. Rupa's
sleeping form, coverless on her floor mat, lay between me
and my side of the bed. I remembered for a fleeting second

the old superstition about how if you stepped over someone you would stop her from growing. But crawling
around Brindha was too much trouble, so I leapt over
Rupa and slipped into bed. I had forgotten to take out the
insect repellent in my luggage. I pulled the sheet loosely
over my head, hoping the mosquitoes wouldn't find out
that foreign blood was so close at hand.

CHAPTER TWO

School Days

MY LINGERING JET lag made it seem natural to be up at 3 a.m. But everyone else was awake too and acting like it was not the middle of the night. Brindha was going to boarding school today, which meant three hours down our mountain and then four hours up another mountain to reach St Helena's in Ooty.

My uncle was sitting with the driver at the table on the verandah. Soft lamplight shone on large tattered maps. I went out and looked over his shoulder. These maps were like high-school geography maps, coloured with patterns to show terrain, mountains and lakes, and desert, but no villages or roads. My uncle said there were no maps for places we lived – at least not ones that were of any use. He was drawing with pencil on the maps, and the driver was nodding. The driver knew the way down our mountain and also the way up to Ooty, but what he didn't know were the places we might stop on the way: petrol stations and tea shops and a four-star hotel in the one real city we would pass through and friends' homes and company people (my uncle had told the company guesthouses to expect us).

I wondered sometimes how long our trips would be without any stops, but we had never made them that way. Long drives, to weddings and airports and beach outings, all required a similar sequence of stops – our own Underground Railroad, my uncle called it. Some were required for the trip at hand – a place to have lunch, a place to use the bathroom, a place just before going to a temple to have a bath, a place just before we arrived at a wedding hall to change into wedding clothes. Other stops – brief ones – were to promise that though we hadn't stopped there to lunch or to bathe or to change this time, we would next time, that they had not been forgotten. Then there were elderly relatives to see – not to take hospitality from, but to receive blessings from and hear stories from and to show them how much you've grown and the new bangles you've received.

My aunt was in the kitchen – she did not want the servants cooking Brindha's last meal. She had made lemon rice and tamarind jelly and aapam, which are pancakes made out of rice flour with a thick lump of batter at the centre and then crepelike at the edges, and stew made from beans that had been soaked and sprouted for two days. She laid the table with ornate dinner china, since those were the only dishes in the cabinet in the dining room. All the everyday things were out back in the cooking shed by the servants' quarters where everyone was still asleep.

My grandmother was re-ironing Brindha's uniforms one more time, as there would be inspection at St Helena's this afternoon. She squinted at a list as she packed Brindha's bag, counting how many shirts, how many socks, how many petticoats, how many hairpins Brindha was allowed to bring. Ammamma looked up from her list to ask me to find Brindha and try to cheer her up.

Brindha was slumped dejectedly on a bench in the garden. She had brought her dog out there to say goodbye, but Boli had gone back to sleep at her feet. He would understand only when he heard the car start up, and mourn when it was too late.

Brindha looked up at me, shining a torch in my eyes. 'Would you like one?' she asked. She beamed the torch down on her lap to reveal a Whitman's Sampler box of chocolates I had brought for my aunt. I had brought Three Musketeers and Snickers bars for Brindha, but the Sampler boxes were for my aunt to serve to guests. Brindha had eaten through most of the top tray of chocolates, though some she had chewed halfway and put back in the box, revealing hearts of caramel or vanilla nougat or syrupy cherry. I picked up the box cover to show her the inside panel that listed the types of chocolate in the box and picked out a chocolate cream–filled one. Brindha was amazed by this directory – it was like being handed the answers for a test in advance. I told her how I used to hide the box top and try to guess the fillings based on close observation of the ridges where a walnut or almond might betray itself, or the sticky red drop of liqueur oozing from another, or the dense compactness of the chocolates that tricked you by having no centre – they were just solid right through.

My aunt would be looking for us for breakfast. I told Brindha we should go inside.

Brindha refused. 'I'm not hungry. It's three-thirty in the morning.'

'You were hungry enough for chocolate.'

'That's different.' She looked at me balefully, like I should have known that. I should have known that.

'How about helping me find something nice to wear for when I meet your friends?' I said.

'I don't have any friends.'

'That's not true. You've told me about Gita and that crick-eter's daughter, and the girl with the dyed brown hair.'

'I don't like any of them. I don't want to go to school.' Brindha nudged Boli with her foot, and he opened his eyes, raised himself on his forepaws, licked her out-stretched hand a few times, and then went back to sleep.

'I thought you liked Helena's.'

'I just say I like Helena's because Amma and Achan need me to go there. Achan has to stay here for his job for some years and there is no school here. He promised at his next posting, there'll be a good school there and I won't have to go away.'

Brindha had been full of chatter since I'd arrived about Helena's this and Helena's that. 'Aren't they nice to you there?'

Brindha was impatient with me. 'Who cares if they're nice? Would you want to leave your mother and father? Not now, but when you were like me?'

By 'like me,' she meant ten years old and in the fourth grade. She meant being tucked in every night and having the wardrobes checked for monsters once in a while. I did-n't tell Brindha that living with my mother and father had been my boarding school, leaving my grandmother and the safe place I knew for a place that had cold dark nights, many wardrobes, and strange, stiff guardians. The other kids at school in America had been pink and blond and fast with everything. My English had felt slow and I had had such an accent. I hadn't known what the teachers wanted from me. And Mother didn't help – she kept telling me I was doing things wrong. I went home with other kids' parents from school without waiting for the school bus, or I lost my milk money in the playground. I hadn't known how anything worked. I didn't tell Brindha that by her age I had wished that I could go to boarding school, where everyone was parentless, and therefore somehow on equal footing.

'Do Sanjay uncle and Reema auntie know you don't like it? Maybe they can find something else.'

'There is nothing else – this is where the girls from our set go. At least I'm lucky I'm a girl – the fifth- and sixth-graders don't bully us like Akash says they do at St Patrick's Boys.'

'They wouldn't want you to stay at a school you don't like. Maybe you should tell them again.'

Brindha put her hand in my hand. 'Nothing will change. It's OK, Maya, I do like that girl with the dyed brown hair, and some others. Let's go to breakfast before Amma thinks we're lost.'

Brindha lifted the sleeping dog and we headed for the house.

WE WERE READY to leave. Brindha gave Ammamma a kiss and hugged her around her waist. Ammamma took the palloo end of her white sari and dabbed the back of Brindha's neck, which was still wet from her bath. Brindha brought Boli over to Ammamma and kissed him goodbye and as she embraced him, she put a collar around his neck. Ammamma got a firm grip on his collar and crouched over him in the driveway. The driver started up the car, Boli's ears pointed up and he arched. Ammamma held on to him tightly, her white sari getting spattered as Boli kicked up mud and tried to get himself loose, and we backed out of the carport and out the driveway. Just as we turned on to the road, our headlights swung over a slim dark figure. Rupa was walking to meet a bus that would take her down the mountain and back home to her village. This was Rupa's last day – there was no more work for her here. Brindha waved wildly from her open window, and Rupa, who could not wave because her hands suppported an ungainly bundle of all her belongings, smiled back.

WE DROVE IN silence for some time, not quite sure if we were awake or asleep, not quite sure if it was night or day. My uncle sat in the front next to the driver, and my aunt sat in the back in the middle so that my cousin and I could each get a window. Brindha first asked to ride shotgun, but she was not allowed in the front seat with the driver. On short drives to the nearby village to get candy or some buttons for sewing, Brindha and I were allowed to go alone with the household driver Ram, and sometimes she would clamber over into the front seat once we were out of view of the house. But this driver today was some assistant at the tea factory just hired for the day who my uncle said he had never used before, so Brindha had slim chance of talking her way into the front seat. Part of the reason Sanjay uncle was coming with us until we reached Coimbatore was so that he could watch the driver, make sure he drove carefully, and treated us respectfully. It might be different after my uncle left, but at least his presence now enforced some degree of accountability, made literal the fact that a man protected our household.

Brindha said we had to take turns being on watch for

the police, and she would go first. She said they might come after us because we had tinted windows on our car. The police had put out an order that until Subha and Sivarasan were caught, no one could drive in Tamil Nadu with tinted windows. But Sanjay uncle said that it was too much trouble to get the windows changed, and the sun would fry us alive. It was still dark , there wasn't anyone on the road, let alone a police ambush. Brindha fell asleep half an hour into her watch.

Sanjay uncle said this was the perfect time of day to see wildlife, but I was too tired to pay much attention to his tour-guiding. After an hour or so, the sun came up, and there were fewer small creatures to avoid on the road as they receded into woods, replaced by the big creatures of the day: buses and lorries charged up at us around blind corners. Since there had been so few cars on the road on the way home from the airport, I had not noticed that there was really only one lane. Each time a lorry came by, hurling black smoke into our car as we pulled to the side to let it narrowly pass us, I erupted in fits of coughing. My aunt took out a handkerchief from her bag and doused it with water (we had four bottles of boiled water to see us through the morning) and handed it to me to put over my nose and mouth. I wiped my eyes with it first, leaving black marks that looked like mascara on the starched white cloth, but I was wearing no makeup – the smudges were all dirt and soot. I held the cloth over my mouth.

Sanjay uncle glanced at me in the rearview mirror. 'You've got American lungs now. The emissions standards are lax here; it's too expensive to burn fuel as cleanly as you do in America.'

Another bus loomed on the horizon, ready to play chicken.

'Why do they come right at us without even slowing

down?' I asked. 'It's like we don't have a right to be on the road.'

'We don't, really,' Sanjay uncle said mildly. 'Those buses are for workers coming up to the tea estates for day labour, and the lorries are bringing supplies and equipment in and tea product out. Fuel and road are both rare resources here, and buses and lorries are more efficient than we are in a private car.'

'Stop lecturing,' Reema auntie said. 'You would never let us go by bus, even if we were somehow possessed with that desire.'

'Correct.' My uncle sighed. 'So we choose, and choose to live with, the luxury of our inefficiency.'

'This is what happens when you live in the only Communist state within a capitalist country. You take care of your own interests, but you feel guilt for it.' My aunt directed this at me, as if my uncle were not there, but it must have been for his benefit, since I hardly knew what she was talking about.

My cousin, Brindha, had been quiet in her corner till now. 'Please, no fighting, no fighting, Amma.'

My aunt looked at her with surprise. 'That's not fighting, it's just disagreeing.'

'But if you keep disagreeing, then Achan will divorce you.'

'Brindha, do you even know what you are saying? How can you say such things?' my uncle said, turning around fully in his seat.

She retreated into her corner. 'That's why Chitra and Padma are at Helena's – because their parents are having a divorce. And also Reshma – her parents are divorced. Her father lives in Dubai now and her mother lives in Madras and she's an actress.'

'I knew we shouldn't send Brindha there. Helena's may be

old and prestigious, but a lot of the girls there do not have good families. What good family would send their daughter away for her whole childhood?' my aunt said to my uncle.

'That's not true, Reema – many good families send their daughters to boarding school, many of my colleagues, everyone at the head office. Some of the families perhaps are too modern or have too much money, but most are good children, good families.'

'Stop fighting, stop fighting.' Brindha covered her ears.

My aunt took Brindha's hands down from her ears and she kissed each palm. 'We're not fighting and we're not divorcing. Everything is OK, you know that, don't you?'

My uncle reached over to the back and ruffled Brindha's hair. 'And you know this is just for a few years and then we'll move, OK? '

'Couldn't I just not go to school for a year? I'll learn fast and catch up next year.'

Sanjay uncle shook his head. 'In a few years, we'll be together again. Don't make this hard for your amma – she will be sad if you're sad at school like last year.'

Brindha unwound the upper part of her mother's sari, and put it over her own head, shade against the sun piercing her window. From under her little cloak, she said, 'You know Maya's parents are getting a divorce.'

'That's not true,' I said hotly.

She said, 'I read it in your letter you were sending yesterday.'

I had been writing to my best friend Jennifer from high school, who I told almost everything to. I hadn't written that they were getting a divorce, just that I worried sometimes that they would.

'You shouldn't have been reading Maya's mail,' Reema auntie said to Brindha.

My uncle looked at me. 'Is something wrong at home, Maya?'

I glared at my cousin, who was still faceless under my aunt's sari. 'Nothing is wrong, everything is like always.'

Reema auntie said, 'Don't pry, Sanjay. She would tell us if she had something to tell.'

Sanjay uncle said, 'Maya, you would tell us, wouldn't you? There isn't anything you want to tell us right now?'

'No. Nothing. No.'

My aunt squeezed my hand, and I looked away, trying to make my pulse slow down. I knew they asked because they loved me and they were concerned, but I didn't want to be pitied. Already, Sanjay uncle and Reema auntie were so delicate about my mother – they knew things were difficult, and I was used to that. I didn't talk much about it, but I didn't try to hide it. Sometimes I thought Sanjay uncle knew more than he let on; maybe he just knew intuitively because it was his sister.

I was glad Brindha was going to school – now no one would poke around in my belongings and go through my letters. A letter from Jennifer was waiting for me when I arrived. I wondered what she had read of my letter to Jennifer. My aunt had given me blue aerograms to write on, and told me to give the letters to my uncle, who could post them at the factory. I had taken a thin onionskin piece of paper out of Brindha's writing pad and written a note to Steve that I had slipped in the aerogram envelope to Jennifer so I didn't have to give my uncle an envelope with Steve's name on it. Steve was Jennifer's boyfriend's best friend, besides being my sometime boyfriend. I wasn't always sure how I felt about him when we were at home, but while I was here, it was nice to hear from Jennifer's letter that Steve missed me. It was nice to be missed, and it was nice to think about someone as being yours, a part of your life that was all your own. He didn't understand some things about the way my family was, like why he couldn't call in the evenings when my parents were at home, or why I could never go to his family's beach house unless Jennifer was going to be there too. He didn't understand why I had said he couldn't write to me in India, but I think on this point he was secretly relieved to be able to just give Jennifer messages and not have to write things himself. It made him nervous how much time I spent writing and reading. Once at his beach house he grabbed the novel I was reading out of my hands and said he wouldn't give it back till I went swimming with him. I didn't go swimming, and we didn't talk for the whole afternoon, and finally he sullenly threw the novel back on to my beach towel.

I didn't like how Jennifer and her boyfriend would sometimes disappear on purpose to leave the two of us alone. I liked Steve, but I partly liked him because the four of us had fun together. It felt awkward sometimes when it was just us. And when it was just us, I was more nervous about doing something wrong, about feeling wrong. Everything we did was wrong by my parents' standards – they would have been mortified if they had ever even seen us kiss or hold hands, but I already made distinctions between my parents' standards and my own. I didn't want to be one of those Indians who lived in America without ever adapting to it. But the problem was, once my standards didn't come from my parents, then where did they come from? And if you didn't keep up to your own standards, then who punished you or told you they were disappointed and made you want to be a better person? I didn't want to be like Jennifer's family either, who let her boyfriend sleep over some weekends; her mother said it was better than having them out in parked cars. There was something tasteless to me about reading the Sunday papers over breakfast in your pyjamas with your mum and dad and your high-school boyfriend.

Even though arranged marriages seemed strange, some things about it sounded nice. My mother often talked about her time in school and college, saying, 'I had the rest of my life for being a couple – those years were for friendships.' She had best friends from childhood, and best friends from high school, and best friends from college, and she still heard from them, from Canada and Kuwait, and Dallas, and all over India. In her school, friends never stopped talking to you because they had a new boyfriend, and they never tried to steal your boyfriend, or use you to go to a party to meet someone and leave you to work out how to get home by yourself.

We knew other Indian families in New York, and there were some Indians in my school. It was different for some of them because they were from big cities, like Bombay and Delhi, where things were modern now, and their cousins dated and went to bars and things. But not in the south, where my family was from. What I liked better about the south, even if other people said it was a backward place, was that at least it was fair to everyone. In Bombay and Delhi, they said you could date, but then many boys still had an arranged marriage when it was time, and they usually didn't want to marry girls who had dated. And also, there were dowries in many marriages there, so even if girls thought they were being independent by dating, they were still going to need their parents to spend a lot of money for them to marry well. In our families, we didn't have any dowries, and dating was equally discouraged for boys as for girls. I was hoping Brindha hadn't read the whole letter.

'Who's Steve?' Brindha piped up after a while. She wasn't trying to cause trouble on purpose, but she was doing a good job. She just wanted to know things, and she knew her only chance was while her parents were there, otherwise I would ignore her questions.

'Jennifer's brother,' I lied. Brothers were the only kind of boys it was OK to be seen with. Or cousins. I tried to change the subject. 'Did you finish your summer assignments for school?'

'Yes, Brindha, have you finished?' Reema auntie said. 'Why don't I check your maths problems to see how many are correct?'

Brindha grumbled and pulled out her rucksack, and took out some papers with crumpled edges.

'You should keep these papers in those nice folders Achan brought you from his office,' Reema auntie said.

'But the folders are plain white and say 'high grade tea' on them. The other girls have pretty ones their fathers bring from Singapore, even ones with pictures of Barbie on them.'

'If someone we know is going to Singapore, we can try to get you some of those, but for now you have to make do. I think Achan's folders are quite nice. I use them in the house for filing letters and bills.'

'Achan, why can't you work in something exciting, like movies or video games? Then we could go to Singapore and all over.'

'I'll see what I can do,' my uncle said wearily.

Reema auntie said, 'Brindha, Achan has a very good job. You see all the people who come to ask him to advise on their tea factories? And his company is happy he took this post, and he is making our factory very productive. You should be proud of him.'

'Yes, Amma,' Brindha said, her head down. 'I'm sorry I say rude things.'

I watched Brindha interact with her parents the way an ethnographer might, studing them, taking mental notes, charting their moments of tension and contentment. There was a naturalness to their rhythms of discussing and resolving, one giving in one time, another the next time. Discord never rose to the level where there were chasms created that no one knew how to bridge.

I knew in my own family, I was not particularly good at being the conciliatory one. But I couldn't help it. I often felt I had got past resenting my mother for the four years I'd been left in India. I pretended we'd been apart for the reasons other children are – because of hardship or poverty, because we were refugees or there was a war or a potato famine. Any of these were more appealing than what seemed to be the truth, which was that my parents had a plentiful life without room for me in it, at least not right away. But even when I convinced myself that those were old grudges to hold on to, new ones cropped up. I resented my mother not only for the four years she chose not to be a parent but for the following ten years during which she was a reluctant one.

Mother travelled a lot, which was fine by me because she didn't know how to talk to me even when she was at home. She had no sense of how to make me feel better when I was lonely or sad or ill. I watched Reema auntie, who was so natural at soothing Brindha, and felt that my mother lacked those primal instincts that told you how to read your children, how to teach them, reproach them, and hold them. Instead, in our house, there was the strained formality and the occasional shrillness of separate and self-conscious people acting out a pale imitation of family.

The road had widened into two lanes, but now there were four cars abreast and a herd of oxen pressing forward. We had reached Coimbatore, and the car crawled along

the main strip of downtown office buildings, until my
uncle said we should stop. The air was dense with grit, and
I smelled petrol and diesel on the roads. The driver and
Sanjay uncle got out of the car, and my aunt also got out
to help get packages from the back of the car, and to talk
to Sanjay uncle at the roadside. They would never kiss in
front of everyone, but he touched her arm fleetingly,
jostling her bangles as they talked. He would be back
home in three days. He ducked into the back seat of the car
to give us both hugs, and to say to Brindha, 'Now, please,
try to be happy there this year. We will write to you every
week as usual, and come for the Visitors' Weekend in two
months' time. Think of your mother, Brindha, and don't
cry today, OK?'

'I wasn't going to cry,' she said in a small voice. 'I
promised already.'

'Say hello to Old Granny for me, will you?'

Brindha made a face. Old Granny was Miss Granville,
who had been headmistress at Helena's forever, people
said, at least a century or two. Everyone mocked her
behind her back, but everyone was a little intimidated,
even the parents.

Reema auntie got back in the car on my side, so I was
now squashed in the middle. I looked at the empty front
seat longingly, with its wide open window, but knew asking would be pointless.

'So, Brindha, shall we go to Aruna's for lunch, or shall
we go to Shantha's or to a hotel?' Reema auntie asked.

'What about that dosa stand that Achan always takes us
to?'

'We can't go there with Maya – it's too much of a local
place, it could make her ill.'

'But you told us it was clean there even though they
serve so many drivers and clerks.'

'Brindha,' my aunt lowered her voice and switched into Malayalam, 'this driver knows some English, so don't just blurt out such impolite things.'

'OK.' Brindha shrugged. 'Then let's go to Aruna auntie's – she serves better food than Shantha auntie.'

'Besides,' Brindha said to me, 'Shantha auntie wants to send her daughter to Helena's, so she pesters me with questions and I have to pretend I have a lot of friends and everything.'

Aruna auntie is Reema auntie's oldest sister's husband's sister. In our family, that's still a close relation. Somewhere in my suitcase with all the other things my mother stuffed in there is a gift set from Estee Lauder or an embroidered hand towel set with a tag addressed to her.

'That's OK,' Reema auntie said. 'You can bring it next time we come down, or Sanjay can bring it to her.'

Aruna auntie used to be a famous classical dancer – she had even been on Doordarshan, the national TV channel. Now she was on the fat side and had four kids, but after lunch Brindha made her show us all of her fiercest expressions, of the temperamental goddess Kali and the snake god Naga and of the evil Kaurava brother Duryodhana. Auntie still moved with stealth and grace when she danced despite all her extra pounds. She could even enlist her plump cheeks to quiver with a demon god's fury.

'Reema tells me you used to dance also, Maya,' Aruna auntie said.

'Yes, Maya studied with guru Padmanabhan near her grandmother's house for five summers in a row,' Reema auntie said.

'You're lucky to have studied with Padmanabhan – he's one of our best,' Aruna auntie said. 'Will you be having an arangetram, then?' An arangetram was a graduation ceremony to exhibit a certain level of mastery in dance.

'We all hoped she would,' Reema auntie said. 'Her mother even found her an instructor in New York to supplement Padmanabhan's instruction. But Maya wanted to stop dancing a few years ago.'

'I didn't have time because I had other activities,' I said.

'Activities? What activities?' Aruna auntie said.

I told her that I wrote for the school newspaper and I did babysitting and I was in the swimming team.

'But this is part of your culture,'Aruna auntie said. 'You should at least keep up practising what you had learned.'

'I really don't remember much,' I said. I liked dancing when I first started and it was about counting out the beats and learning the steps, the intricate footwork, the poses on bended knee. Then my teacher began telling me the best dancing was not athletic, it was expressive. But expressive of what? I had never felt tied to the meaning, I couldn't make my face express things I wasn't feeling. I knew the stories the dances told, about gods and ancient legends – my grandmother had taught them to me, but Kali and Rama had lost their relevance to my present life, they were as remote as Peter Pan and his shadow.

'Aruna auntie, do the Naga pose again. I want to copy you,' Brindha said, standing behind Aruna auntie.

Aruna auntie gathered herself upon one leg, narrowing her eyes to those of a serpent god, and using her arms to create a large ominous hood over herself. Brindha imitated her, drawing her mouth small and mean. But she lost her balance after a couple of seconds and collapsed giggling to the floor.

'I'm going to do that at school the next time the girls say something rude. If it looks scary enough they might think I've put a curse on them,' she said.

'Brindha, don't say such things,' Reema auntie said, tucking Brindha's hair back into some kind of order. 'You have to start out the school year thinking positively.'

'Speaking of school, I took the children to temple on their first day of school last week, and we still have some prasadam. Let me bring it for you,' Aruna auntie said.

'We probably should have gone today, too,' Reema auntie said.

'There's a Vishnu temple not far from here, if you want to go now,' Aruna auntie said, unfolding a banana leaf tied up in string. Inside was a sweet sticky crush of sugar and raisins and lentils. She put some in my hand ('right hand, right hand,' she murmured when I unthinkingly extended my left) and then in Brindha's and Reema auntie's. Aruna auntie herself had a bit, then licked the last of the stickiness from her palm.

'I don't think we have time,' Reema auntie said. 'We're making the drive back tonight, so I don't want it to get late.'

'Shall I give you some tea in a thermos or are you stopping again?' Aruna auntie asked.

'We are stopping for tea in Ooty, so Brindha can change into her uniform there. But thank you,' Reema auntie said.

We got back in the car and Reema auntie sat in the front with the driver so Brindha and I could lie down together in the back and sleep for a while to make the time go faster.

When I sat up again and looked out, everything was green and lush. We'd already gone through the first set of hairpin bends climbing Ooty, my aunt said. And while this summit was higher than the one we lived on, the roads were not carved as steeply or as narrowly. Also, it was cooler up here, chilly even. There was tall grass and soft curves of meadow near the road.

'Stop, stop!' Brindha screamed. She was peering out the

window on her side.

'What is it, Brindha?' my aunt said.

'Look over there, see behind those trees. I think Sushmila Jain is there!'

'Who's Sushmila Jain?' I said. The driver had stopped short and leapt out of the car and was standing at the edge of the road. In the clearing outside Brindha's window, a herd of people came into focus. There were women wearing full peasant skirts and carrying baskets of vegetables on their heads. There were men wearing turbans and white kurta pyjamas with their hands clasped behind their backs holding hoes. They lined up in two rows facing each other, not moving.

'What are they farming?' I asked.

Brindha and Reema auntie burst into laughter.

'It's a movie, Maya,' Reema auntie said. 'Many movies are filmed in Ooty – that's all that's up here besides boarding schools and summer resorts.'

Brindha said, 'That's Sushmila, over there, the tall beautiful one. Amma, can we get out of the car, please, so we can see better?'

'We need to get going,' Reema auntie said, even though she said this without herself turning away from the window.

'Just for one song?' Brindha asked. Reema auntie nodded and we all got out of the car.

The crew was trailing behind the actors and still setting up their equipment, and the director shouted for a run-through of the scene. The two lines of men and women began a dance routine, the women dancing around their baskets, the men running off with them, the women running after the men, the men returning the baskets but only in exchange for a chance to hold their hands. Meanwhile, the star Sushmila Jain, who was wearing a sari rather than

a peasant skirt, danced amidst her entourage, accompanied by a man with slick hair and black knee-high boots.
They mouthed verses to each other, and then the peasant
men and women mouthed the refrains. The songs would
be added in later, but to help the dancers keep time, loud
instrumental music crackled from two speakers. Sushmila
Jain shrieked when one of the cameramen came up to her
and dumped a bucket of water over her head. They started
the dance routine over again, Sushmila's pink chiffon sari
now stuck to her body, her long untied hair gleaming
wetly in the sun.

'I expect the water was cold,' Brindha giggled.

Reema auntie snorted. 'Honestly, these movies are
ridiculous.'

'Jayalalitha wants Sushmila to join her party,' Brindha
said. Jayalalitha, who had been a film star before becoming a politician, had become Chief Minister of the state of
Tamil Nadu last week. The previous state government had
been dismissed because it was suspected of aiding the
Tamil Tiger cause. Jayalalitha and her party were suspected
only of general corruption.

'I wish some of our film stars would just stay film stars
and do what they know how to do,' Reema auntie said.

'Amma, won't you let me ask for Sushmila's autograph
since she might even become our next Chief Minister?'
Brindha asked.

Reema auntie snorted. 'Definitely not. Let's go,' she said.

WE TUMBLED OUT of the car an hour later, in front of a trim
white bungalow. It was a guesthouse of Sanjay uncle's
company, where my aunt and uncle stayed when they
made overnight trips to visit Brindha at school.

My aunt said, 'It might be occupied by some other
company people right now, so be polite. We'll just stop in

and have tea and change.'

Reema auntie walked on to the porch, and a servant came to the door. He took our things and brought us inside. The sitting room had a high ceiling with two overhead fans swirling lazily.

'Do you know who's staying here at the moment?' she asked.

The servant said, 'It is a Mrs Sangeetha Ayengar and her mother, mem.'

'Sangeetha's here? How lovely, I didn't know. Please tell her she has some surprise visitors then. And I think we'll have our tea now – we're in somewhat of a rush.'

The servant came back with tea things, and then a woman wearing a housecoat floated into the room, hugging each of us effusively.

'God, I'm not even dressed, I was just napping, but how wonderful to see you, Reema!' Sangeetha auntie tried to smooth out the many creases in her housecoat. Her eyes were lined with thick black kajal that had got smudgy in sleep and, on her unusually sallow skin, gave her a haunted quality. Sangeetha auntie's husband had worked with Sanjay uncle some years ago.

'Brindha's so grown up, I haven't seen her in at least a year. And, Maya, do you know, I saw you last when you were such a little girl – three, I think, living with your grandmother – you would hide in her sari folds when anyone new came to the house. Do you remember?'

I shook my head and smiled. I didn't remember her. I did remember being shy, not liking new people.

'How is Grandmother now? I hope she's keeping in good health. We all adored her in our old neighbourhood.'

Reema auntie said, 'She's doing well – she had some heart trouble last summer, and high blood pressure generally, but she's been living with us up in the mountains, and it seems to suit her.'

'My husband says that's one of the best postings – he's put it on his list for his next transfer. And my mother, too, is living with me – perhaps we will all be in the same place one day again.'

Brindha made funny faces at me over the top of her teacup.

'It's boring here – there are no children to play with,' she whispered.

'Brindha, why don't you and Maya go and get dressed in auntie's room?' Reema auntie said. 'I'll be in in a minute.'

Brindha changed into her uniform, blue stiff cotton, with a white shirt underneath. And black buckled shoes with white socks. Reema auntie changed from a salwar kameez to a sari and put on lipstick and powder and lined her eyes in black. I changed to a new salwar kameez, and wore the earrings that Brindha had asked me to wear – two big sparkling silver stars.

'I don't think this looks good with Indian clothes, Brindha,' I said. I undid the clasp to remove them.

'The girls at school will think it's cool. Trust me, Maya, okay?' Brindha said. 'Don't you want to make a good impression for my sake?'

I thought of how I interrogated my mother on what she was going to wear before each swimming competition she came to.

'And look, Maya, I brought your scarf – I knew you'd forget it and I want you to wear it.'

'Brindha, that's not going to look right.' It was a red silky scarf that she must have taken from my suitcase. I often twisted it through my belt loops at home and occasionally wore it over my shoulder. I gave in and let her tie it around my neck the way she wanted, Cub Scout-style.

Sangeetha auntie had come into the bedroom too.

'Reema, you almost let me forget. I was going to show you the fabulous necklace that new jeweller made for me. If you like it, ask Sanjay and then let me know if you want to meet him next time you come down here. I'll just get it.'

Sangeetha auntie brought from her wardrobe a bright green plastic box. Inside on two pins lay a heavy gold necklace with paisley cutouts.

'My mother has that same box – maybe she's been to the same shop,' I said. I had seen green boxes like that cluttering her dressing table at home.

'This box?' Sangeetha auntie held it up. 'These are just cheap plastic – all the jewellery shops use them.'

Reema auntie said, 'Sangeetha, you should see the beautiful boxes Maya's mother brings me from New York. Shops there wrap everything so handsomely, with ribbons and velvet and tissue, even if you've just bought a hair grip.'

Sangeetha auntie did not look impressed. 'With our jewellery, you aren't paying for fancy decor in the jeweller's shop or fancy packaging. You pay by the weight of the gold. Feel this.'

She took the necklace off the pins and put it in my hands. It was heavy, like a whole rollful of quarters from the bank.

'When I was your age, I had necklaces already, as fine as this, from my father and mother. But only now, after buying for our three daughters, now that they are married, have I accepted my first one from my husband. '

I hoped the collar of my salwar kameez covered the thin gold chain I was wearing. It was so thin it was more like a shiny piece of thread, really. Steve had given it to me last Valentine's Day. I'd never seen him so bashful before, and I was too surprised seeing him like that to be as appreciative as I should have been. He couldn't have known that in our tradition, necklaces are more important than rings. My mother would take off her wedding ring to wash up or check the oil in the car, but she never took off her wedding necklace. I wore my necklace almost all the time – sometimes at night I reached up inside my T-shirt to glide the tiny links back and forth between my fingers.

'I hope your mother has been putting away some things for your special day?' Sangeetha auntie said, holding the box open for me to put the necklace back.

'I don't know,' I said.

'You don't know? Well, what does your horoscope say? When is the right year for your marriage?'

'I don't know. I don't think I have a horoscope,' I stammered, looking to Reema auntie for help.

'Nonsense! Everyone has a horoscope. Your mother would have seen to it when you were born. Reema, what does her horoscope say?'

Reema auntie didn't look at me, 'Actually, Maya doesn't have a horoscope. Her mother didn't want it done.'

Not having a birth-chart, or horoscope, in India was like missing a basic appendage. Families commissioned a horoscope based on the date and time of their children's birth to guide them in every endeavour: what subjects to study, what medicines to take, what gods to propitiate, what husbands to marry. My mother had not made one for me, and I hated when it came up in conversation. Sometimes I lied and made up a horoscope for myself. I knew what star I was born under, and I would just adapt the formulaic things I'd seen written in cheap Indian tabloids. But I couldn't lie to Sangeetha auntie, not with Reema auntie right there who knew the truth.

'Oh,' Sangeetha auntie said. She looked perplexed. 'But then how will she marry?'

Reema auntie said, 'Hopefully, we'll find a family who doesn't follow these things.'

'Oh,' Sangeetha auntie said again. She looked unconvinced and patted my cheek in a pitying way. 'Oh, well, then I can't really help. But I'm sure you'll find someone suitable.'

WE DROVE INTO the carport at Helena's and were greeted by a line of tall girls, most wearing saris, some salwar kameezes.

'I can't wait to be in the upper school and not have to wear this stupid uniform,' Brindha complained. One of the upper-school girls was dispatched to take us to Brindha's dormitory and introduce Brindha to her room mates for the year. There was silence among eleven watchful girls while the upper-school girl helped Brindha open her suitcase. A teacher checked off a list of requirements – three white shirts, two blue skirts, two blue dresses, two sweaters, one exercise outfit, etc. – and the girl held Brindha's clothes up for inspection. The teacher and the girl conferred over a few items, and when they were in agreement on everything, Brindha was allowed to put her things away in her assigned cupboard.

Reema auntie was asking a teacher some questions, and they walked out into the hall. As soon as the adults were at a safe distance, Brindha's room mates crowded around us. 'So what did you bring for your cigar box?' they asked.

Each girl was allowed one cigar box to keep mementos and trinkets in. Brindha had thought hard over the last few days about what she wanted to bring to school this year. She had pasted scraps of wrapping paper around the outside of the box, and on the lid Reema auntie had drawn a picture of our house. This is what Brindha showed them as she took each item out of the box and lined them up on her bed: her red velvet-covered collar for her dog; a hotel soap carved like a conch shell from a weekend beach holiday to Cape Comoran; a photo of Ammamma from when she was young, black-haired, and shy; a pink embroidered handkerchief of Reema auntie's; a glitter pen that Sanjay uncle had brought from Bombay; and a shiny black locket.

The girls seemed to approve of Brindha's choices. They listened hungrily as Brindha described the new posh hotel in Cape Comoran where she saw not one but two movie stars. She agreed to let another girl try out the glitter pen to make a 'We Miss You' card for a girl who this year had been separated from them for too much troublemaking and put in an older girls' dormitory where she could be constantly supervised.

The upper-class girl, who had quietly rejoined the group, grabbed the black locket off the bed and asked sharply, 'Where did you get this?'

Brindha answered airily, 'I just found it somewhere.'

'Do you know what this is?' the upper-class girl said grimly. She said she'd seen them on the news, these Tamil Tiger lockets. She kept poking at the locket until she found a spring release that unveiled a cyanide capsule wedged inside. She threatened to give the locket to the head-mistress. Brindha begged her not to. She hadn't meant anything by it, and it was only the first day of the new term. The upper-class girl dropped the locket into her blouse as the teacher walked back in to summon the girls to the storeroom to collect their textbooks for classes. Then Reema auntie reappeared and whisked me off with her for an appointment with the headmistress.

I could tell by watching Reema auntie dry her clammy hands in a crumpled handkerchief that she was nervous. We sat in Miss Granville's office for fifteen minutes before she even came in, and when she did she hardly looked at us. Standing at her window, looking off into the distance, she said tersely, 'I don't usually like to meet parents on the first day because there are pressing things that need my attention.'

'Yes, well, I won't take up too much of your time, Miss Granville. There's just one thing . . .' Reema auntie said. Reema auntie had asked the doctor and he said it would be better if Brindha could have a glass of milk every day rather than every other day, the way the school scheduled it.

'So, let me see what you are asking, Mrs Pillai,' Miss Granville said. 'Just your daughter is to have this special dispensation because her bones are more important than all the other girls'?'

'Well, no, the other girls should have equal treatment,' Reema auntie said, weakly.

'So then the whole school is to undergo this additional expense because one doctor has it in his head that we should do something differently? Do you know all the parents who come to see me, Mrs Pillai, asking for the girls to have castor oil once a week or sweet potatoes with supper or only wheat flour no rice flour or only rice flour no wheat flour?'

'Yes, but – ' Reema auntie was cut off.

'I shall think about it, Mrs Pillai.' Miss Granville stood up, dismissing us.

Brindha came to say goodbye to us at the carport. When Reema auntie turned to give some instructions to the driver, Brindha pulled me aside.

'Maya, there is a girl in my grade who is the cousin of that upper-class girl. She says she will get the locket back and make sure I don't get in trouble if I give her what she wants,' Brindha said.

'What is it?'I said.

'She wants your earrings. We can't wear earrings at school, but she wants to have them for her cigar box. I don't want to get in trouble already. Please, Maya,' she said.

I took off my earrings and gave them to her and she jumped up and hugged me.

'Where did you get the locket?' I asked.

'I took it from Rupa – she kept her things in my room. I know what everyone says about the Tigers, but Rupa would never hurt anyone. You won't say anything to Amma, please?' Brindha said. I was tackled in another hug. There wasn't time to ask even the obvious questions. Since Rupa had left the house anyway, it was not that hard to do what Brindha wanted and not tell. Telling would inevitably involve those smug, self-important men from the airport. I didn't feel like seeing, or helping, any of them.

Brindha was downcast and quiet saying goodbye to her mother. Reema auntie waved cheerily to Brindha as we drove out of sight.

We drove in silence for a few minutes, and then Reema auntie asked the driver to stop the car. She asked if I could sit in the front so she could have the back seat – she said she wasn't feeling very well.

'You don't mind, do you, Maya dear?'she said.

I moved to the front seat, not looking at the driver. I was conscious of his dark-skinned, hair-covered arm with the sleeve rolled up to the elbow, lying between us, loosely gripping the gearshift.

Reema auntie lay down in the back, her arm up over her eyes, and cried quietly. Hearing her, I thought: So that is what it would be like to have a mother who loved you. When she had stopped crying, she slept. For the seven hours homeward, I stayed awake, afraid that in sleep I might make an odd expression or look dishevelled, or even accidentally lean into the driver's arm. I was too embarrassed to take off my shoes or open buttons at the neck of my salwar kameez to feel cooler in the heat. I tried to keep before me what I had observed about how to conduct one self with servants – how to project the sense of being the mistress of the house. I sat straight and still and quiet into the night.

CHAPTER THREE

Secret Garden

REEMA AUNTIE'S GARDEN was full of what my mother called illegitimate children. Some of Reema auntie's rose bushes had five kinds of roses on the same bush. My mother kept trying this at home, but the grafts wouldn't take. She had a pathetic-looking branch with other buds taped on to it, like something a kid would do, believing in alchemy. She attempted to re-create a tropical garden – lilies, jasmine, curry leaves, hot peppers – brought from Texas, Florida, Louisiana. Each of our three holidays to Disneyworld included excursions to nurseries and hothouses.

No one brought plants to the US from India because it was against the law, and it was a credible fear that we would bring some plague or pestilence to the Western hemisphere that had never been seen there before. But everyone drew the line at different places; one friend of my mother's brought seeds, but not plants, and some others would sneak plants from Mexico but not from India, arguing that airborne and waterborne diseases travelled back and forth across that border anyway. My mother didn't bother with any of this – she just worked within her constraints, telling us that that was a certain feat in itself, to re-create India from all things American.

In India, you only went to a nursery if you had no friends. Usually, you just took cuttings from everyone's garden. In America, everyone's plants were so small and frail, you dared not ask for cuttings. Except we had grown our curry plant strong enough that my mother was proud to offer cuttings, and people would take plastic sandwich bags with a root and a stem back home to Boston and Chicago and Toronto, where they anxiously abided by my mother's stern instructions as to special light and special food and special soil.

So my aunt's garden had unnaturally created things I didn't recognize, and some that I did: hibiscus, bougainvillea, hydrangea, nasturtiums, foxglove, sweet william, delphinium, jacaranda. Loads of water hyacinths and a few lotuses in the artificial pond, and trellises sagging under the weight of tea roses. And exuberant yellow flowers that a doctor had brought from South Africa a hundred years ago and grafted on to the tree at the far corner where they declared blooming domination over their host. And jasmine everywhere – like our cherry tomatoes at home, it just insinuated itself in every bare patch of dirt.

Jasmine was what South Indian girls smelled like – not soap or spice or perfume, but the heavy honey smell of jasmine, threaded into long necklaces and wound through freshly braided hair in the morning. My hair wasn't long enough for a braid, so my aunt would clip a few stems behind my ear, but it looked silly like that. I usually pulled them off once I was out of her sight.

The special triple-bud jasmine was what my aunt wanted me to wear to the annual dance at the country club. 'This will be your chance to meet everyone,' my aunt said. She said this as if there hadn't been a steady inflow of my uncle's colleagues and friends and local officials whose presence at our home was eventually less notable than their absence.

'I'm still not that close to anyone up here. So it'll be nice to have someone to go with,' my aunt said.

'Isn't Sanjay uncle coming?' I asked.

'Yes, of course,' she said.

'But then you're not going alone anyway,' I said.

'Well no, but the men will be with the men,' she said. I didn't know what that meant.

The dance was on the coming Friday. 'Isn't that Ammamma's birthday?' Some birthday cards had arrived for Ammamma in the mail yesterday and today.

'Yes, that's right,' Reema auntie said.

'Shouldn't we do something to celebrate her birthday then?'

'There's nothing to celebrate about turning seventy-one. Cakes and candles are for children, and for special, auspicious years. The only special year Ammamma has ahead of her is eighty-four, when she's lived for one thousand moons. Then we'll have a big feast. But that's not for a long time.'

'So you think she won't mind on her birthday coming along to this country club thing?' I said.

'She's not coming to the club, Maya. There will be dancing, and loud music – not anything your grandmother will want to sit through.'

'But we can't leave her at home and go out on her birthday,' I said doubtfully.

'It'll be fine with her; you can go and ask her if you want.'

It was true, she didn't want to go, and she didn't seem bothered that we were going. 'You'll have a nice time,' my grandmother said. 'Your aunt and uncle want you to meet their friends – they want to show off their smart, pretty American niece. '

'Everyone has an American niece these days,' I said. There was a time when having a relative in America was a big deal, it meant you had a direct representative on the frontlines of the gold rush.

'It's not because you're American,' my grandmother said. 'It's because you're still ours.'

I felt bad making plans on Ammamma's birthday – she certainly honoured mine every year, not just special years. I was starting to feel, reluctantly, that I should back out from the dance. Then we received a telegram that my aunt's youngest sister had given birth.

'It's her fourth boy,' my aunt said. 'I'm sure she's so disappointed.'

'Maybe they'll have a girl next,' I said.

'No,' my aunt said. 'She's going to have a surgery now so that this is her last one. But she had hoped it would be a girl.'

'When Brindha was born, had you wanted a girl or a boy?' I asked.

'Oh, a girl, absolutely,' my aunt said. 'In our Nair families, you want girls. Girls keep the family together and they keep the family name going.'

'So when do we get to see auntie's new baby?'

'You can go see them in a few weeks if you like. I'm going to go see her now, because the baby came early and needs a lot of care – she asked me to come so she doesn't have to manage with only her mother-in-law and the nanny.'

'You're going to leave now?'

'Tomorrow morning I'll go with the driver down to the city, and then catch a train, maybe book a sleeper compartment.' She was lost in thought.

'So I guess we're not going to the dance, then?' I said. I was simultaneously disappointed and relieved.

'Sanjay can't possibly miss that; it's a big company affair. And how lucky that you're here – at least he still has an escort.'

'I'd been thinking that Ammamma – '

'Ammamma must take some photos when you and Sanjay are all dressed up. We can send them to your parents, too.'

The point at which it was still possible to back out had passed. At the very least, I would tell Ammamma to wait up for us, and when we came back from the country club, we would have a small birthday celebration. Even if it was late and it was just me and my uncle and Ammamma, I would sit with her and tell her about everything at the party and repeat myself if she asked and be very patient.

My aunt wanted to make sure everything was arranged before she left, so she laid out dozens of her saris and salwar kameezes on her bed, and I modelled one after another. I didn't have many sari blouses, so that limited my sari options.

'We'll have to get more blouses made for you this summer. I'll let the tailor know,' my aunt said. 'Try this sari on – I think it will match that blue blouse you have.'

Having dressed me in six yards of blue and grey shot silk, my aunt seemed, finally, satisfied. Then she changed her mind. She asked me to take out my things from home so she could look through them.

We settled on my black dress with a cream coloured border at the neck and hem, with strappy black sandals of my aunt's. Reema auntie was happier with this. 'You don't look natural enough in a sari.'

'Mother never lets me wear black to Indian functions at home. She says it's morbid.' A few times, my mother had brought home her idea of proper, perky dresses from Bloomingdale's. They always had a little bow at the back of the waist: I made her return them. Inevitably, I gave in and wore salwar kameezes to most family parties rather than listen to my mother disparage my clothes.

Reema auntie laughed. 'The older people may say it's morbid, but the ladies at the club read fashion magazines – they know the modern styles.'

Reema auntie took out box after box of jewellery from a safe under her bed. She gave me a set of gold jumki earrings and a gold choker with a teardrop pendant. I hoped she couldn't see Steve's necklace under my dress collar, because she would want me to take it off. She slipped my American gold rings – 14 carat yellow gold rather than 22 carat Indian red gold – off my fingers, saying, 'Better to wear nothing than to wear something too plain.'

Her words stayed with me as my uncle squired me through the grand French-windowed entrance, into the club rooms. There were lots of candles – everyone glowed and glittered in the hazy light. How could my aunt have let me go in there with this shapeless dress on surrounded by ladies in beautiful filmy chiffon things? And yet I could hardly have attracted more attention if I were wearing nothing – I tried not to look back at the many eyes turning to follow us as my uncle manoeuvred us through the room. He introduced me to the club's director, Ravi, and his wife Lalu. Ravi was a big, broad-shouldered man wearing a tight jacket, sloshing a glass with a lot of ice so it made clinking noises. Lalu wore an ice-queen sari of ivory bordered in gold and black, her upswept hair was lacquered and untouchable. Her expertly cut sari blouse framed a heavy diamond choker that climbed high on her thin neck. Lalu had an aimless pink smile and eyes that constantly fluttered around the room. I tried to smile and nod as they talked about cricket, labour disputes at the factory, what kind of tea season the weather would produce.

'Our tasters are concerned – the tea may not be as high-grade from these parts this year, and we hear from up north that Darjeeling is having a splendid growing season,' my uncle said.

'Then we'll all drink Darjeeling tea this year in India and export our low-grade stuff to Chicago or some such place, why don't we?' Ravi said. Everyone laughed loudly. He pronounced the 'ch' in Chicago like 'cherry'.

'Can I get you a drink to start or would you rather play first and drink later?' Ravi asked.

'Lalu, you'll take her, won't you?' my uncle said.

'Of course, Sanjay, she'll be fine with me,' Lalu said. Ravi clapped his hand on my uncle's back and they walked across the dance floor to the long sleek chrome bar. Lalu put a bony hand on my shoulder and steered me in the opposite direction, out through one room into another, and then into a small alcove. There was dark wood and cane, and plush cushions tossed haphazardly on carpets and couches. Ladies were sitting and standing, a blur of saris, and everywhere, the clinking of glasses.

Lalu nudged me to a sofa and sat on another sofa next to a fat lady who looked like she had sunk deeply, irretrievably, into the cushions.

'Lalu, we thought you'd left us,' the lady said, handing a lipsticked glass to Lalu.

Lalu drank a sip, then nodded a waiter over. 'The ice has melted in this drink. Can you bring another one, please?'

'Is it punch, mem?'

'Yes, and also a cola for the girl there.' She pointed to me, the waiter nodded, and walked away. To everyone else, she said, 'This is Maya, Sanjay and Reema's niece.'

'Aren't you the lucky duck?' the fat lady said. 'We've just been talking about them, and we've decided Sanjay and Reema are by far the nicest couple we know. '

'Yes, Reema's an absolute favourite up here,' another lady said. 'It's too bad that they'll be leaving us.'

'Oh, has Sanjay got his transfer already then?' someone else said.

'No, no, it won't come for a while. They like him, and they will give him what he wants, but he hasn't put in enough time yet.'

'If Reema were only tougher, they would do better to stay here. He's well positioned at the company, my husband tells me.'

'Reema's too sensitive about her daughter. We all have our children in boarding school and we manage – she should realize that.'

'What can you do? If your daughter was having difficulties at boarding school, you would have to think about living somewhere else, wouldn't you?'

'But children are adaptable – they can handle anything if they are told that they have to. If the mother's too easy on them, or if she wants the child home for herself, then that's where the problem is – it's the mother, not the child.'

'Strange, too, because Reema and Sanjay seem to get along well. You'd think they would be happy now that they have time to do meaningful things together, not run after homework and dance lessons and such.'

I had to say something. 'There's nothing wrong with Reema auntie and Sanjay uncle. They just want to be able to raise Brindha themselves.'

'Parents are not always the best people to raise their own children. They can't provide discipline and structure as well as a boarding school can. You'll see these things when you're a mother, dear.'

'And children learn so much from their peers. The best thing you can do is make sure they're schooled in an upstanding environment, with the right sort of people.'

I didn't want to argue.

I was brought a glass of ice with a bottle of Limca soda.

'No ice, please,' I told the waiter, and, with a quick turn of the wrist, he simply dumped the ice on to his tray and handed the glass back to me.

'I'm sure the ice cubes are purified – you needn't worry we'll make you ill,' Lalu said.

I hadn't thought anyone would notice my carefulness. I felt my face grow hot. 'Oh, I don't really like ice anyway.'

'In this heat? Ice is the only thing that gets me through the day,' the fat lady said. She held up her glass, fogged and beaded with water, in an imaginary toast.

'Remember how ghastly it was before the company gave us backup power supply through the factory?' said a lady in a sparkly red sari. 'When the electricity used to go off for days at a time, I would go to bed dreaming of ice, and soft drinks, and mango lassi.'

'When I was carrying my second, I had terrible cravings for lassi. My husband would get our servant girl to pour lassi into an airtight whiskey bottle and lower it on a rope down our well so it would stay cold enough.'

It was going to be a long night. There was no one my

age. I hadn't considered before coming that their kids would be at their boarding schools. It was just me and the adults. And my uncle had disappeared on me. I sat quietly and sipped my drink and listened to the prattle: the problems of servants, of finding good courts for lawn tennis, of measles breaking out at their children's boarding schools, of journeying to Mysore or Bangalore or Madras to help some niece or sister or godchild pick out a wedding trousseau, because in this forsaken place you certainly couldn't do anything 'properly'.

I kept thinking about my mother. These women were not so different from her. They all knew English, Hindi, and at least one other language, they were well bred and well educated, with master's degrees in political science or economics or biology. But none of them had jobs – some of them had never had one at all. The one in the red sari was a doctor who had graduated from an elite medical institute. She hadn't practised in over ten years, she said.

'Maya's asking why I don't practise medicine any more,' she announced to the group.

'How could Vandana practice? She was an oncologist; there are no cancer patients here, no hospital here, just the company's infirmary.'

'Would you want to work in the infirmary then?' I asked.

'It has nothing to do with what I was trained for. I don't want to bandage children who fall off their bikes and tea pluckers who are bitten by snakes and wives having false labour. That's not medicine I'm interested in.'

'Sometimes there must be real illnesses, even cancer, up here?' I said.

'Yes, in any population there will be some serious illness.' Vandana spoke with exaggerated patience, like she was talking to someone who was not very bright.'But anything serious would be sent down to the city for treatment at a fully equipped hospital.'

'Do you think we should work just for the sake of work-ing, like women do in America, even if it's menial or not interesting?' Lalu said to me.

'I didn't say that. I was just – '

'Don't jump on her, Lalu,' said a woman who hadn't spo-ken before, coming to my aid. She looked like a large hon-eybee, rounded at the middle and dressed in a black and yel-low salwar kameez. 'Our wealth and our social status come from our husbands' jobs. But we have no embarrassment about that, and I think this is what is new to Maya.'

'In these remote places where our husbands' jobs take us, making life palatable for them is a full-time occupa-tion,' said the fat lady from among the cushions. 'They could not survive up here without us, and they know it.'

'There are men here tonight at this dance who are unmarried, but none over thirty, none rank even an assis-tant manager. The unmarried ones want to marry soon so they can stay here and do well.'

'And the company is grateful to us. There is an unspo-ken understanding that the women will take care of the men and the company will take care of the women – con-tribute to our lending library, open country clubs and throw garden parties, pay our children's tuition, our trips to see family, our medical care. Ask your uncle – he will tell you this is how it works.'

'Come, let's all go back to the main room. There's prob-ably a little time for dancing before dinner.'

In the main room, the one we'd first come into, the can-dles had been augmented with chandeliers. The dance floor was bordered on one side by couches and settees filled with ladies who weren't dancing. The orchestra was on another side, and opposite it were the doors to the verandah, open for the night breezes, through which I could see the staff setting up dinner. Directly across the dance floor from the settees was the bar. There and in the rooms behind it were the men.

I danced with a cluster of ladies to some Hindi film music, and then a Madonna song came on. I tried not to dance the way we danced at home, our eyes blank and unsmiling in a sexy daze, hips slowly rolling. I modified and adjusted my steps to match the women around me so I would not seem so American, so improper. Slow songs were easier. Lalu's husband, Ravi, came and asked me to dance, and I danced with him the way I would dance with my friends' fathers at a wedding or a Christmas party – plenty of air between us, hands held lightly, his hand on my waist, far from my hips.

One of the unmarried twenty-somethings asked me to dance. Suraj wore dark framed glasses, but his seriousness was undermined by his symmetrical dimples. He told me he was a chemist, he was involved with the processing and preserving of the tea. He asked me about New York and whether I'd ever been to the New York Public Library. He said he'd seen it in the movie *Ghostbusters*, and he'd heard it was the biggest library anywhere. He said he'd heard there were a lot of Indians in New York now, in a place called Jersey City. I told him that Jersey City was in another state called New Jersey and there were a lot of Indians now, there and in New York both. He was the first person who asked if I missed home and meant America.

As we made a turn on the dance floor, I saw my uncle standing a few feet away. As soon as the music stopped, he approached us.

'This is my niece. Have we been introduced?' my uncle said.

'I didn't know, Mr Pillai. I am sorry. Ravi suggested ask-

ing her to dance – I assumed she was here with his family,'
Suraj said, his words nervously tripping out on top of each
other. He gave my uncle his business card and said, 'I work
for Mr Sethi and Mr Menon. It is good to make your
acquaintance, Mr Pillai.'

'Likewise,' my uncle said, and led me away, his hand
tightly over mine.

'I thought you'd forgotten about me. Where have you
been all this time, Sanjay uncle?'I said.

'With some colleagues I haven't seen in years. I trust
Lalu introduced you around?'

'Yes, she did, but I was wondering when you'd come
back and rescue me,' I said.

'You don't like Lalu?' my uncle said.

'Well, she's a little cold.' Bitchy was what I meant.

'She can take some getting used to. But she and Ravi
have had us over a number of times, and they're really
quite a lot of fun. Who else did you meet?'

'I didn't catch all the names – there were so many funny
names, like Bunny and Baby and Cuckoo.'

'This set uses pet names more than we do,' my uncle
said. 'Especially the ladies. Your aunt and I have been trying to think of nicknames for ourselves before they think
of ones for us.'

The music stopped and a stocky moustached man
climbed up on the band's platform and announced awards
for the year's events. My uncle took second place in tennis,
within his age group, and first place in table tennis, across all
age groups. The fat lady won two trophies, in golf and in
darts. The bumblebee won for biggest jackfruit in the harvest
festival. Reema auntie won a first in gardening for her tulips.

'Reema will be happy,' my uncle said. 'Her tulips won
last year, too.'

'How does she grow tulips in this kind of weather?' I

said, thinking of our tulips pushing through the last crusts of winter snow in March.

'The tulips bloom in the cool months – in November, December,' he said. 'And before the hot months and the monsoon, by February or so, Reema pulls the bulbs up and puts them in the refrigerator until September. Look in the butter compartment – you'll see.'

Dinner was served out on the verandah and on the patio just beyond it. The food was good, but very spicy, and I couldn't balance my waterglass with my plate. I ate a lot of naan to calm the burn, and then some plain rice too.

I surrendered my plate to an impatient waiter, and went to the row of sinks on the far side of the verandah to wash my hands and mouth. When I came back to the milling people, my uncle had disappeared. I stood on tiptoe and tried to find his slightly greying head among the others. I went back inside, where the dance floor was empty except for a few bedraggled flowers. The musicians having a break, wiping instruments clean, readjusting music sheets, getting drinks from the bar.

I went behind the bar towards the dim lights in the next rooms. This side of the club was much darker – less lighting, more wood, with smoke thickening the air. Bottles of imported liquor stood on side tables, clusters of men were playing billiards, or playing cards, or standing and talking. Some were smoking cigars and pipes and, because they were planters and this was not Bombay or Delhi, chewing tobacco. Everyone looked up as I walked past them, but anyone whose eye I caught politely looked away.

'I'm trying to find my uncle, Sanjay Pillai. Do you know where he might be?' I asked the group encircling a billiards table in the middle of the room.

After a long awkward silence, one man said, 'I just saw

him step out. I'm sure he'll be back soon.'

'He's not in this round, but he's in the next one,' another man volunteered.

'Would you like me to go and find him for you?' said the first man, pausing as he chalked up a stick.

'No, thanks, you look like you're in the middle of a game,' I said, venturing closer to the billiards table. 'Is this like pool?'

'A little. The scoring's different. And the size of the table. Do you know how to play pool?'

'My friend at home in New York has a pool table in her rec room. So we play sometimes, but I'm not as good as she is. She can even beat her brother and he's really good.'

'So you're Sanjay's niece from New York?'

'Yes, I'm Maya,' I said. 'How do you know Sanjay uncle?'

He didn't answer me, calling over his shoulder, 'Come here, Ravi, Chirag – see, here is another example. This girl is Sanjay's niece, pure South Indian, and see how light-skinned?'

Ravi and Chirag came over, ice clinking in their glasses, liquid sloshing over the edge, I moved back a little to keep my dress from getting stained. All three were my uncle's age – married, moneyed, confident of their charms, confidently in charge of this club, this company, this evening. They peered at me and, sensing their open appreciation, I stood taller, kept my hands still at my sides.

Chirag said, 'She's light-skinned, yes, Giresh, but not that light-skinned. I still say there is no way to tell a Sri Lankan girl from a South Indian one.'

'You're wrong, I tell you, Chirag. Our girls are much fairer. That woman Dhanu – they should have known right away from looking at her that she was a Sri Lankan and kept her away from Rajiv Gandhi. She was so dark, almost black. They should have known.'

Ravi spoke. 'Listen to yourself, Giresh. You're saying just by looking at her I can know whether she's the type of girl who will strap a bomb on a belt around her hips under her nice clothes and blow us all up?' I felt them looking at me, as if they were trying to imagine what it would all look like – the bomb, the belt, my hips.

'Of course she wouldn't,' Giresh said. 'It's not the pretty ones who become killers, it's the dark, homely ones who don't have any other way of getting attention. Blowing up leaders is the only way dark-skinned girls will ever get to have their picture in magazines.'

'You don't need to do something like that, do you?' Chirag said. His voice was low, intimate. I shook my head no, tried to smile. There was a certain tension, but I felt unafraid in this room full of men, full of ice and warm gin. It was the first time I'd felt really awake, alert, all evening.

'Are you going to play or talk?' another man said to Giresh. Giresh gave me an apologetic smile and stepped up for his turn.

'If he loses he's going to blame it on you, you know. He'll say it's because he was trying to keep Sanjay's niece entertained, and he was too distracted to play well,' Chirag said to me.

'If she plays, maybe she'll trounce you,' Giresh said to Chirag.

'I'll play if you teach me the scoring first,' I said.

'Sanjay, what do you say? Shall we all play?' Ravi said to my uncle, who had just come into the room.

'I don't think so,' he said, coming to stand next to me. 'If you're tired now, the driver can take you home – it's no trouble.'

'I'm not tired, Sanjay uncle. I'm fine.'

'Are you sure?' my uncle looked steadily at me. 'You look tired – maybe we'll get some fresh air.'

My uncle walked me to the verandah out back. The remains of dinner littered the fabric-covered tables. Light, filtering through the windows of the club, brightly illuminated the porch, the patio, the sprawl of gardens beyond.

'These are colleagues of mine,' my uncle said. 'Please be careful.'

'What do you mean, Sanjay uncle? What have I done wrong?'

'It's not just what you do, it's what everyone else does. You don't see any other ladies in the billiards rooms, do you? If the men are drinking a lot, or if they are talking freely, some will be embarrassed that you are there, they will be less comfortable, have less of a good time. This party is for everyone to relax among friends. Do you know what I am trying to say?'

'They came up to talk to me, I didn't make them,' I said. I felt defensive.

'I know, Maya. I just don't want anything to go wrong. I will bring you here some other night and teach you billiards, maybe next week,' he said, his tone softening. 'It's probably a dangerous thing to teach you – you'll be better than me in no time, won't you?'

'Do you want to send me home now?' I asked stiffly.

'Stay if you want to – there'll be dancing for another hour or two, and usually there are games for everyone together, charades or something. We can go home together. Shall I take you back to Lalu or to Bunny or someone?'

'No, I can find my way. I promise I won't cause trouble. I'll see you later at charades,' I said.

My uncle left the verandah and went back to the billiards room. I was tired of adults, tired of trying to make sense of them and make sense around them. I didn't want to go sit with Lalu or anyone else. But going home felt like admitting defeat. I looked out from the verandah at an enormous grid of half-grown trees. A maze was mapped out there, but the bushes were only waist-high, so it wasn't much of a maze yet. I opened the patio gate to walk out to see it up close.

'I don't think you should go out there.' It was the chemist.

'Why not? I always walk in our compound at night.'

'But this is much nearer to the woods, and there are wild boar around here at night,' Suraj said.

'Wild boar? You're serious?'

'Yes, absolutely. Look, they've destroyed these flower beds. Look here.' There were deep jagged furrows through the flower garden just outside the gate. The blossoms were mashed and the roots bared to the sky.

'A wild boar did that?'

'Yes, and see over to the left of that tuberose – you can see the footprints, hoofprints actually.'

'Where are you looking? I don't see,' I said, leaning over the gate next to him. He was pointing to the left and I pointed at what I thought was a tuberose. 'You mean over there with the pink buds?'

'No, farther to the right, the one with the white flowers, see?' Suraj said, touching my hand lightly in a leftward nudge to direct my vision. It was so quick and light it almost seemed as if it hadn't happened. He had held my hand earlier when we were dancing, but that was just part of dancing. His hand touching mine out here in the quiet half-light half-dark felt like a whisper, a question, a declaration.

'Yes, I see now,' I said, even though I didn't.

'Then do you see the footprints. They're just next to the rose,' he said.

'Yeah, I do,' I said, trying to sound like I did. 'But I want to see how the maze works. Why don't we go out there just for a few minutes? I'm not ready to go back inside the club with those stuffy people.'

'But the boar could come back. That's what I've been trying to tell you.'

'If you're there, there'll be two of us. We can warn each other if it's coming and run back inside the gate, or we can make some noise and scare it away.' I lifted the latch on the gate and took a couple of steps. If he wanted to be alone with me, this was his chance.

He hesitated, but he followed me to the gate, saying, 'You know, my father climbed his first tree when he saw a boar, and he didn't even think he knew how.'

'I've never seen a real-life maze,' I said. 'Whose idea was this?'

'Mr Sethi, one of the senior vice presidents – he was posted in England for a few years, and he was taken to all these fancy homes and gardens, and he wanted to try to make one like what he saw there.'

'Right now, it's too easy to see the exits. I wonder how long it will take for the trees to grow and knit together.' We walked through the first few turns and twists of the maze.

'Not very long, everything grows fast here. They started growing these trees two years ago, and they're already three feet. Come, let's go back to the clubhouse, Maya. People might wonder where you are.'

'Do you think when it's finished, we could actually get lost in here – or only kids would?'

'I saw the blueprints that Mr Sethi had given to the club to work from – they're pretty complex. Of course, there's only a certain number of options, and with adults, they'll try each one and narrow it down to the right way out. The difference with children is that they aren't logical like that.'

'Let's crouch down so that the hedges are over our heads, and see if we can find our way out.' I knelt down on the ground and waited for him to do the same.

He reached down and put his hands around my waist. He pulled me up off my knees so that I was standing facing him. I thought he was going to kiss me then.

'Maya, what are you doing?' he said. 'Now you've got mud all over your dress, what will people think?'

'Oh, it's OK,' I said, brushing at it with my hand. The dirt faded into the black part of the dress, but the cream-coloured border showed the grass stains and dirt in high relief.

He took out a handkerchief and handed it to me.

'I don't think that'll make a difference,' I said, handing it back to him.

'You could at least try,' he said.

I took the handkerchief from him again and rubbed it across the border, where the brown and green were already set like indelible ink. 'See? It won't come out until it's washed or dry cleaned. But I don't think it's ruined.'

'Who cares if it's ruined. How can you walk back to the clubhouse like that?' His voice was tense and clenched. 'Do you understand what your uncle will think? Do you know who your uncle is? He could have me sacked, and I won't even have a chance to explain. Not that I would blame anyone for not believing me. I should never have been out here alone with you.'

'I can tell them nothing happened.' I looked at him, I tried to make him look at me. 'Why are you so mad?'

'They'll think you're lying when you say nothing happened and they won't blame you for lying. Because you would want to protect your reputation. They'll think I came after you.'

'But they know you – they won't think that once we explain.'

'I was doing so well at the company, I might even have

been posted abroad, away from these riots and government problems and whatnot. Maybe Singapore, or even America, somewhere with good laboratories where I could do advanced work. And now . . .'

'Stop it. You're being ridiculous. Look, I'll fix everything, don't worry,' I said.

'You can't 'fix' it, you don't understand how things work here. God, the longer I'm out here with you the worse this looks. At least go back inside now, and I'll work out by myself what I'm going to do.'

There had to be a way out of this. I was starting to realize even if I'd done nothing wrong, I'd have to explain to my uncle what I was doing out here in the first place. After I'd already told him that I would be careful and not cause trouble! He was just like my mother when things went wrong – he never got mad at me, he got disappointed. They were both like that, they would just close up and back away from you and they wouldn't want to share with you or laugh with you about anything for a while. 'Maybe they didn't even see you come out here,' I said.

'No, the bar staff saw you going into the gardens. They told me to stop you. I should never have let you force me to come out here.'

'I forced you to come out here?' I thought he came out here because he liked me, but now that was too embarrassing to say. 'I thought you wanted to be out here, too, away from all those boring people.'

'Those people are people I work for, people whose respect I want. I only came out here to keep you from getting into trouble. Which was a big mistake.'

'Look,' I said. 'I'm sorry it's a big mistake to be around me. If you can just stop hating me and listen for a second, I'll tell you what to do.'

'What?' he said.

'Go bring me food from the tables on the verandah – anything dark, like chicken curry or black bean curry. I'll say a waiter spilled a plate of food down the front of my dress. In case anyone is looking, go by the side and stay out of the light and I'll wait here.'

He brought back a heaped plate of food. I scooped some black beans into my hands and smeared it across the border of my dress. I held the dress away from my body as I dipped the hem of it in the plate to soak up the curry. I squeezed the hem to get out the excess liquid, and the fabric bled oily dark reds and browns on to my hands. I threw the plate of food into the hedges, and dried my hands by wiping them through the grass.

He held out his handkerchief again and I used it to blot the last of the curry off my fingers.

'That should do it,' I said. 'Should we walk back now?'

'I'm sorry you had to do that to your dress.'

'Yeah, well, it's just a dress.'

'I'm sorry I was getting rude. I was nervous. Can you understand?'

'I guess,' I said, not looking at him as we approached the exit to the maze.

'Maya,' he said. He tipped my chin up with his hand so that I had to look at him. 'I don't hate you. You're a nice girl. Maybe sometime over the summer you can ask your aunt and uncle to invite me over for tea or dinner or something.'

'Is that because you want me to like you or you want my uncle to like you?' I said.

'That's not a very polite question,' he said.

'I like honest people more than polite people,' I said.

'I want you both to like me. That's honest, isn't it?' he said. 'I went to college up north – that's the only reason I even know how to talk to a girl like you. We don't talk about 'liking' girls here, not unless you're marrying her.'

'I know that. I just meant like me as a friend,' I said, although I hadn't really.

'I like you as a friend already, OK?' he said, but there was a long silence after that and he looked at me in a way that made me feel giddy and tremulous. 'But even as friends, I can't invite you anywhere that will be proper to your aunt and uncle, so I'd like very much for you or your uncle to invite me to see you at your house or here at the club sometime.'

'That's only if my uncle ever invites me to the club again after he sees what I look like tonight,' I said. We closed the gate behind us and started across the patio. 'I think it's better we go in separately. I'll stay out here and come in later.' He nodded, his face composed, distant, a different person already from the one who had just said all those things. He didn't even glance back at me as he swung open the doors and shut them behind him.

There was charades but I didn't play. Around four in the morning, the kitchen staff at the club were awakened and brought from their cottages across the greens to make an early breakfast. When we reached home, it was still dark but there was pink edging over the next hill. Vasani was mopping the dew off the windows, and Matthew and Sunil were in the kitchen grinding the rice flour for fresh idli batter for breakfast. I took off my dress and threw it somewhere in the dark at the foot of the bed, too tired to care. Lying in bed, half-asleep, I remembered that we hadn't done anything for Ammamma's birthday. We'd come home so late and we'd let it pass. Doing something tomorrow was not the same thing.

I went to her room and she was still sleeping, though she was usually up at this time. How late had she waited up for us? I shook her, and said, 'Happy birthday,

Ammamma, I didn't know we'd be out so late.' She looked at me sleepily, reached up and pulled the drooping jasmine out of my hair, and asked me if she should have Matthew walk Boli or would I be up in time to do it. I promised her I'd be up in time to walk him, and she nodded drowsily, sinking back into sleep. I returned to my room and my bed and lay face down so as not to see the streak of sun at the window.

CHAPTER FOUR

The British Are Coming

IT WAS ALREADY hot at five-thirty in the morning. In New York, I could hardly get out of bed before checking the weather in the papers or on TV. In the winter I called the seventy-five-cents-a-minute ski weather bureau to get exact predictions as to winds, amount of precipitation, time of day the sun would go down. I liked to be prepared.

None of that was necessary in Tamil Nadu. It had been an unusually hot and dry summer. The nights were cooler, just enough to tease me into sleep, but the heat came crashing back again before six every morning. I could hear my grandmother's rustlings in the next room as she unlatched the windows and pushed them out. The other day I was up this early, I thought I would go sit on the front porch and read magazines. I liked being up alone – at home, I ruled the house until my parents woke. But Ammamma broke her morning prayers to fuss over me, to prepare tea for me and make breakfast without the servants. I hadn't even been able to go out to the porch, because Ammamma pointed out all the slugs that had crept up on to the smooth red stone in the night and would need to be salted and swept away when the servants arrived.

Today, I decided to stay in bed until a more reasonable hour. I watched the birds that nested in the jackfruit tree outside my window organize themselves for morning chores and take flight, find worms, and return. I wondered why the birds didn't just live off the jackfruit. Maybe the newborns didn't like jackfruit. Or maybe they needed protein. I watched them take turns, one guarding, the other flying away. Matthew and the gardener were talking as they walked towards the back door, and the frightened birds rushed up into higher branches, their nest pitifully exposed. I got up to go ask Matthew to heat water for a bath.

My cousin Madhu must have already boarded the flight from Bombay to Coimbatore. She was supposed to land at eight o'clock, and Sanjay uncle had stayed in Coimbatore last night on business so that he could be there today at the airport. He was good about that, being there right when the flight landed, as if he knew how nervous it could make her, standing by herself wrestling with turbaned porters who were probably trying to mount her suitcases on their heads before she had even agreed to purchase their services.

Of course when Madhu arrived, I realized she wouldn't have been nervous at all if Sanjay uncle had been late; she wasn't the nervous type. She had come with lots of luggage, she was not interested in being self-sufficient, she knew people would help her; they would want to help her. She was beautiful in a way that demanded notice – tall, wearing high stacked heels and a short lime-green dress, a polyester one, the kind that cool girls at my school recycled out of their mother's seventies wardrobe, but that Madhu or I had to buy in a flea market to make up for a lack of history. Why didn't she worry about twisting an ankle in the customs line with all those wheeled carts around? Why didn't she think about how cold it usually was on international flights? Or wearing a dark colour in case of spills? Or being dressed more like a nice Indian girl walking into this house?

Madhu begged off from having lunch right away and went out on the porch with a pack of Camel Lights. She looked so American that I was continually surprised by her British accent.

She laughed when I told her that. She said, 'It's your accent that's off, you know. That American advertising voice – you sound like you're selling laundry detergent.'

I asked her whether my aunt and uncle were coming from England anytime soon.

'Mum and Dad hate the heat, and Dad got ill last time we came four years ago - hepatitis B from eating mussels during the monsoon. They're too busy to go on holidays that disrupt their schedules like that. They'll come back only for big things – births, deaths – but not just to come say hello.'

'Don't they miss it here?' My parents had come every year since they'd emigrated twenty years ago, except for these last three years when I had wanted normal summers like other kids. They used to keep a calendar in the kitchen marking the months and days until our next trip.

'Sometimes it's five or six years between trips for us. It's expensive to come out here, and there are other places we want to go—we went to Sweden a year ago, and to Russia before that. Mum wants to go to Greece for a few weeks next summer, maybe even go sailing out there.'

I'd never been to Russia or anywhere like that. After going to India every summer, my parents never had many holiday days left over. Some years we went with my parents' friends the Bavnanis and their daughter Rena on a driving trip for a long weekend. We'd gone to Williamsburg once, Saratoga another time. My mother liked it to be historical so we would learn something. The only time I had been abroad, not counting India, was one summer when we were en route to India and we used the stopover to stay in Paris for a few days. I remembered crying at the Eiffel Tower because my mother thought it was too dangerous to go all the way to the top. Because she didn't like heights, none of us got to go up. I dropped Mother's camera cover into the Seine when we were on a boat trip. I don't think she believed me that it was an accident.

'Do you know how to sail?' I said. Sailing seemed very glamorous, and very upper-class, to me.

'I can't, but Mum and Dad were learning with some friends who sail. They like the idea of it, I think – being far from people, independent, relying on your own resources. When they retire in a few years, they want to sail more, go on more trips. What are your parents going to do when they retire?'

'I don't know,' I said, thinking hard about whether they had said anything about it. 'I think they have a while, because I have to go to college and stuff. I know they want to come back here, because Sanjay uncle bought some property for his family and our family near the coast.'

'So they're going to come back and relive the past. Doesn't sound very adventurous. Maybe they'll change their plans, hopefully for your sake.'

'I kind of think it's nice if they come out here,' I said. It was better than picturing them in some old people's resort in Florida or Arizona.

'But you'd have to come here and visit them and feel guilty whether you do enough for them or see them enough, just like our parents feel. Why go through that?'

'I like coming to India,' I said, believing it more as I heard myself say it, reacting defensively to Madhu's disdain. 'I like seeing my aunts and uncles and going places with them. Don't you?'

'Well, of course you like coming here. Sanjay uncle and Reema auntie are sweethearts, I like staying here too. And the rest of Dad's family live in pretty nice setups – I don't mind going to see them. But Mum's family lives in a miserable little village. My brother and I always beg not to go there – there's no septic system or anything and the whole town reeks. And everyone stares at us because we have shoes. Sometimes, Mum gets her sisters and their husbands to come and meet us in the city nearby, and we pay for them to take the overnight train in and stay at a lodge with us. But one time her oldest sister asked if she could just have the money instead to use for her son's school fees, and Mum was hurt that they didn't even want to see us.'

'Are you going to go see them next?'

'No, this is my holiday – I'm just seeing who I want to see. Just you all, and my cousin Deepa who lives in Bombay – I don't think you know her. And I'm meeting my flatmates in Goa – they wanted to do India for Margy's

hen party. It should be a good time.' The Canary Islands
used to be the place to go, Madhu said, but now it was
tacky, and India was hot – bhangra rock, mehndi,
Hinduism. They were spending some days in Goa at the
beach, and then they were trekking for a week.

It made hanging out here seem boring. My whole day
yesterday – walking around with Brindha's dog Boli and
helping him chase birds, playing cards with Reema auntie
and her friends – seemed kind of lame.

'I love going to the beach,' I said. 'I go to my friend
Steve's beach house a lot back home.' I decided in that
moment to edit out the fact that Steve was sort of more
than a friend, because he wasn't exactly my boyfriend
either, and anyway, Madhu would probably think it all
sounded very teenagerish.

'You can come to Goa with us if you want. You can't
come trekking – no offence, but I don't want to be responsible for you. If you've never trekked before, you should go
with a beginner group, not with us.'

'That's OK, the beach sounds better to me anyway,' I said
quickly, glad she had invited me even on part of her trip.
'That would be really nice.'

'Ask Reema auntie first. And let me know soon, OK?'
Madhu put out her second cigarette and crushed the
empty cigarette pack. She threw it off the porch on to the
pile of scraps heaped up on one side of the yard. The servants lit a match to the trash, and they stirred the pile of
trash with a big stick, like they were stirring a pot of oat-
meal, so it heated evenly, and burned without much
smoke. It was a daily, conscious objective, not to create too
much waste. All the food remnants were taken by the servants at the end of the day, to feed milkcows kept by some
of their families. They took the newspapers, too – some for
their children to practise reading, and some they used for

wrapping fish or vegetables they bought at the market. There would be that burned rubber smell all day from the few plastic containers that my aunt could not recycle for some other use, the few that defeated her imagination.

'The tailor will be here soon, so why don't you both come and have lunch?' my aunt said from the doorway.

Madhu was on a special diet – she ate nothing cooked at lunch, and nothing raw at dinner. This made for an odd assortment on her plate: yogurt (heated and fermented she didn't count as cooked), bananas, mango, tender green beans and carrots. My aunt had prepared a regular lunch for me, I ate rice and pullishery and potatoes and beans. My uncle, who missed work all morning because of the airport trip, would not come home for lunch today, so Reema auntie sent the driver to the factory with food for him.

As the table was being cleared, my aunt said, 'We might as well let them come in even though they're early.'

I looked out on the front porch, and there were two people standing there patiently, carrying string-tied bundles on their heads. It was the tailor and the seamstress, and my aunt told Matthew to take them to the guest bedroom. As we followed them into the room, I saw Madhu's clothes strewn across the bed, and realized that meant she was sleeping there. I wondered how this was decided, that she would not sleep with either me or my grandmother. I felt a little indignant – that Madhu was guest enough to warrant the guest room and I was not – and also a little hurt that Madhu didn't want to share a room with me. It's one thing my not wanting to share a room with my grandmother, with all her particular ways. But I would have liked sharing a room with Madhu, watching her do her hair in the morning, put on her makeup. I had even cleaned up my room in preparation, moved my clothes to make space for her, stuffed some of my things into Brindha's half-full drawers. I had found in the bottom drawer of the bureau more of Brindha's stash of movie star pictures clipped from magazines. And also pictures of the terrorists Subha and Sivarasan, clipped from newspapers and newsweeklies, close-ups where I could tell his glass eye from the real one. And pamphlets with inscrutable Tamil words in runny green ink, and diagrams too, like the ones that came with a bike or a computer printer that my father would stare at for hours. I wondered if Rupa realized Brindha must have taken these pamphlets, and whether she felt safe anyway. I wondered who had provided Rupa with these instructions in the first place and if she had ever tried to put together an explosive or a poison compound. It was so far out of the realm of what girls were normally allowed to do that I could imagine feeling proud to occupy such a central role. When Dhanu had been entrusted with killing Rajiv Gandhi, did she feel proud to be chosen? It had come out in the papers that Sivarasan had been also wearing explosives on his own body and was loitering nearby as a backup. Dhanu must have felt the pressure to perform, to not be shown up by a man who was older and more experienced. I put the clippings and the pamphlets in my empty suitcase under the bed, and cleared two more drawers in the cupboard for Madhu.

My aunt brought Indian fashion magazines from her bedroom and gave them to Madhu. Madhu took some magazines out of her suitcase and gave them to my delighted aunt – *Elle, Vogue, Mademoiselle*. They were sold only in Bombay, and they were expensive – my uncle sometimes brought one for my aunt as a gift from a business trip. We sat on the bed and pored over the pages, scratching at perfume samples, tossing the postcards and inserts on the floor. The seamstress and tailor unrolled a

straw mat on the floor and then unpacked and arranged
their bundles on the mat. In the magazines she had
brought, Madhu had circled the dresses and outfits she
wanted the tailor to make for her, and my aunt went
through them, trying to figure out which ones he could do
a decent imitation of and which ones were beyond him.
The short swingy jersey dress she said would be easy, so
would the long straight column dress.

'I don't think you should ask him to make trousers,' my
aunt said in a low tone to Madhu. 'He doesn't have expe-
rience with that.'

'Who makes trousers for Sanjay uncle?' Madhu asked.

'Sanjay gets his trousers made down in the city, but that
tailor is a men's tailor.'

'Can't we ask him anyway?'

'I don't think so,' my aunt said. 'He's very respected. He
would be embarrassed.'

'Everyone's so prissy about everything,' Madhu said, as
she swung the lime green dress over her head. Underneath,
she had on a silky beige slip.

'Maya,' my aunt said. 'Will you also go and change, put
on a petticoat, and bring Madhu my dressing gown. She'll
be cold.'

I could tell my aunt did not want Madhu in lingerie in
front of the tailor, who was openly staring at her, but
Reema auntie refrained from saying anything directly. I
went to my aunt's room and got her robe off the back of
the wardrobe door. Then I went to my room and took off
the salwar kameez I was wearing, and put on a sari petticoat and a sari blouse. I went back to the guest room and
gave Madhu the robe. It didn't really cover her – she wore
it loose and open, and you could still see the shape and
bounce of her full breasts, the darker nipples outlined in
silk. My sari blouse was grey, and I wore a bra under it, but

I felt exposed with even just my stomach bared the way it was. I knew I was pretty enough for men, but not enough to feel secure around girls like Madhu.

The seamstress approached Madhu first with a tape measure in hand. Round the neck, then the upper arms, the wrists, across the fullest part of the breasts, then just under the breasts, at the waist, lower at the hips, then the length from waist to ankle. Madhu let the robe drop and stood tall and straight, the slip loose at the small of her back and then stretched tautly over her hips and thighs. Madhu went on talking serenely about the dress on page seventy-two, the one on page seventy-nine. My aunt started writing down a short list of the things Madhu was going to order. Then it was my turn. I tried to stand equally straight, to ignore the firm and yet indifferent hands travelling over my body. The seamstress called out each measurement to the tailor, who wrote them with a pencil stub in a dingy notebook. Madhu had picked up some of the bolts of fabric from the mat – day silk and heavy brocade silk, and cotton, linen, chiffon – and draped them against herself in the mirror.

'I had them order lots of light cottons from Coimbatore to show you girls because I thought that's probably what you wear more often than silks, since everything's so casual there.' By 'there', Reema auntie meant the *west* at large – London, Westchester, more of the same.

With a burgundy cotton held against her neck, Madhu frowned in the mirror at herself. 'The only problem is, none of this cotton has any lycra in it.'

'Spandex?' my aunt asked, confused, 'You mean like swimsuits?'

'Sort of like that. Look at the photo of that V-neck dress again. It could never be cut so smoothly if it didn't have lycra in it – how would she put it on?'

'I just thought it had side seams with a zipper, or snaps. You can get the same effect, the tailor can show you,' my aunt said.

Madhu looked sceptical, but the tailor showed how he could run extra folds down the seam of a skirt that could be kept open or shut for a billowy or straight look. He told Madhu good sewing was better than lycra because you had more choices. He made a face, saying, 'One size fits all, what they say in America, no?' He said lycra was the easy way out for selling clothes without fitting them or doing much work. My mother would have agreed with him – she said tailors in America had lost any sense of ingenuity. Most American tailors could only do minor adjustments on what you started with, like hemming a pair of trousers, or putting an elbow patch on a jacket. They were shocked when Mother brought them an old dress I'd outgrown and told them to cut off the skirt and put an elastic at the waistband and add velvet trim. Mother said only the Chinese tailors still knew how to invent things.

'OK, so that's four dresses and two skirts for Madhu,' my aunt confirmed the tailor's list. 'Maya, do you know what you want?'

I was kneeling on the mat, feeling the different textures of the fabric. 'I like this one,' I said, holding up a dark green nubby silk, but I had no idea what to make with it.

'We can talk later and I can show you more patterns. For now, let's get what Madhu wants because she's leaving soon and you have all summer. So four dresses and two skirts. That's it for the Western clothes. And now what about salwar kameez or ghaghra cholis or lehengas? You can buy readymade sets in Bombay, Madhu, but those will only be the current trend, so I thought you might want a few traditional full sets sewn that won't go out of style.'

Madhu didn't want full sets. She said she mixed and

matched Indian clothes with her usual clothes, that it
looked cool like that. She proposed a sari blouse out of
black satin for wearing with a miniskirt or jeans. She wanted red crepe made into a blouse and a dupatta; she said
her friend Sonali had made a similar blouse when she
came to India which they took turns wearing to college
parties. The green silk I was holding, Madhu wanted to
turn into a kameez shirt, but she wanted the tailor to sew
up the slits on the sides halfway, so she could wear it without the trousers as a dress.

Madhu said, 'Maya, you should have the same thing. It
would look good on her, don't you think, Reema auntie?'

My aunt looked doubtful. The things Madhu wore
would never be in good taste here. 'Let's make Maya a
proper salwar kameez out of the rest of the green silk.
You'll like that, won't you?' she asked.

I nodded, glancing apologetically at Madhu. I'd never
tried wearing my Indian clothes to parties and out with my
friends the way Madhu did. I wore salwar kameezes to
temple or to Indian holiday events at the homes of family
friends. I tried to imagine walking into temple with my
parents wearing only a kameez top and no trousers. I did-
n't think it would go down well.

The tailor was suggesting modifications to Madhu's
instructions. 'Puff sleeves are the fashion this year – you
must try puff sleeves on one of the blouses.'

Madhu looked horrified. 'I can't think of anything more
awful. Let's do three-quarter sleeves on one and traditional sleeves on the others.'

Now the tailor looked horrified. 'But madam, I haven't
done a three-quarter sleeve for anyone in at least two
years.'

'That's what I want,' Madhu said curtly. They went on to
negotiate over each neckline, on the front and the back of

each blouse, and then on the length of the blouse. The tailor couldn't understand how she could wear a sari blouse so short. If she wasn't going to wear a sari to veil her stomach, he wanted to make the blouse more like a fitted Punjabi jacket.

Madhu held her ground. As the tailor and the seamstress were discussing the final pricing with my aunt, Madhu sat down next to me on the bed. I thought she would be annoyed after wrangling with the tailor, but she was smiling. She said to me, 'Did you hear him when we were arguing? Did you hear him?'

'What do you mean?' I asked.

'While we were arguing, he picked up a British accent. I don't think it was conscious, but he was trying to sound superior, and he heard my accent – he was trying to match it. Listen to him talking to Reema auntie – he's still got it.'

And he did. I could hear the false English pitch as he said, 'Very good, madam, very fine, madam.'

'I get a kick out of that when I come to India. People are still in love with the English. It's the ultimate irony. I bet no one is trying to sound like you.'

That was true. My aunt and uncle made fun of me for the way I said my *t* like a *d*, in words like *party*, or *motorscooter*. And their friends sometimes had a hard time understanding me, whereas they understood Madhu perfectly, even though we both sounded foreign. But her intonations were what Indian English attempted and fell short of – they were the intonations Indians hoped to achieve.

'Face it, Maya. Indians respect Britain much more than they respect America. Every Indian still holds a candle for the Queen.'

'I don't wish I was British,' I said defensively.

'No, but you don't find it enough to be American, do you? All of you who went to the States, you come back here more than we do, like you're looking to be something more than American. In Britain, we know who we are, and we're not Indian. '

'I had an Indian passport until a couple years ago, so did Mother and Dad. Why can't we feel like we belong here?' Didn't Madhu, too, sometimes wish she belonged here?

'But it's not your future, is it? Are you really going to give up everything you have there so you can eat mango all year round and have a washerwoman do your laundry? It's quaint and beautiful here, but it's not real.'

I thought of what Madhu had said when I was looking through the bookshelf in the drawing room later that night. There were rows of leather-bound books, some fat, some thin, but all the same height, by people like Sir Oliver Goldsmith and Arnold Toynbee Thomas Hardy and Charles Dickens and Anthony Trollope. My uncle settled into an armchair nearby and put an oil lamp on the floor between us. 'What are you looking for?' he said.

'Something to read. How come all these books are British?'

'That's Macaulay's shelf,' my uncle smiled. 'We go in phases.' He said some years the education minister would proclaim global standards, and then the schools and colleges emphasized British textbooks and exams, so people could gain acceptance abroad. And then some years, a new party would Indianize everything, and then, Sanjay uncle said, the schools scrambled to replace their Hardy and Austen with Tagore and R. K. Narayan. And then it swung back the other way again.

Sanjay uncle explained, 'When I was in college, they were in a British phase – that's why we have those books. We have lots of Indian authors, too, but the books made locally are on poor-quality paper – they don't hold up to the heat and humidity well, so we keep the Indian books in the cupboard in our bedroom. You can ask Reema if you want – she'll take them out for you.'

'What about American books?' I said. My aunt came into the room just then, and curled up on a sofa across from us with a sketchpad in her lap. She was working on something new she wanted to send home with me for my mother.

'Like what?' my uncle said.

I thought of my reading assignments for the summer. 'Like the books I have to read for school, *The Old Man and the Sea* and *Huckleberry Finn*. Why has no one I talk to here read them?'

'Some people have, I'm sure,' my uncle said. 'I can read them while you're here to help you with your homework.'

'But why not your friends? Why not kids my age?'

My aunt spoke over my uncle's voice. 'Kids your age in America aren't reading Indian novels either. When America looks outside itself, it doesn't look to India, it looks to France and Germany and other places. When India looks outside itself, why should we look to America either?'

'Why look to England when you fought for independence against them?' It seemed so contradictory to me.

'England and India still have strong ties, and much to learn from each other,' my uncle said. 'America is too young to learn from. Those books you're reading, Americans read them because they are still working out how to tame nature, how to form a society. Those are not new things for us.'

'And America's problems with race, it consumes them, and it doesn't speak to us,' my aunt said. 'Class – we think about class, and England thinks about class, too. '

My uncle said, 'India does want to learn a couple of

things from America – how to make money the way Americans do, how to build a nuclear bomb. But those aren't things Americans are willing to teach anyone.'

'I thought India already knows how to make a nuclear bomb,' I said. 'Isn't that what Devi auntie's husband works on?'

'Yes, that's the Atomic Commission. We can build some things, but nothing like what America can build right now. Indians will never forget how America used the atom bomb to end World War Two. We never want to be in the position Japan was in, of total devastation. America was ruthless.'

'But Japan was with the Nazis,' I said, remembering my history class last year. 'India was on the same side as America and England. Isn't it good we won?'

'But what about when India's not on the same side as America?' my aunt said. 'How would we stop America from destroying us if they wanted?'

'You know,' Sanjay uncle said, 'some people are saying Subha and Sivarasan are not the real assassins, that it does- n't make sense for the Tigers to do this and lose their sym- pathizers here. Some people are saying it was America and the CIA that killed Rajiv Gandhi.'

'Why would America want to do that?' I said. I was care- ful to not say 'we' for America.

'Why wouldn't they? The CIA has plotted to kill other strong leaders before – even your president Jimmy Carter admitted as much when he passed a law to stop funding political assassinations.'

'So then it's outlawed already. They couldn't have done this,' I said, relieved.

Sanjay uncle scoffed. 'Do you think the Reagan-Bush empire obeys the law, especially a law passed by a Democratic president? The CIA might not want a strong

leader here in India. They might want to keep us impover-
ished and weak.'

I didn't have an answer, I felt like I didn't know enough
to keep up with them.

'Sanjay and I don't really think it's the CIA, Maya, but
it's certainly a possibility. You shouldn't be naive about
such things,' my aunt said.

'We don't want you to be brainwashed living over there.
Your parents wouldn't want that either,' my uncle said.

'You've been Indian longer than you've been anything
else,' my aunt said. 'Don't forget that.'

My aunt waved me over to sit next to her on the sofa.
'Do you think your mother will like this? I might add
another figure behind the well. What do you think?' My
aunt had sketched a stout woman carrying an urn of water
away from a well. She sketched a lot, and occasionally she
would expand a sketch into a full work, an oil on canvas.
There were two matching oils of Krishna's milkmaids in
her living room, and we had others at home in New York.
Houseguests had asked my mother if she would sell one,
so my mother was encouraging Reema auntie to send
some new pieces to us to see if anything might come of it.
My aunt hadn't tried selling her work in years. When she
had, the only thing people had bought were her art school
training canvases – copies of old masters, Renoirs, Titians,
Botticellis. Some rich people in India wanted Renaissance
infants in their living rooms. But my aunt didn't want to
paint any more of those, and so she'd gone back to just
painting for herself. The figures she had sketched recently
looked like they came from one family – they had beautiful faces, but their bodies were claylike, they had heavy feet
and legs that weighted them down. And they were always
in the act of doing something, moving, carrying, or pulling
something, and it always looked exhausting. You were

supposed to see the strain of the labour in their bodies, my aunt said, but their faces were to remain serene, inward-looking.

'My mother will like this,' I said. 'But don't add another figure – it's better this way, not cluttered.'

'Do you think so?' my aunt said, erasing and drawing a new figure farther back on the horizon line, then another even farther back, barely visible.

'So,' I said after a few moments of quiet, my aunt making marks on her sketchpad, my uncle's head hidden behind the newspaper, the lights and the oil lamp flickering. 'I was thinking I would go with Madhu to Goa when she goes.'

My aunt and uncle looked up at me, at each other.

'Do you know anything about Goa? Why do you want to go?' my aunt said.

I said, 'I like beaches. I want to go swimming.'

'You can't go swimming there this time of year,' my uncle said. 'The water's too turbulent.'

'Then I'll hang out on the beach and meet Madhu's friends from England. I'm sure we'll find things to do.'

'That's what I'm afraid of,' my uncle said. 'I don't think it's a good idea.' My uncle looked back at his newspaper.

'Why not?' I said. My aunt looked at my uncle, and he looked up from his newspaper again to find her looking at him, waiting for him to rejoin us. He folded up the newspaper noisily.

'Why don't you tell her why not, Sanjay?' my aunt said.

'Well, it's not somewhere for you to be, that's all. There aren't any families there, it's not for family holidays any more. It's these Europeans, young people – not even young, just foolish. They come to Goa and stay for weeks and weeks, doing nothing meaningful.'

'No one does anything meaningful on holiday, right?' I

focused on being agreeable, though it was starting to seem like I wasn't going to get what I wanted. 'I'll be with Madhu the whole time. And I'm not even asking to go on the trek or anything.'

My aunt said, 'Don't you have summer assignments from your school? Those book reports and everything – you have a lot of work.'

'But I have the whole summer. I can get it done, I'm not worried about it.' I kept the edginess out of my voice and stayed polite; they weren't my parents, after all.

'Maya, this is also a good chance to spend some time with your grandmother. You were fully occupied by Brindha when she was here, and then you've been meeting our friends, we had those two dinner parties, and took you to teas and things, and now Madhu's visit,' she said.

Sanjay uncle nodded in agreement. 'Your grandmother's hardly seen you because of all that. Your mother was hoping you'd keep your Ammamma company and talk to her and maybe even improve your Malayalam with her this summer. I know she wants to teach you.'

I was getting impatient. They were trying to get me to lose sight of what I wanted. 'I can do those things later, all summer. I'm talking about one week with Madhu. Isn't it good to be close with my cousin, too? She'll go back to England and it could be years and years before I see her.' I tried to sound forlorn at losing Madhu for years and years.

'It's nice that you and Madhu are close. But your uncle and I would like you to stay here, especially because we are leaving to go to a wedding in Bombay the same day Madhu leaves. And we'd like to stay in Bombay for some weeks and stay with my relatives. Ammamma isn't up to a trip like that right now, so we were hoping you'd help her look after the house and manage the servants and everything.'

Not only would I miss out on Goa, I would miss out on Bombay, too, because of my grandmother. I wanted to appeal to a higher court, but I wasn't sure who that would be – my mother had made it clear before I left that while I stayed with my aunt and uncle, they were in charge.

I decided not to pursue it now. Maybe I'd come up with a new line of reasoning in the morning. I reshelved the jumble of books I'd pulled down from the bookcase. I said goodnight and walked down the hall to my bedroom, and then realized I'd left my glasses on the coffee table. As I walked back towards the drawing room, I could hear my aunt and uncle talking. I stayed just outside the room and listened.

'My brother told me about Madhu's schoolmates – they're a wild crowd,' my aunt said. 'Madhu's boyfriend might be there, and they're probably drinking all weekend. And smoking bhang. What else do Europeans come to Goa for?'

I stayed to listen for my uncle's response.

'Madhu's too old to control. I don't pretend I understand how your brother and his wife have raised her,' my uncle said. 'I'm just glad Brindha wasn't here when she came, because I wouldn't want her being influenced.'

'I don't know what to say to Maya,' my aunt said. 'She really seems to look up to Madhu.'

'Well, we have the rest of the summer with Maya – she'll work out what's right. She has time to learn.'

I turned away quietly and walked back down the hall. They'd been trying to make me feel guilty about leaving my grandmother, when it had nothing to do with her. I felt hurt for Madhu, and for me. Did they think I hadn't been around people drinking and smoking pot before? Did they know what an American high school was like? Madhu or I could be so much worse if we wanted – everything was there for the asking.

I felt outraged. I went to Madhu's room, wanting to talk. She was sleeping, and I shook her shoulder. She turned over, away from me, and fell still again. She looked younger sleeping, her fingers curled up, no makeup on, her hair liberated from clips and styling spray, pillowing her face. 'Madhu. MA-dhu. ' No response. She breathed softly, evenly. I gave up and went to bed.

Madhu was unsurprised by everything I told her in the morning. I wanted more of a reaction, but she was calm, not particularly mobilized by my indignation. We were walking in the bright morning sun in the garden, trying to stay out of the way of the gardeners, who, in turn, were trying to stay out of our way. They were pouring big buckets of water at the base of the parched plants, the puddles vanishing, as if sucked into quicksand, within seconds.

'This is what I meant – this isn't the real world for us,' Madhu said. 'They don't respect us.'

'But there's nothing wrong with us,' I said. It was unpleasant to be under suspicion. At home, I was a model to my friends' parents. They would say to their own kids while I was in their kitchens, staring at my shoes, 'Why can't you be like Maya, and do well in school and swim at the state finals, and dress nicely and have only one earring in each ear?'

'You're still young, but you'll get the picture soon. Last time I came to India, my grandmother, the one on my mother's side – sat me down and told me the whole Sita story to warn me to be a good girl. Your Ammamma seems nice, but watch out for what you tell her. Grandmothers are the worst. They don't understand that things change.'

I wished Madhu wouldn't keep thinking of me as so young. But I hadn't understood what she was saying about Sita. Sita was the goddess who was the wife of the god

Rama. There were many stories about their courtship and their marriage, and the epic battle against the evil demon-king who abducted Sita and held her prisoner. Rama, his brother, and a whole army of celestial monkeys rescued Sita and brought her back home to their kingdom. Everyone knew these stories – they were constantly retold as bedtime stories, television serials, dance dramas, comic strips. When Madhu didn't elaborate on her own, I finally asked, 'What does the Sita story have to do with being a good girl?'

Madhu settled herself on one of the stone benches at the far end of the garden, and I sat down next to her. She said, 'Do you know what happens after Sita is rescued from the demon world?'

I thought that was the ending. Sita and Rama went home to rule their kingdom happily ever after.

'That's what all children think,' Madhu said. Her grand-mother had told Madhu that after Sita's long imprison-ment, Sita had to prove she was still pure. She was not fit to be Rama's wife again if she had been with any other man, even against her will. Sita gave her word of honour that she was pure, but they made her take a test of purity – she had to walk unscathed through fire. She passed the test, but there were still rumours spreading in their king-dom that she had sinned. She lost the trust of her people, and, eventually, of her husband. Sita was heartbroken and she asked Mother Earth to swallow her up. Mother Earth took her in. Rama went on to have a long and prosperous reign by himself.

'Your grandmother told you that?' I had never heard this ending before. It wasn't enough that Sita was good. Everyone had to believe she was good, and they didn't.

'I'm sure your grandmother will soon too. Mine wanted me to know that's how much purity matters in India. She

warned me about preserving my morals in that underworld of England. After that, I wouldn't exactly come back
here with my boyfriend on my arm, would I?'

I couldn't remotely imagine bringing Steve here either.
His hair was never clean, and it was too long, and he was
always wearing a baseball cap. And he was not Indian, not
Hindu, not Malayali, not high-caste.

'Is your boyfriend Indian?' I said in a casual voice, like it
was just another quality like any other quality, like having
red hair, or being tall.

'No, his name's Perry.' Madhu laughed. I could tell she
was thinking about him, about some happy memory.
'Definitely not Indian.'

'So he'll be there in Goa with your friends?' I said.

'No, I told you this is a hen party – all girls before
Margy's wedding.'

'So maybe Reema auntie won't mind, since it's all girls,'
I said. It was my first glimmer of hope.

'God, they see everything in this narrow way,' Madhu
said scornfully. 'I know I can only come back here a few
more times before my life will be too incomprehensible to
them.'

'What do you mean?' I said.

'Like when I'm thirty, what if I'm not married? I won't
come here and let everyone feel sorry for me. They'll say
my parents neglected me by not arranging a marriage for
me. Or, worse, what if I marry someone Pakistani or poor
or both?'

'Your mother's family's poor, so maybe that's OK?' I
said. As soon as I said it, I realized maybe I wasn't supposed to know that, but I'd heard it from one of Reema
auntie's sisters. And Madhu had mentioned how they had
no shoes or anything in that village.

Madhu paused, looked at me, and decided not to feel

insulted. 'Well, they weren't poor when she married my dad – her parents lost their family business later, otherwise I'm sure his family wouldn't have let the marriage happen. Listen to Reema auntie's friends talk about marriages for their daughters. They talk about a marriage between equals. That doesn't mean education, or equal rights for women. That means money.'

'But arranged marriages aren't so bad.' Sometimes Madhu seemed ready to get rid of everything, and I wasn't sure what would be left to hold on to, to be proud of. 'I mean, look at my parents or yours. They're happy,' I said. Thinking of my parents, I said, 'Or at least as happy as my friends' parents are in their non-arranged marriages. '

'I'm not saying it never works, Maya. I'm just saying it leaves a lot of people out. In England, we're all the same – Indian, Pakistani, Bangladeshi. We're more the same than we are like anyone else in England. But here, if I married a Paki, some of our relatives would never talk to me again.'

'Paki is for Pakistanis?' I said.

'You've never heard that before? It's not a very nice word for Pakistanis. I mean, there's nothing wrong with the word, but people say it in England as an insult. Not just to Pakistanis – to me, anyone dark.'

I didn't know any Bangladeshis. I knew some Pakistanis, but I'd never thought about whether that was important, to my parents or anyone else. Sumeer at school was Pakistani and Muslim, but I didn't find out until we were all at a baseball game and we had to ask around for kosher hot dogs.

'What do Americans say? What do they call you?' Madhu asked, curious.

They didn't call me anything. Or not usually. There weren't enough Indians around for us to be noticed. When I was in the first grade, I remembered making headbands out of construction paper to stick paper feathers in for recreating the First Thanksgiving. Some kids asked me if I could bring in a real headdress from home, since I was Indian. Now there were more Indians, people knew who we were, that we were from somewhere else. I wasn't sure that was a good thing.

'I've heard them say 'Dothead' to other kids at school,' I offered. 'And when I was walking home from school one day last year, a kid yelled 'Hindu' at me, from the window of a schoolbus.'

'Hindu?' Madhu thought that was funny. 'That's just like Paki. It's not intrinsically demeaning – in your case, it's actually true. But people use it in this hateful way. Imagine if I started yelling 'Italian' on a tube platform in London! They'd think I was another crazy homeless person. '

I remembered when that kid had yelled 'Hindu', I didn't feel like it was true about me, it seemed like a curse-word. In my head, it looked like 'Hindoo', the way it looked in old racist history books and Walt Whitman poems.

After Madhu went inside, I made one last attempt with my aunt. She was at the other end of the garden, instructing the gardener on how to space newly whittled wooden stakes among the chilli pepper plants. Reema auntie was using cloth rags as mitts to pluck the chillis – they were so hot they would burn her skin. She was wearing sunglasses that were large and round on her face, like Jackie O. She showed me the chillis nestled in the rag in her hand – two gnarled green ones, and one firm-skinned, shiny red one.

'If you even look at these for too long, your eyes will start to water,' my aunt said. 'Sanjay likes pakora made from these peppers. I was thinking I would tell Matthew to serve that tonight before dinner.'

'Reema auntie, I was talking to Madhu about Goa. And

she says her boyfriend isn't even coming. It's all girls, so won't it be OK if I go?'

My aunt paused, then leaned forward across the row of plants towards me. 'I'll come in with you. Take my glasses, will you? I don't want to touch my face.'

I reached out and slipped the glasses over her ears and off. She walked with me to the door, motioning for me to open it. I trailed her to the kitchen, where she put the peppers next to the sink and lathered her hands with soap.

'These things are difficult to talk about,' she said.

'What things?' I said.

My aunt took my hands in her chapped wet ones and looked straight at me. 'We love Madhu, but she is not any kind of example. We could never take her to a company party or the nice places we take you. She would make too many people upset with her opinions and the things she does.'

'But – '

'Look, Maya,' my aunt said, with an edge of exasperation. 'It's up to you. You can come here and be a tourist, do whatever you like to do, or you can come here and be a member of this family, with responsibilities and obligations. You choose.'

My aunt's watch had accidentally got wet. I took my hand out of her grip to use the hem of my kameez to swab at her watch. My aunt took the watch off her arm, shaking it, holding it up to her ear.

'Can you hear something?' I said.

'No, I don't think so. I always think I should be able to hear the sound of time passing, but I don't think this watch ever made sounds. I think it's working still.'

'That grandfather clock in the hall makes enough sound for everyone to hear time passing,' I said, trying to find something safe to talk about.

'We bought that last summer, at Brindha's request. When your grandmother had her heart problems, Brindha was upset, she was afraid Ammamma would leave us at any time. She wanted a clock that rang out the hours, so she could break from her games and her studies and go and check on Ammamma and make sure she was resting and breathing easily, that everything was OK. Brindha wanted to sleep in Ammamma's room, but she's too restless a sleeper, she woke Ammamma too often, so we persuaded her to stay in her own room.'

I felt bad about the last few weeks, about not having paid more attention, been more aware of my grandmother's presence. I would be better about it, even if it meant staying home more, doing less fun things.

'So maybe I should stay here with Ammamma while Madhu and you and Sanjay uncle are away?' I wanted to make peace with Reema auntie.

'That would be good. It would make us worry less about her.'

We didn't talk about what she had said about Madhu, and I didn't tell Madhu either. I wanted to tell Reema auntie she didn't understand. One day would she say about me what she said about Madhu? 'We love Maya, but . . .' But what?

Everyone was leaving. On the verandah were Madhu's luggage and big orange steel-frame backpack, my aunt's carpetbags and vanity case, my uncle's lone black carryall looking like an oversized sports bag. The assembly of servants and Ammamma, and me. I held on to Boli, waving good-bye as the car muttered to itself, slowly gathering speed.

Watching for the car to come up over the neighbouring hill, I saw movement among the teabushes. The pluckers, who worked section by section throughout the day, emerged en masse like a cloud of grasshoppers. I finally saw the car pop up on the horizon, just the profile out-lined sharply by morning glare, and then it was gone.

I turned to go back in the house, and my grandmother was standing in the doorway, her eyes on the same hori-zon. We were alone now.

She asked, 'Shall I ask Matthew to serve breakfast?'

I was not hungry yet, and preferred a bath first. But I wanted to keep her company, start things out on the right foot. I said, 'Yes, sure, we can eat now.'

'Actually,' my grandmother said, 'today is a fast day for me.'

I had forgotten this. I realized that meant all day I would eat my meals alone.

'But come and have breakfast,' my grandmother said. 'I'll sit with you, drink some water.'

'No, that's not necessary,' I said. 'Besides, won't it be tempting to sit in front of food? When Mother's on a diet, she never comes to the dinner table – she says it's too dan-gerous.'

'It's not like a diet,' my grandmother said.

'Oh,' I said, as if I understood. If I was the only one eat-ing, and I wasn't keeping her waiting, then I'd do what I wanted. I said, 'I think I'll bathe first.'

'Of course,' my grandmother said. 'Whatever you want to do is fine.'

I told Vasani to bring hot water into my bathroom. I was out of shampoo, and I looked at the shampoo bottles Brindha had left on the window ledge, 'Fair Beauty' and 'Beautisoft'. I opened one and it smelled strong, the way a perm smelled the first day you washed it after the salon and there was still a lot of chemicals.

I went to the guestroom and the bathroom there to see if Madhu had left any good shampoo behind. There was nothing on the countertops or on the sink. I looked on the shelf under the sink, and there were some things there. No shampoo, but a bottle of sunblock. I also saw Madhu had left her hairbrush behind. It was a nice wood-handled one with a wide paddle – it made her hair straight and smooth. Looking at the brush closely, I saw blonde hair mixed in with the black. There was also a wheel of pills on the shelf, and looking at the dates, and the punched out spots for each of them, I could tell they were birth-control pills, just like the ones Jennifer brought home after trips to the doctor with her mom.

Madhu thought I was so young. She wouldn't think to tell me – she would say sex wasn't a big deal anyway – but I sort of wished she had. Just to talk to someone. I collected the sunblock, and the hairbrush, and the pills, and took them to my room. I dragged out my suitcase from under the bed, and I dumped Madhu's stuff in a side pocket, alongside Brindha's Tiger clippings and her movie magazines. Then I took my bath, resigned to the noxious shampoo.

CHAPTER FIVE

Solitude

THE HOUSE WAS quiet. No kids, no guests, no visitors. My grandmother and I talked in low tones. Boli was subdued. The servants still came every day. Even with just us here, they had a lot to do. Less laundry and less ironing, but the house needed cleaning every day – dust and insects resettled on every surface soon after it was swept. And the garden still grew at its furious pace – fruit needed to be picked, flowers to be weeded, grass to be cut with the shiny dull-bladed scythe. And food – Matthew still cooked as if we had a full house. Ammamma and I sat down to tea and

Matthew had made banana appam, two kinds of vada, and three kinds of chutney.

'Ammamma, you have to tell him to stop making so much food for us.'

'He must know we can't eat all this. I think he's calcu-lated so that Sunil can eat to his heart's content while Reema's away,'Ammamma said. Usually Matthew and Sunil and the other servants would eat whatever rice or vegetable we ate, but not the chicken or fish at dinner, unless there was some small piece left over, not the teatime snacks or the desserts. Now, because Reema auntie was not here to oversee the cooking, they were getting five-course dinners out of it.

'Wouldn't Reema auntie want us to say something?'

'She might, but I can't be bothered, it's not that big an infringement. They don't mean any harm, they never steal outright from us. When Reema's back in three weeks, she can run a tight ship again, but it's not in my nature.'

My grandmother said things like that, 'it's not in my nature.' It sounded permanent and immutable, like no one could ever make her be a different kind of person. I could not say things like that. 'My nature' could change at any time. I felt like I was made up of the drops of mercury that were inside a thermometer that could move – shoot rapid-ly up or down, break into pieces, re-form – when you least expected it.

We'd had two days already of breakfasts, lunches, teas, and dinners. Four-hour blocks of time in between each of those meals needed to be filled. I tried sitting with my grandmother, but I was nervous that if we talked between meals then we might run out of things to say at the table. Food, the servants, the weather. My mother, my father, my school, my summer assignments. I had to think a few sen-tences ahead, so I didn't say anything stupid. I spoke slowly and made my vowels very round and my consonants very hard so she followed everything. She was polite and nonjudgmental about everything, but when I talked about New York to her, it was watered down, drained of life. I told her a version of my life filmed in black and white.

She was also nervous with me – she was worried she didn't know how to entertain me. She was relieved when I told her I was going to read or listen to music – these were things I liked doing, and they didn't require anything of her, and we were both happy.

She was less happy when I went outside. The garden was OK, safe enough, but I liked to go outside the gate, to walk around, check things out. She wasn't able to keep up with me and she didn't want me out there alone. She feared I would lose my way or maybe get hurt.

In the early evening on the second day, I went jogging. I'd done almost no exercise since coming here, and swim team tryouts were the week before school started. There was nowhere to swim, but at least running helped my breathing, my endurance. To remember my path home, I ran directly into the sun, picking the westward side of every fork.

On the third day, after breakfast, there was a girl on the front porch. It was Rupa, Brindha's nanny.

'What's she doing here? She must know Brindha's back at school,'I asked.

'I called Rupa here to show you around when you go walking,' my grandmother said.

'You mean, to follow me around? I don't need her – send her back down the mountain.'

'Maya, please, it's better to have someone with you.'

'A babysitter? Brindha's ten, Ammamma. I'm fifteen. I don't believe this.'

'She's not babysitting you. When you're here at the house, you can go about as you please. But when you go outside, she'll go with you, I'll tell her to stay ten steps behind if you want, so she won't disturb you.'

'I can't even talk to her, she doesn't speak any English. This is a crazy idea.' It was an even crazier idea that Ammamma was inviting a Tamil Tiger back into our home. Or someone with Tiger connections. But I couldn't tell her that.

'Maya, we're five miles from any neighbour, and there's snakes and wild animals out there. Someone should be with you.'

'There's snakes out there when Reema auntie goes walking, too. She just takes her chances. That's what living's about, Ammamma.'

'But Reema knows what to look for, and she's lived in places like this all her life. Please, Maya, I don't want anything to happen while we're up here alone that will make Reema or Sanjay or your mother have to worry . . .'

'OK, OK. But how will we talk?'

Ammamma said Rupa could speak a little English and decent Malayalam, besides being fluent in Tamil and Kannada. Like most servants, she adapted to her employers, and picked up languages like new uniforms as she moved from household to household.

Rupa sat on the porch all morning. I was trying to make a compilation tape on my uncle's stereo from his old albums so that I could listen to it on my Walkman. He had old Simon and Garfunkel albums, and the Beatles and the Carpenters. He had tapes too, of recent stuff, but nothing I liked.

After tea, I changed into Nikes and a T-shirt, and put on light cotton salwar trousers, wishing I could wear shorts. I went out on to the front verandah and, without even glancing at Rupa sitting there, walked down the steps to the driveway. She got up, folded the clothes she was mending, and left them on a cane chair. She walked after me as I opened the gate. I didn't wait for her, but I left the gate open behind me.

I started with a light jog. I took light rabbit steps, trying to keep from kicking up dust. The sun was far down in the sky, but it was still hot, and I felt wetness at my ears, my neck, under my arms. Rupa was not far behind me – if she walked at a brisk pace, she was able to keep up. I thought about the bright red, rubberized track at my high school, and I stepped more deeply, pretending that the ground gave energy back to me, charged me for the next forward motion. My heart pulsed rapidly, trying to keep up with my lungs, absorb all the air I took in, pump air through and out, heart contracting, squeezing. My legs moved effortlessly, leaving me to concentrate on breathing, on trying to keep my mouth lubricated with saliva, resisting and finally giving in to the dry sharpness. My tongue was heavy in my mouth, tasting the dust and the tears that the dust brought to my eyes.

After another mile or so I stopped, my hands on my hips, my skin hot. I held my T-shirt away from my body, blew air down the neckhole. I turned around, and Rupa was far behind, panting. As she came closer, I could see she was drenched in sweat, her breathing loud and laboured. And she was limping. Thinking she might have hurt herself, I stayed put to let her catch up. But she was limping because the heel on her left chapal had broken. She reached me and stood bent over, taking heavy, heaving breaths.

'Why don't you stay here and I'll finish my run and come back here?' I said.

She looked at me not comprehending. I pointed at her, and pointed for her to sit where she was. She sat. I pointed at myself, then at the horizon, moved my finger in a circle and then pointed at the ground. She said nothing.

I turned towards the horizon and started running. When I turned around, she was many paces behind me, running, her chapals held out in front of her. I kept going, and we ran like that, like the engine and guard's van of a train, changing speeds in tandem but with hundreds of feet of a long invisible link between us, over and up and down and through the hills.

RUPA CAME THE next day again. As long as she was here anyway, I wanted to do something adventurous. I'd seen a waterfall on our car trips – Brindha had told me she'd been in the water at the base of it, and that it was cold and clean. I didn't want my grandmother to worry herself, so I put my swimsuit on under a salwar kameez and didn't tell her what I was planning. On the verandah, Rupa was playing with a deck of old cards. I beckoned for her to come, and we started walking.

I walked the same path that we'd taken the previous night, even though I had no idea which direction the waterfall was in. After we'd got some distance from the house, I stopped and said to Rupa, 'Please take me to the waterfalls.'

She stopped short right behind me. She had been staring at the ground and walking mechanically, and now she raised her eyes up to look at me.

'Is there problem, mem?' she asked in English.

'I want to go to the waterfall,'I said slowly. 'You know, where Brindha swims in the water?'

'Water, mem?' she asked.

'Pani, water, do you understand?' I said. She looked at me without any recognition in her eyes. I remembered *pani* was water in Hindi, not in Malayalam. What was the word in Malayalam?

'Kuli,' I tried the word for 'bath', not able to remember the word for water.

She understood this, but it did not explain what I wanted her to do.

I made swimming motions with my arms. I held my nose as if I was going underwater. She giggled. I said 'Evda?'

She looked back to where we had just come from, towards the house, as if seeking permission from my grandmother. I repeated my question more insistently. I could tell she was trying to decide what kind of violation this was, what size the crime, and what size the possible punishment.

Finally she nodded and said 'ba,' and I followed behind her on scratchy dirt paths through the thick teabushes. She gestured for me to walk very close behind her, so her shadow would protect me from direct sun. We walked for a long time, almost an hour, and I was beginning to doubt she had understood me after all. Then I heard what sounded like wind chimes tinkling, and Rupa pushed through another few bushes and the waterfall was there in front of us. It wasn't much of a waterfall right now – the water slowed to gentle trickles over a wall of rock, splashing into the basin at the bottom. On the surface, perfect circles rippled away from unseen magnetic forces, and ended up as lacy foam decorating the point of division between water and shore.

I stepped out of my salwar trousers and pulled the kameez off over my head. I threw these on the ground, but Rupa picked them up and folded them. She sat on a rock nearby with my clothes on her lap, watching me in the water. The water was shallow, five feet in the deepest part, and I tried to stay afloat as much of the time as possible so as not to scrape my feet on the rough stones at the bottom.

'Why don't you come in the water,' I said. Rupa shook her head and looked at the ground. She seemed uncomfortable at the thought of having any fun while she was working. She was only a couple of years older than me, though I hadn't really noticed that before. After the long hot walk, her dark navy salwar was covered in chalky dust up to the knees.

I splashed her with some water, and it made spots on her clothes. She looked up and smiled, wiping her face clear of the spray with the back of her arm, her face shiny in the sun.

'Come in the water,' I said in a loud, commanding voice. I wanted her to feel the force of my voice, to relieve her of responsibility for her actions, so that she could just say later 'Maya told me to.' She hesitated, put my clothes down on a flat part of a rock, and stepped out of her chapals. In quick motions, she undressed, and then leapt into the water so that it enveloped her nakedness. She stayed some distance from me in the water, and I kept to my side to respect her modesty, but gestured to her to race me across the basin from her parallel position. I swam a butterfly stroke across and she paddled, but she was strong, and kept up with me until the halfway point. Then, determined to win, I pushed hard into the strokes, breathed deeply, lunged back for the starting side and reached it first.

Rupa dived under a few times and came up with beautiful purple pebbles and a translucent white stone with one dark vein running through it. She moved right under one of the streams of water coming down so that it was like a tap turned on over her head. 'We can come after rains,' she said in Malayalam. 'Real waterfall then.' We settled into a routine of her speaking Malayalam to me and my speaking English to her with a few Malayalam words thrown in. Her Malayalam was basic – you could see her making the mental translations in her head, but I envied her unselfconsciousness. I understood everything said around me, but I had not tried to form a whole sentence in Malayalam in years, embarrassed by my childlike grammar.

We swam around for a while. I got out first and walked a little way with my back to her so that she could get out and get dressed. I came back to the water's edge and sat on the rock next to my clothes, waiting for the sun to dry me a little before dressing. Rupa pointed at my legs, and there were two black marks on my left ankle and one on my calf – black marks that were the length and width of large industrial-strength staples. I peered at them closely, lifting my leg across my lap. She pointed to her own wrist, where there was a similar black staple, and with a quick pinching motion, she pulled it off, and threw it in the sand where it began to wriggle. A wave of repulsion came over me. They were leeches. I asked Rupa to take them off my leg. She looked at me strangely. 'Please, mem,' she said, shaking her head. 'Your family would not want that I do it. Better your grandmother do it when we reach the house,' she said.

She was from a low caste, she wasn't supposed to touch me. I couldn't imagine walking the whole way back with those leeches on me, or putting my clothes on over them. 'Please,' I asked, looking into her eyes.

'You are ordering that I do this?' she asked. She did not want to get in trouble.

'Yes,' I said. She pinched the first one, then the second one and they were gone. The third was stuck in more deeply – she pinched and dug in her fingernails and pulled and it was gone. The soft white underside of my calf, where the last leech had been, had a little blood running from it. She took a leaf and trimmed it down and stuck it on the cut.

Rupa's braid had come loose in the swim. As she gathered her hair up off her shoulders to tie it up, I noticed, just at the bottom of the back of her neck, another black staple.

She tried to look at it over her shoulder, but she couldn't see it. I swallowed hard, and reached out to try to remove the leech. Rupa moved out of my reach when she saw what I was trying to do.

'Please, don't,' she said. 'I can't let you.'

'You must let me,' I said. I hoped it would come out in one pinch. I tried to picture my nails under it – would it feel soft and slimy or hard and brittle?

'I will wait. Vasani can help me at the house. I will wait,' she said. 'Please.'

But I want to show you I don't care, I thought. I'm not afraid of your skin, your blood. She looked frightened as I came towards her, moving back as I moved forwards. 'Please,' she said. Respectfully, but there was real pleading in her voice. I stopped.

She picked up the smooth pretty pebbles she had col-lected and offered them to me. I took only one so she could have the others. She tossed them into the bushes, and started walking. She turned to see if I was following close, and I was. I walked in her shadow, my eyes trained on the black mark slashed across the coffee skin all the way home.

WE WENT ON walks with Brindha's dog; he was much more demanding now that Reema auntie was away, too. He wanted to stay out on the hills for long periods of time, and he wanted to play games. I liked him – he was a good medium-size dog. The small ones were too much like rats, and I was afraid of the large ones. At five I had been chased around a park by a fierce German shepherd that got close enough to rip off a piece of my winter coat. The owner finally caught up with us and leashed his dog, and then he tried to help me find my mother. We found her inside a phone booth, with her back pressed up against the door. She had seen the dog running loose and taken refuge in the phone booth. Somehow, she hadn't stopped to wonder where I might be; we had to knock a few times before she turned around slowly and came out.

Boli had a nice white coat, and I didn't mind feeding him table scraps at dinner or petting him when he came and sat by me on the verandah. Ammamma said he was calmer than he used to be: he was so hyper as a puppy that they would throw a blanket over him to make him quieten down. Even though he'd grown up, I didn't think he had much composure. As soon as he saw me, he flipped on to his back and offered me his belly, his eyes glazed in a foolish stupor. Or he tried to get attention by licking my arm, my foot, the buckles of my sandals – anything within reach. It's in his nature, Ammamma said, but he wanted more from me than I wanted to give. He had the run of the house, he was never locked up. If I wanted some peace, I had to tell Sunil or Vasani to come drag him out of the room and then I had to lock myself in. This was not so bad, because it became an excuse for privacy – otherwise the doors were never kept closed, everyone coming and going without knocking or asking.

The one time I wanted Boli around was for walks. The tea pluckers loved him, and it made it less awkward when we ran into them, because I couldn't talk to them, and Rupa wouldn't. She held herself apart from them. They were country people, she told me. She at least was from the village. Boli ran round and round their skirts, and they put their baskets down, brimming with tea leaves, and picked him up and nuzzled him. He liked this, though he squirmed out of their clutch at the first glimpse of bird or mouse. The youngest of the girls who worked on the tea were probably younger than me, and the old-est women had white hair and earlobes stretched from half a century of wearing thick gold earrings. They were shoeless, with brown paste spread over their feet and hands. Rupa said this was a mix of tobacco paste and herbs that kept insects from biting them. They wore sari blouses that stuck to them with sweat and dark cotton lungis wrapped around their skinny waists. They worked quickly, each taking a bush, picking only the tender tips – the bud and the first two leaves of each stem.

Soon after the women worked through a whole section and moved on, two men appeared with machetes. They pruned the bushes with a few deft strokes, and then dropped their knives by the side of the road and smoked and called out teasingly to the women bent over at work. Rupa said if the tea shrubs were not pruned, they would grow into trees. It would be too hard to pick the leaves then, and there would be fewer tender buds.

Just then, Boli started barking loudly, and as we looked to see what had claimed his interest, he was drowned out by the approaching helicopters. The tea pluckers shielded their eyes to stare up at the sleek silver insects. As they passed directly over us, papers rained down on our heads. I unfolded a square of white paper to stare at the faces of Subha and Sivarasan. Beneath their pictures was a picture of a wad of bills, making the cash award for their capture clear even to illiterates. The pluckers clutched the photos and chattered excitedly, and I looked at Rupa, who would not look at me. What did she know? Would she ever tell me if I asked? The more I knew her, the less I hoped she knew. Yet, the more I knew her, the more I hoped she'd share what she knew. She was no longer a remote person, no longer an anonymous brush with danger, and history.

She crumpled the paper in her hands and then thought better of it, opening it and smoothing it out. She made herself busy collecting the papers littering the path, putting a rock on top of a sheaf of them. As if the outdoors were a great big house she could tidy up and bring some order to.

Boli bounded into the bushes after one of his favourite girls and we waited on the path for him to come back. After some time passed, I called his name loudly, and then Rupa did the same. We waded through the bushes, and saw far ahead of us the bobbing heads of the women working farther down the hill. Rupa told me to wait, that she would go down and bring him back, but I went with her, trying to hold my arms in close to my body to keep from getting scratched up.

The women were entering a straw hut. The baskets of green leaves were lined up neatly in the clearing. Rupa and I heard Boli barking and we walked into the hut. There was incense and clouds of smoke and torches lit at a stone altar. Women were kneeling on the floor chanting, and each went to the altar and prostated herself before leaving. I squinted to see the altar through all the smoke, looking for a statue of Shiva or Vishnu or Lakshmi. But all I saw was a little pile of twigs, lying on a faded piece of silk. Boli was crouched on the floor between two women and I tried to reach him without stepping on anyone. I gathered him in my arms and headed for the square of daylight at the back of the hut. We were outside again, with fresh air, and light.

'What was that?' I said. 'Who is that temple for?'

'It is just an altar they've set up for praying at the end of the workday,' Rupa said.

I'd never seen an altar like that. There was no icon or anything, just those sticks. 'Who are they worshipping?'

She didn't understand me. I reeled off names of common gods, 'Shiva? Parvati? Vishnu?'

'No, it is not for any of our gods. These are country people, I told you. It is just for some god of theirs, the spirit of sticks or sun or tea leaves – who knows.'

I thought of temples I'd been in with my family, the elaborate architecture, marble pillars, gold and silver necklaces and hundred-rupee notes lying on big trays in front of statues of our gods. Statues painted in blues and reds and blacks, glossy from butter and oil, with aggressive, sometimes leering smiles. People crowded between the rails, leaning into those in front, waiting to drop coins in little boxes before making a full circle around each statue's shrine. My mother hunted for enough change in her bag, my father stood in another line to pay the priest the fees listed on a big menu for special prayers with our names in them. You could purchase prayers for specific good things, like good grades, good marriages, many children. If you paid a little extra, my father said, the priest would recite prayers for good things you didn't even know to ask for.

RUPA CAME EVERY day, and as we embarked on our various excursions we built a vocabulary of our own, mostly laughter and nudging and nodding interspersed with broken Malayalam. We rarely spent any time indoors because Rupa would not sit on the living-room couches or lounge on my bed or eat at the dining table, and it strained my idea of our friendship to see her crouched over her food in the corner of the kitchen or watching a television programme squatting at my feet. So our world was the world out of doors, where we were equals before birds and snakes and fish. Ammamma would let us eat our lunch on the veran-

dah, and when we were finally exhausted, we descended on
to the twin porch swings and rocked ourselves into afternoon naps. Rupa went home to her brothers at the end of
the day. I was not Brindha's age after all, and Ammamma
had not hired her to stay the nights and ward off monsters
in wardrobes. Some days, we were so caught up in whatever we were doing that Rupa would have missed the last bus
home if I didn't make Ram drive us to meet the bus.

Rupa was crying on the verandah one morning when I
went out to join her after breakfast. She wouldn't be able
to work for a few days, she said. It was hard to understand
her through her tears, and hard to get her to speak more.
She started backing away from me, turning to go. I made
her sit down with me on a swing. I wanted to know and,
unprompted, I promised not to tell. Her eldest brother was
in some trouble and he had got himself to Madras, and
from there he would get a train to go far away. She was
going to go meet him in Madras to give him the family
savings, though how she and her other two brothers
would manage, she didn't know and couldn't think about
right now. Her tears were subsiding, and she dried her face
on her sleeve.

'What kind of trouble is he in?' I asked.

She looked at me. I had asked too much, seemed too
curious. She stood to leave, and I could sense her distrust
and her regret that she had told me anything. She was leaving now, and she was never coming back.

'Ammamma hasn't paid you for the week yet,' I said. 'I'll
go and ask her and bring it for you.'

She stood there uncertainly on the verandah. I needed
her to know she could trust me. There was money
Ammamma kept in a vase for household spending, and I
took all of it, but it wasn't that much. I went into my own
room, and took out the handbag I hadn't touched since

the day I arrived. I removed two crisp twenty dollar bills from a wallet. I gave all of this to Rupa, but she gave the twenties back to me – she said you couldn't change money without the right papers. But she saw that I was trying, and she seemed calmer and more friendly.

'You will come back?' I asked.

'Yes,' she said, smiling a little. 'I don't much like Madras.'

While Rupa was gone, I watched my grandmother to see how she filled her own days. She was on an unwritten but unvarying schedule. She studied and read Sanksrit verse in the early morning, before even the servants came at six. She helped them make breakfast and decided on the day's menu. After we had breakfast, she bathed and performed morning prayers. She used to bathe and pray as soon as she woke up, I remembered as a child creeping into her prayer room and climbing into her lap, helping her offer fruit and flowers, light incense sticks and triple-tiered velakkus, feeling against my body the vibration of hers in quiet chanting. But now the bathing and the praying had been moved to the midmorning hours – she was afraid of catching cold bathing any earlier. Everyone thought it was damp and cool in the morning, before the sun found our hill, but to me, even at that hour, there was a mugginess, a latent heat, just waiting for its cue to take centre stage.

Then she sat in her room and wrote letters and responded to mail. She had an address book with every page filled in and stuffed with slips of notepaper with more names and addresses scrawled on them. My mother was the beneficiary of one out of seven of those writing sessions every week – the letters came with the predictability of credit card bills. Mail going the opposite direction was nowhere near as dependable. Our letters from the States often took two or three weeks to arrive, and sometimes they didn't arrive at all. But we were also not dependable ourselves, and so, when we called on the phone, we would lie, and Mother would say, 'You haven't received our New Year's card yet? But we sent it three weeks ago at least.' The thing with Mother was, she never forgot anything – she knew everyone's birthday and anniversary and she checked all the holidays in advance on the lunar calendar. But just because she knew didn't mean she would do anything about it unless she decided it was a priority. Which was why sometimes we sent out our Christmas cards in February, and why sometimes, when she was away or working late on my birthday, she wouldn't even bother to call. My father and my friends taking me out to dinner and the cards and telegrams from India could almost – but not quite – disguise the stark fact that Mother had little interest in commemorating the one day in her life that had been totally consumed by my entry into the world.

After taking care of her correspondence, and reading the newspaper, which the boy on the bicycle never brought as early as he was supposed to, Ammamma and I had lunch together. Then there was the afternoon rest for us and for the servants too – an hour of rest in the dead still heat. My grandmother sometimes lay on the floor in the afternoon, because the doctor had told her it was good for her back. The floors were wonderfully cold, ice cold. Sometimes I lay there to read, though I couldn't sleep.

In the afternoon, Ammamma knitted. Right now she was making a sweater for her sister's new granddaughter. And she listened to music – bhajans playing on a musty small radio in her room with crackly speakers. I told her the stereo in the living room was much better, but she said she didn't know how to use it and she didn't want to ruin anything. Anyway, she said, she knew all the songs, she was mostly listening to them in her head, and she just used the radio to fill in the gaps, check on certain verses, remind her of the rhythm and the count.

If Vasani and Matthew had finished their work, they would come to her to have her write letters to their villages for them. She only wrote after they scrawled out a few alphabetic characters for her, to show her they had made some progress. She drew lines on the blank paper before she gave it to them, so that they would write in straight lines across the page. Then she took a couple of lines of recitation from each of them, and added to the letters that were already in various stages of completion. She said if she wrote a letter in one sitting for them, they would have no reason to come back to her for a week or two. By then, they would have forgotten anything she taught them.

Then, after teatime, Ammamma walked around the garden, saw what work had been done that day and what work there was to do. She walked around the entire compound, but always within it, never outside the gate. She peered up at our trees for ripe fruit that could fall and hurt someone. She called Sunil, just home from school and full of energy, and he scampered up tree trunks, to cut coconuts, or mangos, or jackfruit. Sunil would bring down green coconuts if we asked him. He hacked them with a knife in such a way that he always created a perfect spout for drinking from, like the triangle cuts the kindergarten teachers would make in Hawaiian Punch juice cans at snacktime. One cut and the juice went all over the place, sprayed our play tables, but two cuts, and the juice poured smoothly, miraculously.

Ammamma had another bath then, but with her hair pinned up on top of her head to keep it dry – and then evening prayers. It was always at the twilight hour during which mosquitoes and fireflies started their day, they would hear her chanting, smell the sweet spicy incense, and try to insinuate themselves into the house, to sneak in through a torn screen window or a gap in the caulking.

I lingered on the porch some days, covered in insect repellent and a long-sleeve kameez, to watch the fireflies, which were bigger and shone brighter than any I'd ever seen. It was as if they knew they had an extra burden. Some nights, the electric company dimmed our lights, and other nights, we'd have no electricity at all, and the fireflies tried to do their part, offer bright burning light to see the night, the world.

We would watch the evening news on the television, the broadcasters usually beautiful pale Bombayites, talking about mining scandals, cholera epidemics, the new census report. There were updates on the Subha and Sivarasan manhunt every day, which was not really news at all. The government owned the only television station and had banned it from independent reporting on the manhunt, saying that too many fresh leads were getting out. But people were clamouring for news, especially the millions who could not read the newspapers. So the government allowed the television news anchors to regurgitate the headline articles from that morning's papers. The newscasters were not allowed to interview anyone or film anything live for the updates either. They showed the same stills everyday. Subha and Sivarasan of course. And Sonia Gandhi at the funeral pyre of Rajiv Gandhi. And the one I was most fascinated by, Dhanu bending to touch Rajiv's feet. To pay her respects. To blow him up. Concentrating on performing flawlessly.

They had caught other Tamil Tigers even though they had not caught Subha and Sivarasan. So far an actress and a prostitute, a pamphlet printer and his mother who was a nurse. The hard part was catching Tigers before they took their own life. Two killed themselves just before arrest, another hanged himself while in prison. The police carried cyanide antidotes every time they broke into a suspected hideout. We watched and listened carefully, in case the broadcast had any sliver of information that our papers had missed. But it was usually all old news.

Then Ammamma would help with dinner, both her own meal and whatever was being cooked for me and the household. Matthew and Sunil and Vasani and Ram would kneel on the floor in the drawing room, and Ammamma would put the television on for them. When Sanjay uncle was home, he only allowed television programmes once or twice a week – he wanted quiet after the factory day. Ammamma let them watch every night. Then she would fill and light the oil lamps and put them in the halls throughout the house, and one for me if I was reading. Around ten or eleven, we would go to bed. I would often lie there, not tired enough to sleep. But if I stayed up, my grandmother would feel obliged to stay up with me. We both tried to accommodate each other, pretended things were natural. But I had no way of sharing in her quiet, slow days. I didn't know how to knit or write Malayalam or sing bhajans. So we just went on with our separate lives in this house where we had been left together.

I WANTED TO take pictures today, with the camera I'd borrowed from my father. His camera had seemed ungainly and awkward to me, set up on a wobbly tripod at my dance recitals and school award ceremonies. But when I sprained my ankle last year and couldn't take gym, I took photography with Mr Thompson. And he was impressed with my father's camera – he showed me how many settings and options it had. I wanted to see what I could do with it here, with the light so extreme, the house full of shadows and ledges and silhouettes. Look for contrasts, Mr Thompson said. Contrast can be the heart of the picture. He didn't always like my pictures. I liked to overexpose my film, make everything look bleached and harsh, as if all my subjects lived under this Indian sun. I thought it was nice when a picture unfolded, when it didn't tell its whole story right away. When you overexposed a picture, it made the person looking at it see that light could hide things as much as darkness.

When my mother left for a long business trip last year, five weeks in California and the Pacific Rim, I turned her home office into a darkroom. I painted the walls black and papered the windows over with grocery bags. She came back a few days early, before I had a chance to explain. But she didn't say anything until I brought it up. She thought she would wait to talk to me until she had talked to the counsellor at school, she said. She had told the counsellor she thought I'd joined a cult, because of the black paint, and no light, and tubes of chemicals. That's how little she knew.

Over breakfast, I asked my grandmother about going to the tea factory to take photos. I remembered seeing huge blowers there, with steel screens placed over them, the wet tea leaves taking flight as they dried. Workers jumped up on top of the screens, to try to catch and remove leaves that looked blackened or damaged. The workers' hair would fly around, and their sarongs would whip around their legs, and they would suddenly look startled, like Marilyn Monroe on that subway grate.

'I think you should wait till your uncle returns,' Ammamma said.

'Why? He wouldn't mind, would he?' I said. I hadn't expected her to object. I had wanted her to call someone

at the factory who could walk me around and get me
through the gated areas.

'He might not mind, but the company might. They
might have rules about photos and things,' Ammamma
said.

'Rules? It's just a tea factory.' She wasn't going to help, so
I'd have to wait for my uncle. Maybe I would take pictures
of the kitchen, the indoor one and the outdoor one, the
open fire, brass pots burnished by flame, the stainless steel
trays lined up for dinner.

'Why don't you take pictures of the garden? It's looking
quite nice. Reema and the gardener are having a good
growing season.'

'The garden's too pretty. The pictures wouldn't be interesting.'

My grandmother looked puzzled, but she let the subject
drop.

'Could we ask the driver to bring new shampoo the next
time he goes down the mountain?' I asked. 'Brindha's
shampoo is ruining my hair.'

'Your hair does look dry,' Ammamma said.

Brindha's shampoo had dulled my hair, made it chemi-
cal-smelling and rough. Ammamma said Brindha had very
different hair. Mine was more like Ammamma's – wispy
and fine. She said, 'When you were small, I would put hair
grips in your hair, and by the evening, they had slid all the
way down, dangling around your chin.'

I wasn't surprised. When I went to the junior-high-school
prom, and we backcombed each other's hair, within minutes all my locks sat back down flat against my head. But
people said I had good hair – at least it was soft and silky.
Secretly, I often thought it was my best feature.

Ammamma said Ram could bring a good imported
shampoo from the city when he went at the end of the

week. For now, she suggested using hair oil. I was reluctant. I remembered how greasy and heavy it felt.

Ammamma said, 'We used to put it in your hair when you were little – that's how your hair became soft. Just try it. Do you want me to comb the oil through your hair?'

'No, no, I can do it,' I said, standing up from the table. Anything I accepted from her she took as a sign to push for more. It was like a foot in the door trying to wedge a larger place to occupy.

Matthew came in to clear the breakfast dishes. When my aunt and uncle were here, Matthew stayed in the room to serve, but when it was just us, we served ourselves. My grandmother had taken her small portion from the serving dishes first, and then she slid them towards my side of the table, where they remained lined up like a row of ducks for the rest of the meal.

Sunil brought the hot bath water today. He carried the big stainless steel bucket, his head and shoulders stuck far out to the right to balance the weight on his left side. He didn't pay much attention to me. He was eleven, and to him I was an irrelevant in-between age. The significant people in his life were either his own age or the ripe old age of his parents, his teachers, his employers. He was dressed for school, wearing a stiff white shirt that had gone greyish in the wash, and blue shorts. He hated school, but my aunt and uncle paid his fees at the village school, so Matthew forced him to go. Sunil preferred being here, helping the mechanics who came from the factory to make repairs to our car, or the gardener to chop down a tree that had cracked in a rainstorm.

He set the bucket down gently in my bathroom. In bare noiseless feet, he padded back to the hall, leaving wet footprints across my bedroom on the soon-to-be-swept floor. I closed the heavy wood door to the bathroom, and latched it. The sun escaped from behind rainclouds, and morning light sliced across the small square room, surprising moths that were settled in sleep on the window ledge. I hung my fresh clothes on one hook, and the clothes I'd taken off on the other. I was out of everything I had brought from home: soap, lotion, toothpaste; now there were no familiar smells. I brushed my teeth with baking soda. I bathed with resin-coloured sandalwood soap. I cleaned my hair with half a capful of Brindha's shampoo, and then I conditioned with the oil. Everyone left the hair oil on after bathing, but I couldn't leave it in my hair. I would never sleep. I could picture the dark greasemarks on my pillowcase. I left it on for some minutes and then rinsed. It had the smell of boiling sugar, before you whisked it into peaks of frosting. When my friends would play house when I was little, and I'd have to be the husband because I was tallest, I used to pull the end of my ponytail under my nose to make a moustache, and my hair would smell just like this.

I turned the tap too far. Cold water thundered into the smaller mixing bucket, silver drops shooting up off the stainless-steel bottom, a fountain catching the light of the sun, until I managed to steer the tap back. Each day, I made myself use less and less hot water in the mixing bucket and more and more cold water. One day soon, Vasani was going to come with a brimming bucket, and I was going to say, maybe at the breakfast table in front of everybody, that's OK, Vasani, I won't be needing that. I can withstand what you can withstand, I don't need to be accommodated.

I poured the last of the water out. Soap bubbles slid across the purposely ever-so-slightly tilted floor. The sun played over me now, reaching places it usually never reached, and I felt unexpectedly intoxicated, droplets of water glistening on my stomach, my richly soft hair exotic to me. I imagined growing it really long, so it could be braided and flowers would stay in it. I took talcum powder from a lower shelf and dabbed it everywhere, a translucent white sheen.

I reached for my clothes on the hook, just to the left of the sink. And I slipped. I felt the oil slick underneath, and heard my head hit the sink. The sharp sound of a single clap, or a snap, or a smash. The sound of a baseball bat making contact with a baseball. Then I was down on the floor.

I didn't pass out. I felt a sticky, oily feeling in my hair, but it wasn't oil. I had rinsed all the oil out.

'Ammamma,' I called, uncertainly. I wished there was someone else to call.

I tried to stand up. I unlatched the door, and called again, louder, 'Ammamma.'

I put my clothes on, underwear, salwar, pulled the drawstring tight, bra, catching the eye with the hook, twice. Then the kameez, over my head, and when I brought it down over my shoulders, and smoothed it down over my hips, the kameez was stained with red, and my hands were stained with red. My grandmother walked in, and she caught me as I slumped towards the ground. She sat right on the floor, the wet floor, and as I sank into her lap I was engulfed by the white of her sari, and watched as her sari became batiked red with my blood. And then I passed out.

CHAPTER SIX

The Lying-In

I WAS CONSCIOUS for most of the drive, but dazed, like I was wearing my grandmother's thick glasses and everything had receded into wobbly figures in the distance. At the company infirmary, I was lifted off my red-saried grandmother's lap in the back seat of the car by nurses and our driver and the doctor. The infirmary was adjacent to the tea factory, and I could smell freshly ground tea dust in the air.

The doctor asking my grandmother what happened. The nurses ushering patients out of their beds, in their house-

coats and rumpled hair, and escorting them to the two other
wards, so that the factory manager's niece could have her
own private ward. Me in a room of fourteen empty beds,
green scratchy blankets and grey-white starched sheets.

The doctor saying it looked like a bad fall. He would
take care of what he could and the rest would have to wait.
A nurse holding a white cloth on my head, until the white
was dyed red, and then applying a new cloth. Clumps of
my black hair descending on to the floor and across my
lap. Half-dry hair, wavy on one end, cut crisply on the
other end. A steel tray with sharp things, with black wiry
thread spooled around a card.

The doctor asking if I felt any pain. I felt nothing, but I
tasted blood in my mouth. Asking if I knew where I was,
who had brought me, what month it was. The infirmary,
my grandmother, July. Repeat after me: monkey, rowboat,
hat. Monkey, rowboat . . . hat.

He looked into my eyes, flashed a light on, off, on. He
asked me to follow his finger. He asked me to stick out my
tongue.

He asked if I had had a tetanus shot. Did I remember?
He was burning a needle in a flame that the nurse was
holding out to him over a steel tray. What I remembered
was the stapled folded set of medical records that my
mother had sent with me sitting in the suitcase under the
bed. Right next to the hypodermic needles and syringes
my mother had also sent with me, that my paediatrician
wouldn't give her, and that she got instead from my
father's Gujarati podiatrist. I said to my grandmother, 'Go
to the house, look under the bed. Someone must go and
look under the bed.' The doctor said to my grandmother,
'She is in shock; she is speaking nonsense. Sometimes it is
like this for some time,' and he walked towards me with
the shiny needle burned black on the tip. The black tip was

submerged in the plump soft skin of my upper arm, farther in and farther in, and then out. It was happening to someone else's arm, I felt numb, and far away. My hair was in my face, but my arms were too numb to reach up and push the hair out of the way. I pursed my lips and blew air out of my mouth upwards to try to move my hair off my nose and eyes where it was itching me.

Then the card with thread stretched tightly around it, unwound by the nurse, who flipped the card over for each length of thread, threading it on to a hooked instrument. The buzz of an electric razor, small fuzzy pieces of my hair flying around us. I felt the weight of hair bunched over on my left side, enveloping my shoulder, and the lightness of no hair on my right. There was a shooting icy pain, like a popsicle in my mouth bumping into a tooth that was sensitive to cold. I shuddered. 'That's the betadyne. It'll feel cold. We're just cleaning up the area.'

The nurse gathered all my hair to the left side and pinned it. She put a plastic drape on top of my head with an opening the shape of a diamond that she moved around until it was over the wound. The doctor came at me with a long thin needle, and he said, 'Have you ever been stung by a bee? This won't be worse than that.' I had been stung by a bee – it had hurt a lot. I braced myself for the needle plunging into my arm, I made a fist, clenched my jaw. Then I realized he was aiming the needle at my head. That taste of blood in my mouth, of blood and metal, and the burned sugar smell of hair oil, rose up, and choked me, and I started to gag. My grandmother reached out to stroke my back and the nurse readjusted the drape on my head. The doctor said, hiding the needle behind himself, 'Please be calm, child. We'll be finished soon.'

I closed my eyes. There was a rain of bee stings – not one, but two, three, four. I counted in my head the number of lockers down one long hall in my high school – fifteen between each classroom, six classrooms on that hall, twelve more lockers before you reached the stairwell, ten more by the exit sign. I heard the sound of them rattling open, slamming shut in those six minutes between classes.

There was the quiet sound of snipping. I saw the glint of scissors that the nurse handed to the doctor and that he handed back to her, and then the whole thing again. Each time, small pieces of thread fell on to the steel tray the nurse was holding out in front of me, like an airline stewardess proffering peanuts before dinner. The doctor cursed under his breath when the nurse said the surgical tape he wanted was out of stock. 'These Tiger supporters, they are swiping even my most basic supplies,' he said bitterly. The doctor opened a roll of wide tape, the sound of the adhesive back unsticking from itself. Scissors flashing, he cut the tape into smaller rectangle strips. Then gauze taken from the tray, then a bandage. Then a long white strip of cotton wrapped around my head like a Martina Navratilova headband to hold the bandage in place.

The doctor said, 'The most serious injuries are not always the ones that hurt the most.' He set my throbbing right arm with long wooden splints and then covered it with tight vicelike bandages up and down the length of my forearm.

The nurses disappeared with their trays, and the doctor told me to lie down. He and my grandmother talked. I heard some words and not others: *scan equipment, receptive language hearing, neurochecks, mental status changes, nerve fibres.*

'You can go home now – you will be more comfortable there than in this infirmary. I'll come and check on you, and I've explained to your grandmother what the next few days will be like,' the doctor said.

I looked at my grandmother standing there, her sari
bright, moist red only in parts now and mostly a dark,
dried, brown, her hair straggly and meagre. She was wearing ratty pink bedroom slippers my mother had brought
two trips ago. I looked at the hospital, at the nurses in their
stiff uniforms and the beds made with square corners, and
the green blankets each folded down at the same precise
angle.

'I'd rather stay at the hospital,' I said. I looked at the doctor and did not look at my grandmother.

'This isn't a hospital, child – it's an infirmary. There's
not much here for you. We called a hospital in
Coimbatore to see about sending some imaging equipment up here for you, maybe tomorrow as we see your
case develop. For now, go home with your grandmother. I
will look in on you.'

'Do you have trunk lines to make telephone calls?'

'Ours aren't working, but the tea factory has lines that
are working.'

'I want to call my parents in New York,' I said.

My grandmother looked at me, her eyes frightened, her
hand over her mouth. The doctor looked at her, then said,
'You know what, let's not call your parents right now.
They're on the other side of the world, they're sleeping,
no?'

'I want to call my aunt and uncle then. They're supposed to be in Bombay for another two weeks.'

The doctor said, 'We'll know more in a couple days, so
let's wait, shall we?' He said this like it was a question that
had only one answer. 'We'll worry everyone by calling. It
was a bad fall, but it has already happened. Now you need
bed rest. A lot of bed rest. Be a good girl; go with your
grandmother. Everything will be taken care of.'

Taken care of by who? My grandmother and a country

doctor? I wanted to call someone, anyone who lived any-where else, just so I wasn't swallowed up by this mountain place, forgotten here. But I was tired, and nauseated, I longed for cool clean sheets or, even better, a cool clean floor.

'Nausea is natural after an insult to the brain. Yes, and dizziness too, and fatigue. Look, if I tell you a list of symptoms you'll start being anxious, and you'll make yourself have them all. We can talk more after you've had rest,' the doctor said. To my grandmother he said, 'Nothing to worry, auntie. Do as I've told. Nothing to worry. '

We headed home. My grandmother put her arm around me in the car, but I squirmed away. I couldn't look at her, at that sari, and the fear in her eyes. I sat primly apart, near the window. But as the car gained speed, I was scared of being jostled. I leaned into her shoulder, let her absorb the friction of the car for me, from me.

I was crying without thinking about it. My grandmother said, urgently, 'What is it? Are you in pain? Should we go back?'

'No, no.'

'Then, what?' she said, her arm around me, holding me securely.

'I feel alone.' Her being here did not make me feel not alone. But she was all that I had right now. I knew this.

'Maya, you must believe me. I will do everything possible. I will do everything Dr Murugan says.'

'What if he's not a good doctor? Mother always gets a second opinion and a third opinion.'

'Then we can get more doctors for you, from Coimbatore – anything you want, Maya. But you have to be calm, and rest, and trust me. The doctor said if you're agitated, it's not good. Please. Will you?'

'I'm not agitated. I'm not,' I said. Now she was crying

too, the driver was eying us in the rearview mirror, some of her tears fell on me, dripped on to me leaning on her shoulder. I gave in. 'Don't cry, Ammamma.'

'I will. I will do everything. I know you think of me as an old woman. But I can do this. You'll be better, you'll see,' she said, speaking into my hair. I nodded drowsily, falling off to sleep.

I WAS TIRED all the time. I couldn't sleep for more than a few minutes before feeling uncomfortable. Then my grandmother and Vasani would come and help me change position in my bed. I felt nauseated, and the painkillers I took at regular intervals made me more nauseated, until I was entirely unable to eat. My grandmother fixed all kinds of concoctions, but I couldn't eat any of them. The doctor on his next visit brought electrolyte fluid. It tasted like flat orange soda mixed with baby aspirin and salt. Every five hours, I drank a whole teacupful, usually in two large gulps. Right after, Ammamma gave me a pinch of sugar to hold on my tongue to chase away the bitter and the salty with sweet.

I was moved into Ammamma's room, so she could watch me. The two double beds had been separated; she slept a few feet away so that she did not turn and wake me or disturb my sheets. My bed was under the mosquito net. My grandmother didn't want me using the chemical repellent while I was taking strong medications, and while I couldn't bathe. Every time I woke in the night, she was standing there peering at me through the white netting.

Not bathing contributed more to my discomfort than my injuries did. My hair hung limply, my face was covered with a thin film of flaking skin. With one of my grandmother's handkerchiefs, I wiped my forehead and came away with grey smudges. My grandmother brought a bucket to the side of my bed and she helped me soap my face, my hands, then rinse, dry. On the third day, the doctor let me have a 'half-bath.' I sat on a low bench in the bathroom, and Ammamma filled one bucket with soapy water and one bucket with warm clear water. She soaped a washcloth and handed it to me. I waited for her to leave – she stayed just outside the door, worried I might need her – and then took off my robe, managing everything with my left hand, my right hand limp like a scarecrow's. Ammamma had covered the bandages with the bubblewrap Mother had cushioned Reema auntie's perfumes in. I soaped everywhere with my one good hand. Then I poured pitchers of clear water over myself from the neck down. I put the robe back on, and called for Ammamma. She came, helped me rise from the bench, and walked me back to my bed. She left me sitting on my bed with fresh clothes laid out. It took me fifteen minutes to manoeuvre into a salwar kameez. Ammamma came back then to do up the snaps on the back of the kameez.

It was delicate, this matter of staking out a little territory of privacy, even though I needed help eating and cleaning and dressing myself. Ammamma tried to respect my wishes, appearing and disappearing at a moment's request, but I still felt self-conscious, awkward. I suggested having Rupa come to help, it would be better. With her, I knew there would be the unembarrassment of sisters, the easiness of those who have swum and played together and know the other's body instinctively because it is so much like one's own. But Ammamma brushed my request away, not seeing what was behind it, saying, 'I can manage everything you need, Maya. I want to do everything for you myself – you have only to ask.'

Each time the doctor came, two or three times every day, we played twenty questions, sometimes with my grandmother, too. I had to be able to guess what they were talking about, identify the name of my high-school teachers, of my cousins, of different countries, different kinds of fruit.

It was hard to stay in bed all the time. My legs cramped up, and my back hurt. Sometimes I would lean on Ammamma and walk around a bit, but I would get dizzy and tired and have to lie down. Each time she walked me to the bathroom, and waited just outside, she talked the whole time through the door, nervous that I would be dizzy or lose my balance. Walking felt strange, my weight supported by another. I felt gravityless, only touching on the earth, but not bound to it.

A Dr Mani came from Coimbatore. He was a neurologist and a professor on faculty at the medical school there. He made me play more games, word games, puzzles, add numbers together, count backwards. I liked him better than Dr Murugan; he talked to me, told me what he was thinking. He said I had good long-term memory and good short-term memory, and was processing information well.

'It is important to talk openly about gains and abilities,' he said, sitting on the side of my bed. Boli barked indignantly on the other side of the door; he had been banned from my room, and he was incensed that there was a visitor who had not yet passed muster with him.

'Is everything going to be normal?' I said.

'Everything looks pretty much on track. But tell your grandmother immediately if the headaches get more frequent or more intense, or if you feel like you are forgetting things or not able to think of words for things you know.'

I told him how I kept trying to think of things I wanted to make sure I didn't forget. I kept repeating my name over and over silently, so that it wouldn't go away from me. I wanted to write things down, but I couldn't because of my arm. It made me dizzy to think of everything in my head. 'Is that strange?' I said.

'It's normal to be worried about failure of memory in a situation like this. But try not to be obsessive. Hopefully, you will have everything up there' – and he tapped my head – 'that you used to have.'

My grandmother came in with a glass of tea for Dr Mani.

'I am going to suggest to your grandmother that she help you explore your memory so you're not worried about it by yourself. If there are gaps, I can come back and talk to you and see if they are significant.'

'Like those questions Dr Murugan is always asking?' I said.

'This is different. This is not testing abilities per se, this is about talking and exploring a whole range of memory,' he said. Picking up a picture frame from the bureau, he said to my grandmother, 'Use photos of family, friends, possessions. Speak of familiar names, places, interests, and activities. And, Maya, these things you're worried about losing, tell your grandmother. She can write it down and remember it for you, so she can remind you if you need it. If there's anything you don't feel fully comfortable sharing with her, you can give her keywords or names, so you can use them to remind yourself. This should help you relax, I hope. Is there anything else you want to ask me?'

Yes, I thought. Will you stay? Will you take care of me? Will you be my confidant, my comrade, my partner in memory? I would tell you everything, so easily.

But instead, there was my grandmother. Over the next days, I told her things. She did not comment – she just wrote, asked me to repeat things, go slow. She filled page after page of a notebook, front and back.

I told everything – my first treehouse, my first swim

team medal, my first period. The only time Mother ever slapped me, the only time I had detention at school, the only stuffed animal I still slept with. The walk home from junior high school to my house, the muddy field we cut across, red maple leaves in our hair, the races to the stop sign, and then running back to pick up the books and lunch bags we'd deposited on the side of the road. The bus to high school where everyone picked on the new girl from Hungary who wore the same clothes three days in a row and had crossed eyes. How my lab partner in chemistry class was known for breaking things – pipettes, flasks, microscopes – so that everyone thought it was her fault our experiment caught fire, but it was mine. How the girls at my last slumber party wouldn't talk to each other by the end of the night.

My best friend, Jennifer. My rival on the swim team, Samantha. The year I took horse-riding lessons until a horse threw me, and then I stopped. The summer I worked at the movie cineplex and gained seven pounds from subsisting on buttered popcorn and Raisinets.

My friend Steve. How I taught him the whole periodic table. And binomial equations. And trig. How he ran for student council and made a speech in front of the whole school. And lost.

And how I kissed him in the school parking lot that day to make him feel better. I wanted to say this, but I didn't. In the pause, as I thought of what to say instead, my grandmother looked up from the notebook, shaking her pen to bring more ink down.

'Maya,' my grandmother said. 'Pretend I'm not your grandmother if it helps. I know in your life, like in anyone's life, there might be things you are not proud of, or things you are proud of that you think your family would not accept.'

I didn't say anything.

She continued. 'I am old, and I won't to try to tell you what is acceptable or not. Tell me everything, so you can have everything back that was yours. These notebooks you can take, and the things I know I will take to my grave.'

'Don't talk like that, Ammamma. You'll be alive for a long time. Mother says half of it is positive thinking. She worries about you.'

'Does she? What your mother doesn't understand is that I'm not afraid to die – it's more natural than to live beyond everyone you know.'

'Seventy-one is not that old, Ammamma. We know lots of people older than you.'

'Yes, but unfortunately, not so many I am close to. Your grandfather's family, they have weak hearts. His three brothers died in their sixties soon after your grandfather. And my two brothers, they're not well. I would rather not live than be bedridden like them.'

'I'm bedridden,' I said, trying to make her smile.

'It's not the same. I sit by your bed, and each day I see you more lively, less tired, light in your eyes, restlessness in your legs. It's not like that when you're old. Lying in a bed when you're old, it saps the strength, the light leaves the eyes.'

My grandmother opened her cupboard and took out her stuffed black leather address book. She opened it and ran her finger down a page, sight-reading, and then tore the page out. Then another, and another. 'I should have done this a long time ago,' she said. I picked up one of the pages on my bed, and looked at the people listed there, some with many addresses, some with maiden names and married names both, the names of children and grand-children written in the margin.

'Are all these people . . . gone?' I said. She nodded. Just before tearing out another page, she stopped.

'Look here,' she said. 'This is the doctor who delivered you. I wonder if she is still alive.'

'Who was she, Ammamma?'

'Dr Bose. She was the only lady doctor in our town, one of the first who was granted entry into India's best medical school. Your grandfather was impressed with her – he wanted your mother to grow up to be a doctor like Dr Bose. We were all dear friends.'

'Then why don't you know where she is now?'

My grandmother would not look at me. She spoke in a flat voice. 'Some things are too old to talk about. Shall we go back to the writing, to your memories?'

'These are my memories, too, Ammamma,' I said. 'The ones I couldn't forget because I had never known them. These years before I was born. And the years I lived with you when I was a baby. How did that happen?'

'When your mother was six months pregnant, she came back to us from America. Your father brought her and had to go back in a few days. He didn't have much leave from his job – he'd only been at that company for a short time.'

'Didn't Dad mind not being here when I was born?'

'I'm sure he wished he could be, but he couldn't come here for a longer stay, and we didn't want her to be in America for her first child. We wanted her to come even sooner, but she had her job and had to stay on to finish some things. She came near the end of her sixth month, for her lying-in. In those days it was customary to have a time of confinement, when a girl would be with her mother and the women in her family, and everyone could watch over her.'

'I must have missed my mother when she went back to New York.' I said it as both statement and question. I couldn't call up memories of what I had felt as a baby, but I often suspected I could still know what it had been like.

'I think you missed her, but you were so young, only three months. Your mother had been breastfeeding you, so it took some time for you to adjust to milk powder. You lost a few pounds and made us nervous. But you were eating and making sounds and banging on toys in no time.'

'And Mother just left me like that. Just went back to New York.'

'At the time, it seemed like the best thing. Your mother and father came to visit once every year. We sent them pictures of everything – your baby steps, your pretty dresses, your blessing at the temple. We did everything for you that we imagined they would do.'

'But Ammamma, I didn't even know really that you were not my mother. When I went to America, I kept wondering why you sent me to live with this nice auntie and uncle who used to visit us.'

'We tried when they visited to explain to you who they were. You were shy, and we didn't want to push you. We hoped in time you would understand.'

'Understand what? That my mother didn't take me with her because I would have been in the way?'

'Maya, don't be so hard on your parents. They want everything to be good in your life.'

'Ammamma, you don't have to protect them. Sometimes, I see Mother look at me like she's reminding herself she even has a kid. I wonder if she didn't really want to have one. I've never said that to her because I know she'll deny it.'

'It's not true, Maya. They very much wanted children. They were so happy when your mother found out she was expecting, I remember the phones were down and your mother reaching us by telegram to tell us.'

'But having a baby doesn't mean just having it. They tell us that over and over again at school. You're supposed to stay around and take care of it. That's how you prove you're a good mother.'

'You have to believe your mother loves you.'

'Why should I believe that, Ammamma? We don't talk, we're not close, it's just not that way.'

'Maybe it will get better, when you're not a teenager any more and there aren't so many things to have conflict over.'

'The older I get, the less I need them. When I did need them, when I was a kid, they didn't bother. '

'Was it so hard for you back then? I hoped you would like it in America.'

'Everything was so new. I was scared of sleeping in my room. I'd never slept without you. I kept waiting for my real life to start again, to come back to our old house here with you and Sanjay uncle and that old monkey we had – remember Kiki?'

'How could I forget Kiki?' Ammamma extended her arm, where there were still sharp scars of the monkey's teethmarks at her wrist. 'Maya, it's been a mistake to let you think these things for so many years. When I hear you blame your mother, I realize it's not right to let this continue. A lot of what happened back then was my fault.'

'Your fault, Ammamma?'

The servants had come in many times to ask us what to do about dinner. Ammamma sent them away again before she turned to me.

'It was my idea for you to stay with me. I thought that would be best.'

'But why didn't Mother stay here too?'

'Because she wasn't well. We thought it would help for her to go back to New York.'

'What do you mean she wasn't well? What was wrong with her?'

'She was in a depression after your birth. It wasn't

improving even after a few months.'

'So she felt better by being far away from me?'

'You're not understanding . . . maybe I'm not explaining properly. Your mother doesn't talk about this, so I never thought I would tell you. But if it makes you resent her less, it is better for everyone.'

Ammamma looked so serious. She got up to arrange the netting around my bed, it was getting darker and the insects were coming out. She sat on a chair next to the bed. But I wanted to see her face as she talked, so I picked up a corner of the net and made her creep under it and sit on my bed.

'It was my fault.' Ammamma put her hands over her face.

'What, Ammamma?' I said, sitting up straighter. My bad arm lay stiff on the blanket next to her, but I reached over with the other arm to touch her. She shivered for a second when I did that.

'When your mother was pregnant with you, I was the one who said she must come to India for your birth. That she should honour tradition. She offered to fly me to New York or to come in the months after your birth, but I told her that was not enough. Your father urged her to do what I wanted. He had only been married two years – he felt he knew nothing about children being born, and that she was safer with us.

'She came, and in the last six weeks of her pregnancy, she wasn't well. I was glad she was with us. She had complete bed rest as the doctor instructed, and we could look after everything. I prepared her food by myself, not trusting the servants to cook without butter or ghee or any kind of nuts or tomatoes or the other things your mother was sensitive to. She was like you are now, only able to walk for a few minutes before tiring, thirsty all the time, sleepless at night because she had lain in bed all day.

'We had Dr Bose, who I told you we thought was a very good doctor. I still think she was a good doctor. There are some things no doctor can control . . . There was another baby, Maya, besides you – your twin, and she died nineteen days after you were both born.'

I took my hand back from Ammamma. Part of me wanted to know everything she was saying and the other part of me kept chanting This is not real, this can't be real. Ammamma got out from the netting and went to her cupboard and pulled out an old rucksack. She brought it with her back to the bed. She emptied the rucksack out and there were two sunbonnets, two rattles, two bibs, two tarnished, streaked silver spoons.

'Your mother took it very hard. She was afraid to get attached to you. And she didn't want comfort from any of us, especially me. Your mother believed if she had been in New York, they might have saved your sister. And your father was far away; communication was difficult. He did not even know the other baby had died for another three days, and there were still presents coming in the mail for weeks after that he'd already mailed – presents that came in twos. Your mother would cry every day when she saw the mail carrier coming to the house.

'The more your mother pushed me away, the guiltier I felt. I tried to do everything for you. I wanted to still be good at mothering someone, even if not my own daughter.

'I don't know if anything would have turned out differently in New York, I only know that I disregarded your mother's wish to stay there, to have her babies in the new country she had come to know and trust. It seemed so important then that she be here, that she share this birth with the family. I wanted you – and your sister – to be ours, not just hers. It was selfish, and everything might have been different.

'I read in the paper about miracle babies in America, five babies born at a time, at three pounds, two pounds, each. I think how our other little one might still be alive over there.'

'What was her name?' I tried to ask in a regular tone of voice but it came out in a cracked whisper.

'Shivani would have been her name. But she died before the name-day ceremony.'

'Everyone knows? Sanjay uncle, Reema auntie, Daddy's whole family?'

'Yes, everyone knows. Because they were either there for your birth or they were coming for the name-day ceremony. We had it still, but your mother couldn't take part. She was sedated by the doctor for most of it. She refused to talk to the guests in the house.'

'And no one thought of telling me?'

'Your mother never wanted it talked about. Many people are superstitious about things like that – she did not want them to say your life would be marred by it. That's why she never had a horoscope made for you. She did not want you to find out anything that would make you think your life had been unlucky.'

'But you could have told me I had a sister. I should have been told that.'

'When would we have told you, Maya? When you were four, and screaming in your parents' arms? Or when you were nine and had an imaginary friend you told us was because your parents never gave you a brother or sister? When you were here in the summers and seemed happy and at home?'

'I don't know when. But maybe I wouldn't feel like I didn't know myself now.'

'Don't blame your mother for that. Blame me,'

Ammamma said.

That would be much harder. I had spent too many years thinking of everything a certain way. I didn't want to talk any more. I slipped down lower on the pillows and closed my eyes. Ammamma gently lifted the net to exit, then tucked it back. She went to the kitchen and came back in a little while.

'Are you hungry? Do you think you might be ready for some food or do you want another electrolyte drink?' she said. She had a thali plate with her. There was rice in the middle, and on the side compartments, yogurt, dal, a piece of lime pickle, and a small mound of coarse sea salt.

I was hungry. She lifted the mosquito net and sat next to me. At first Ammamma mixed the food in the palm of her hand, and lined it up in spoon-size lumps for me to eat myself. But when I lost interest in eating after a few spoonfuls, she insisted on feeding me by hand. With each clump of rice, she alternated a dab of dal or a dab of yogurt, and touched it against the salt and the pickle for flavour. She scooped too much in her hand one time, and dal dribbled on my chin and the front of my salwar. I wiped my face with my good left arm, and tried to pick the lentil pieces off the front of my shirt. I put the remnants on the side of the plate.

'I'm sorry,' she said. She swabbed at my shirt with the end of her sari.

'Can you bring me another salwar kameez, please?' I said plaintively.

She brought me clothes from Reema auntie's wardrobe and then stood outside the door. I was wearing my aunt's oldest salwars, the ones that were out of fashion now, because they were the loose flowing style and easier to pull on and off with my one good hand. Once I had it on I got under the covers, and Ammamma came in, tucked the nets around me, and sat in her chair knitting blindly in the dark, watching as I went to sleep.

AFTER BREAKFAST THE next morning, Ammamma brought her chair near the bed and filled her pen with ink.

I didn't want to do the notebooks and the remembering any more. I wasn't sure I wanted to keep the way I remembered things the same.

'I'm bored,' I said. 'Can I walk around?'

We walked out of my room for the first time, just the length of the hall. There were good smells from the kitchen. 'Let's go in there,' I said. My grandmother walked me there, and Sunil and Matthew jumped to their feet. Ammamma told Matthew to bring me a mat to sit on. After watching me for a few minutes, Sunil and Matthew went back to squatting on their haunches. Sunil was sifting rice on a fine cane mat, separating out the husks and stones. Matthew was grinding spices, making garam masala for the week's curries. Coriander seeds and leaves, cumin seeds, whole peppercorns. Cardamom teased out of its jacket, cinnamon sticks, whole cloves, fresh nutmeg.

'Write these things in the notebook, Ammamma,' I said. 'How much garam masala for alu gobi, how much for channa. And write the way you make okra. Daddy says his favourite way is the way you make it. And bitter gourd fritters, too.'

Ammamma brought a notebook to the kitchen and flipped to a clean page. She took out a teaspoon and the sugarbowl and kept putting sugar into the spoon with her fingers. She said she had to figure out how many pinches of things equalled how many spoons.

'Tomorrow, can we have okra so I can learn how to make it?'

'Maya, you're not well enough to eat that yet. You still have a weak stomach.'

'Then I don't have to eat it. Sunil can eat it. I just want to see how you make it. If you wait till I'm better, Reema auntie won't want me hanging around the kitchen. So let's do everything now.'

Ammamma told Matthew to pluck some green plaintain for tomorrow. And to bring some okra from the market for the day after that. And some chicken.

'But only a small portion. For two people only,' she said gravely in Malayalam. She whispered to me so he wouldn't hear, 'Wait until he sees it's all for them!'

Ammamma helped me to the front porch for a few minutes. This time of day, the sunlight was directly on us. It was the first time I felt sun warm my face since the day of the fall, and it felt good, a warm, glowing reunion. Then I saw black spots before me, black and purple flashing spots, and my head hurt. We went back inside.

Ammamma asked in the afternoon if it was OK that the servants came into our room and she finished their letters home. Their families would have missed hearing from them these days that she had neglected them and been occupied with me. Matthew and Vasani sat on the floor at the side of my bed, and Ammamma sat in her chair. She did not try to make them have spelling lessons or drag out the dictations today. I wanted to sit up and watch, so another chair was brought for me.

When the letters were finished, Matthew brought cooked rice from the kitchen to use to seal the envelopes. Ammamma wrote the destinations on the outside in her graceful hand, and gave Matthew and Vasani their letters. They received them gingerly, like they were being entrusted with sacred stone tablets. As they got up to leave, Vasani shyly extracted a folded-up piece of paper from her skirts, and showed it to Ammamma. Vasani had traced out her alphabet letters just under Ammamma's handwriting. Each letter had many bumps, where the pen had lifted off and returned to the paper, and the ink was thick from pressing the nib hard. Ammamma was pleased – sometimes she had to push Vasani to complete her lessons. Ammamma wrote out five more letters, large and looping, and took Vasani's hand in hers, tracing over the letters so that Vasani started and ended in the one sweep that Ammamma used. Matthew and I looked on, and Ammamma took out more paper for him to write on. I took a piece of paper from her lap and drew the same letter Vasani and Ammamma had just drawn – a planet with a ring around it and an upward pointing tail. Then an oval-shaped planet, with two rings and a diagonal. Ammamma corrected the angle of the tail. Once I had the shape of it, she told me to shrink it down to size. I repeated the downscaled letter five or ten times in a row. We filled up sheets and sheets like that – big bulky letters followed by their offspring of baby letters. Afraid of dampening my interest, Ammamma only told me afterwards that I'd been learning to write Tamil, not Malayalam. She taught the servants Tamil so they could communicate with their families; she suggested separate lessons in Malayalam for me, and I agreed to try it for a while.

At night, Ammamma came into my room with a pickle jar covered with cloth. I was not sleeping but the lights were off in the room. They had been so dim that night because of the load-shedding that they were not useful at all. The nets had come down for the night, and I was lying there listening to the wheezing ceiling fan.

'Sunil helped me with these,' my grandmother said. She ducked under the netting and sat cross-legged at the foot of the bed. She removed the cloth cover and waved the jar through the air. Blinking lights tumbled out and took flight. Fireflies winged through the air, occasionally bumping into the nets and falling in straight vertical drops, then readjusting themselves. It felt magical.

'We used to do this for your mother to appease her when she wanted to sleep on the roof with her brother and his friends,' Ammamma said.

'I wish there was a flat roof for sleeping on this house,' I said. 'I would sleep out there.'

'That's why I'm glad there isn't one,' Ammamma said. 'I hope you can be back outside soon. I know it's hard for you to be in here like this.'

'The stitches come out in two more days. I can't wait,' I said.

Ammamma said, 'And this weekend, Reema auntie and Sanjay uncle come back. And everything will be the way it was.'

'At least we can think about other things and forget all this,' I said.

'Yes,' my grandmother said, picking up the nets to get out. She repeated softly, not resentfully, but with wistfulness, 'At least you can think about other things.'

IN THE MORNING when I woke up, my grandmother was tiptoeing around my bed. She had the pickle jar with her. She was collecting the fireflies, some dead, some comatose in sleep, to take away.

'I didn't want you to wake up and see them here. I find them depressing in the morning. They don't have any place in the day,' she said, plucking one off the net near my head.

'I feel aches all over from lying down all the time,' I said, sitting up in bed.

Ammamma led me to a chair. She said, 'Why don't we try some dance steps?'

Dance steps? I could still hardly walk around the house.

'You can do it from the chair. It's good for stretching,' Ammamma said.

She opened the wardrobe. The side that had been cleared out for me at the beginning of the summer now held my clothes, my medication, my books. Ammamma rummaged through her side and found in the back of a lower shelf what she was looking for. She pulled out a hand-pumped harmonium, and began to play.

I danced whatever I remembered, from the edge of my chair. I stretched my arms above my head, to the right, to the left, forming lotus leaves, holding tea lights, hiding behind peacock feathers. I bent my legs at the knees and pounded out the steps on the floor, my feet slapping the floor loudly, echoing through the room. She played the harmonium and kept time. We counted together, 'one-two-three, one-two-three, ONE-TWO. Thid-thid-they, thid-thid-they, THID-THEY. Thid-they, thid-they, thid-they, THID-THEY.'

In the afternoon, we worked on my summer reading, *Huckleberry Finn*. Ammamma read me chapter eleven, where Huck discovered that men were coming to look for the runaway slave, Jim. Huck told Jim to hurry, 'they're after US,' even though they were only after Jim. I told Ammamma to read this part slowly, and I told her which sentences to underline in the book. I was going to use it as an example of Huck allying with the runaway slave who has broken with society, even though it meant jeopardizing his own safety. I had to write a paper on the topic: 'Discuss Huck Finn's choice between the freedom of the raft and the restriction of the society on the shore.' It had to be done before the first day of school.

It was Thursday, the day the stitches were to come out. I didn't even want breakfast. I wanted to go to the infirmary as soon as I woke up.

Ammamma coaxed me to drink tea and sit at the table with her. 'The doctor won't be there this early, Maya. Ram is also mending the tyre, so even our car is not ready. Wait an hour or two and then we'll go.'

Dr Murugan was still saying his morning shlokas when we arrived, so we waited with the nurse. We sat in his office, and I leafed through one of his dusty medical books, shaking out the dead spiders to look at the colour plates of the brain. His home adjoined the infirmary, and the chickens that his wife kept in their backyard were making loud fighting sounds.

Dr Murugan came into his office, still buttoning his blue bush shirt that he wore to say his prayers. He pulled a white coat over himself, and moved his glasses down from the top of his head to sit far out on the tip of his nose.

There was another nurse, but no sight of the two that I had seen previously. She knew the routine: steel tray, steel instruments, and collecting the bits of thread on to the tray as the doctor worked. I could feel him manoeuvring on top of my head, and I thought that I could even feel the stiches being undone, the threads coming loose. It felt like floss being moved between two tight teeth. It had to be wedged slowly through the tight part, and the rest was easy. The bandages that the doctor had stripped away lay in my lap. They seemed wholly foreign to me – yellowed from my betadyne, browned from my blood. I closed my eyes.

I opened them and the nurse was standing there with a mirror.

Dr Murugan was washing his hands as he talked to me. 'Don't worry, child, the hair will grow back. Not right where the scar is, but all around it. And until then, you can use hairpins to pin your hair over it. You can wash your hair but be very careful – ask your grandmother to help you. Keep the splints on your arm for another two weeks and then we'll see.'

In the mirror, I saw a small, pale clearing at the top right side of my head. I touched it tentatively, and there were raised scars in the centre of the clearing. I closed my eyes.

WE WERE HOME. Vasani carried hot bathwater to my bathroom. Ammamma said, 'Look what Ram brought you.' He had brought five different kinds of shampoo from the city, afraid of choosing the wrong one. I didn't recognize any of them.

'You pick,' I said. Ammamma picked one and put it on the window ledge in the bathroom.

She filled a bucket with cold water, and then poured hot and cold water together in a third bucket. She swirled the water inside the bucket to mix the water from bottom to top, hot and cold melding into warm.

'Are you ready?' she said. I took the robe off, keeping my arm stiffly in place. I remembered Ammamma giving me baths when I was little. I would clutch her sari-covered leg at the knee. I would reach out and try to grab her gold wedding necklace, which would be fluttering just out of reach as she bent to pour water over me. She would keep a hand as a brim over my forehead, to keep the soap from my eyes. Her sari would be soggy and bedraggled by the end.

Now I was taller than she was, by two inches. I sat on the bench, and she poured water over me. She kept a hand as a brim over my forehead, to keep the soap from my eyes. I felt a shiver travel over my spine, my arms bristling with goosepimples, my breasts rising up under her touch.

She moved quickly, smoothly, soaping, then rinsing, shampooing, then rinsing. She worked her fingers through my hair, massaging gently, pouring pitchers of water at a slant to fall away from my face. And then, wrapping a thorthu deftly around me, avoiding my limp right arm, she applied another towel to my hair, not rubbing, but sponging, pressing lightly.

Afterwards, I sat on my bed, and held a mirror up as she combed my hair. We parted the hair on the side, and clipped it over the pale white empty patch. It looked unnatural, lopsided.

'Let's try something,' Ammamma said. Rather than pushing hair from one side over to the other, she pulled all the hair upwards into a ponytail on the top of my head. It did cover the white spot more naturally. But because my hair was short, there was no nice ponytail at the end – just a true pig's tail, a stubby, bumpy knot of a tail. Ammamma opened and closed different drawers in her dresser, and then she came back to the bed with one of her British cookie tins. She opened it, and inside was red tissue paper, and inside that was a coil of hair.

'Your mother's hair,' Ammamma said. 'Extensions were the fashion when she was your age.'

She undid the ponytail and braided my mother's hair into mine, starting at the nape of my neck. She braided it halfway and swept up the end into a ponytail, and rubberbanded it in place. A sleek shiny ponytail nodded at me in the mirror when I moved my head.

'I've never worn fake hair before,' I said. 'But it does look better than without it.'

'In another two weeks, the hair will grow back enough to cover the whiteness, then it won't be that noticeable. But for now, if you want, we can do your hair up like this. It's easy.'

A new thought occurred to me. 'Maybe we don't have to tell Reema auntie and Sanjay uncle this all happened. They'll make such a fuss, and their friends and everyone will ask about it.'

'It's impossible not to tell them – the servants know, and everyone at the infirmary, and probably some people at the factory. Just tell what happened, and how you've been taken care of.'

I took Ammamma's hand from my hair where she was still smoothing the ponytail, wrapping my fingers over her soft wrinkled hands, feeling the skin and the bone of her hand as distinctly discrete things. Her eyes looked tired and shadowed; she had not slept through a whole night since I'd been injured. I felt sleepy from the exertions at the infirmary, the bath. I drew Ammamma down next to me on my bed, and we slept the afternoon away.

CHAPTER SEVEN

Harvest

THE HOUSE WAS full of sound again once Reema auntie and Sanjay uncle returned from Bombay. Sanjay uncle was frustrated with the factory mechanics whom he'd summoned to repair the phone line to the house. He asked us how long it had been out of order, and we shrugged. At least the last two weeks, we weren't sure – we hadn't needed to phone anyone. Reema auntie wanted the furniture in the drawing room rearranged to make space for the inlaid marble table she had bought from a Bombay antiques dealer. Neighbours came to ask for news of Bombay movies and restaurants and sari emporiums.

Ammamma and I sat in our room and made faces at each other. We'd both been put to bed the second Reema auntie and Sanjay uncle spotted my artfully arranged hair and found out what had happened. Neither of us felt like we needed to be in bed, but we took our punishment quietly. They were furious that we hadn't called them in Bombay. They would have come home earlier, sent friends and company people to look in on us, and consulted all their doctors in Coimbatore.

Ammamma bore the brunt of both their reproaches and their concern. I looked healthy enough now, sounded good-humoured about my injury; I was surely getting better. But Ammamma should have been responsible and called them, and she should have arranged full-time help to take care of me, a nurse or an nanny or both, rather than doing it herself. They were worried that she looked tired, that she hadn't been eating properly, that she hadn't even reordered some of her medicines when she had run out. As soon as the phones were fixed, they were calling their doctors in Coimbatore to come up the mountain to look at both of us.

By the second day of their return, I was restless. Ammamma and I weren't allowed anywhere near the kitchen, nor in the drawing room with the visitors, and certainly not outside where we couldn't be watched over. They didn't want us to exert ourselves or have undue excitement. Even our food had no excitement – just rice and yogurt and dal, even though Ammamma in the days just before their return had let me graduate to eating the vegetable curries we cooked together.

I tossed my book aside and disentangled myself from

the bedcovers. 'Shall I go protest our confinement?' I said to Ammamma.

'I don't know if it will do much good,' she said, looking at me over her book.

'The doctors aren't coming for another two days and we can't just lie here until then,' I said. 'We can at least try to campaign for more rights.'

'You go then. You'll be more effective. I'm in more trouble than you are,' she said, smiling.

I slipped my feet into my sandals, saluted her, and walked down the hall towards my aunt and uncle's bedroom.

They weren't there, but I heard voices in the drawing room. As I crossed the dining room to join them, I caught a glimpse of my aunt on a sofa, with blue letter paper strewn across her lap. I stopped in my tracks in the dining room, hearing my aunt crying. I stood outside their view, listening.

'Reema, she'll manage, she will. She is growing up, and she will learn how to be on her own.'

'Sanjay, I can't bear leaving her there with those children. They sound cruel and awful. She's the first one to start her periods, she's still a child. She writes that they taunt her, and say that she is polluted and dirty.' My aunt covered her face with her hands. 'They're calling our daughter dirty, Sanjay.'

My uncle reached out to her on the sofa. 'Reema, what can we do? She has to go to school, and it's a good school. Do you want me to call the headmistress and say something?'

'Don't call. If she reprimands any of the children, they'll take it out on Brindha.'

'We'll go and see her. In three more weeks is the Visiting Weekend. I've booked the company bungalow, and we'll have a nice stay.'

'I don't want to wait three weeks. She didn't even know what was happening to her. I never thought to tell her – ten is so early.'

'She was making friends, wasn't she, this year? That letter we got before we went to Bombay said she was trying to choose between two girls for who would be her new best friend.'

'But these letters that came while we were away, she sounds lonely. And the letters I wrote her from Bombay were about stupid films and parties. I couldn't even write her about these things she's upset about. I didn't even know.'

'It's not your fault, Reema. These things happen. You can't sit here like you did when she first went to boarding school last year. You can't spend the whole day waiting for the boy to bring the mail. That's not the answer.'

'Then what's the answer? Maybe I'll go and stay at my parents' house in Palgaat, and she can go to school there.'

'Then what will I do? I have to stay on here. This job is important. In a few years, I have to think about sending Brindha to university, even abroad if necessary. And look at how my mother is. Her health isn't good – I can see a difference even in this short time we've been away. What if she needs to go to hospital or what if my sister wants me to send Amma to an American hospital? I have to think of these things. What do you want me to do?'

'Nothing. Nothing.' My aunt breathed heavily, her tears coming under control. 'There's nothing we can do.'

'Look here in this letter, she doesn't sound so sad. Did you read this one? She's talking about the state education minister coming to the school assembly, and she was asked to do a recitation. She says the minister gave her a sandalwood letter opener.'

'Yes, I read that,' my aunt said.

'And see here, she is helping in a celebration of Onam. Reema, read this part, from here.'

My aunt cleared her throat, reading. 'She says 'the other Malayali girls here are 'too Mallu' to be good actresses, so I am the only Malayali taking part. The other girls don't even know what Onam is but they are happy for any excuse for a party. I am going to play King Mahabali, and my Punjabi friend, Jyothi, is going to play God. I think Mahabali is a better role because I get to wear a lot of makeup and gold and silver robes, and God is only wearing a cotton kurta."

'See, she is getting through. I know the children can be cruel, but they seem to have short memories.'

'Brindha doesn't have a short memory,' Reema auntie said.

'Yes, but learning to live with insults, that's part of school.'

'Not for me. It wasn't like that at my school,' Reema auntie said.

Sanjay uncle said, 'Then you were lucky. They were merciless to my sister – they said she would never marry because she was too busy studying and she didn't even know how to wear a sari properly or cook a payasam. There's always something.'

'What should we do about Onam? I don't feel like celebrating since Brindha's not here. '

'Yes, but Maya is here, and for us too – we have to have a full life, Reema, just like we tell Brindha to have at school.'

'They wanted me to run the Onam festival at the club, but I haven't given an answer yet.'

'Tell them you will. We'll have a big show of it – it will be good for you.'

I crept silently back down the hall to my room.

Ammamma looked over at me as I slipped into bed.

'No success?' she said.

I shook my head no.

'That's OK. I'm a bit tired, anyway. I hope the doctors will soon release you from captivity.' Ammamma looked quite settled in her bed. Her thin grey hair was unpinned and smoothed out on the pillow behind her head. There was another pillow under her lower back so she could sit up at a slight incline to read, and another pillow under her knees, which she'd rubbed with herbal ointment to ease the arthritic aches. When I had been three or four, Ammamma used to have me walk on her legs and lower back to relieve her aches. Walking on uneven territory like that, I would slip and stumble in her sari folds and fall giggling on top of her.

The doctors came, one for me, one for Ammamma. They were both dour-faced, but they admitted we couldn't stay in bed forever. They told both of us to take bed rest whenever we felt the least bit tired. The doctor for Ammamma brought loads of pills for her – big, hard-to-swallow ones in pastel colours. He laid them out on a magazine cover and reminded her what each one was for and how many times a day to take them. Ammamma dumped the whole collection of jewels in her lap, and wrapped each colour of pills in separate pieces of brown paper, and then tucked them snugly into the British biscuit tins where they belonged.

Reema auntie said to my doctor, 'I am chairing an Onam festival at our club, and I was thinking Maya might take part if it's not too much for her.'

The doctor said, 'A doctor doesn't like to say his patients know more than he does, but in a situation like this, only she knows what goes on inside her head. The external wound is healing correctly, so it's more a matter of headaches, continued dizziness. Maya's the best judge of what she can manage.'

Repacking his medical bag, Ammamma's doctor said, 'So will you be having grand Onam celebrations this year in the hills?'

'I don't know about grand,' my aunt said. 'But you must come and join us if you can.'

Reema auntie was being modest with the doctors – she was planning a grand celebration. The harvest holiday of Onam would begin next week and it would last for ten days. We spent hours planning the feast, the flower decorations, the performances of song and dance. We talked about whether to have party favours, and whether to have place cards. We spent one morning writing up announcement cards – everyone at the club was invited, so this was more to remind them. Reema auntie was handpainting fleshy red anthuriums on each card, and I was writing in my best handwriting.

When Sanjay uncle came home from the factory at lunch, he brought with him a mousy girl who was a few years older than me. She looked at the floor shyly and twisted and retwisted the straps on the handbag she was carrying.

'I have a surprise for you both. Do you know who this is?' he said.

I didn't, so I waited for Reema auntie to answer. Reema auntie had a pleasant but blank smile on her face, and I think she was trying to decide whether to lie and pretend to recognize her.

'That's OK, auntie,' she said. 'You might not remember I was small then. I was in Maya's dance class that summer she was visiting her Ammamma and learning from my guru, Padmanabhan.'

'And you've come for touring up in the hills? It's good

you missed the bulk of the rains – now that it's August, they're almost over.'

'Reema, she's not touring. I've brought Ajitha here for you. Padmanabhan of course can't leave his students, but I thought Ajitha could teach a dance to the ladies for the Onam performances.'

Reema auntie brightened with pleasure at her husband. Since I'd overheard their conversation about Brindha, I'd been noticing how valiantly Sanjay uncle was trying to keep Reema auntie happy. 'I was going to teach them something simple myself, but this is much better. Ajitha, I'd love to do some traditional kaikottikkali dancing with a group of ladies, all dressed in white with gold coin necklaces – you know, the old way, very classic.'

'Of course, auntie, whatever you like. I'm eager to prove that I am worthy of being guru Padmanabhan's student.' She had twisted the straps of the bag so tightly that her right hand was now caught in it. She pulled at the straps to extricate herself, and then embarrassed, stopped struggling with it, and left the bag dangling awkwardly.

'The guest room is to the left. Maya, show her. We have twelve days to rehearse, we shouldn't waste any of it. I'll send a boy out to deliver a message to the ladies to come after tea today.'

I helped Ajitha unpack and put her clothes away in the guest room. She was stiff and shy, but I felt the glimmer of friendship beginning. It was nice having someone around who was young – like Rupa, who I wondered about often – but who spoke English, and would be able to join in things with everybody else.

The ladies came in the late afternoon, and we rolled the cotton dhurries off the floor in the guest bedroom. We took turns standing with our backs to each other to see what our heights were, and then arranged ourselves in a balanced circle of ten. The instructor and I were the youngest and smallest, so my place in the circle was exactly opposite her. It made it hard for me to remember to do exactly what she was doing, not mirror it looking at her. Her left was my right, left is right, right is left, I kept reciting to myself. At guru Padmanabhan's dance class, we would stand in rows behind the guru, and it was easy to trace his steps. Only the Onam dances were in a circle like this.

Everyone had heard about my injury; they asked lots of questions about how I was. Even Lalu sounded so empathetic that I decided to try to like her more. The oncologist, Vandana, peered at my head, and said that the doctor had done his stitching neatly, that there wouldn't be much scarring. In the circle, they were careful not to bump into me or step on me, and they would help me prop my bandaged arm in an approximation of the poses I would be able to make properly in two weeks' time, when the splints could come off. When I was out of breath from dancing, everyone promptly stopped and took a break with me and called for soft drinks and snacks to be brought. I basked in their attention, conscious of being somebody to them now beyond just my aunt and uncle's niece. I had my own distinct role.

When Matthew came to clear the dishes, I asked him to send Ammamma in. We ran through a step sequence three more times, and she still hadn't come. I went to her room.

'Ammamma, don't you want to see us practise? Why lie here by yourself?'

'I'm tired just now – I'll come and watch maybe tomorrow. You know I'd love to see you dance. Onam is my favourite festival, I'm glad you'll be here for it this year.'

'Are you sure you don't want to come see right now?' I

asked, as I edged towards the door. She shook her head and lay back on the pillow. I went back to the ladies.

Ammamma didn't come watch us the next day either, and she didn't come to meals, or go walking in the garden. But the day after that, she did say she would visit with our guests who were coming that evening. The chemist, Suraj, had sent a note to Sanjay uncle, saying that his parents were visiting from Madras and would like to make our acquaintance. Since Suraj lived in the bachelor's apartments near the factory, his parents were staying at a company guesthouse nearby. The guesthouse had limited furnishings and staff, so Sanjay uncle said the right thing to do was to invite them here. He asked me if it was all right if they came to tea.

'Sure,' I said. Why not? I hadn't seen Suraj since the party.

'And you want to do this? You feel up to sitting with them and making conversation?'

Everyone seemed more interested lately in what I wanted. It was nice for a change. 'Yes, it's fine, it's just tea, right?'

'Yes, tea and snacks. That's usually how it's done when we don't know them. Dinner would not be expected.'

'Whatever you decide is fine.' My uncle and aunt had entertained countless guests. If they thought tea was the right thing, then it was.

When Ammamma was asked to be there, and she agreed, even though she'd avoided socializing all week, I should have noticed these were not regular guests visiting in a routine social way.

Even when Suraj's parents aimed their conversations and questioning at me, it didn't seem unusual. I had been getting a lot of attention, from doctors and visitors, so this seemed like more of the same. We sat in the living room; I sat between my uncle and my grandmother. Suraj hardly looked at me, while his parents were friendly and his mother especially wanted to know all about me. I answered question after question:

'I'm going into the eleventh grade next year, then I have college in two more years.'

'Maybe NYU, or Princeton, or University of Chicago, although Dad doesn't want me to go far away.'

'NYU and Chicago are not Ivy League, only Princeton is. But not every good school in America is in the Ivy League –'

'Yes, I'll work. I think maybe a lawyer or a diplomat. I'd like to live in Washington, D.C.'

'Dancing? Well, I'm taking part in Reema auntie's Onam dance. No, I didn't have a dance graduation – I never got that far. I haven't learned classical dance in years.'

'I can understand Malayalam, but I don't speak it that well. Hindi I never knew.'

'Children? Yes, I like children – how many? I don't really –'

My grandmother interrupted, 'Shall we have our tea now?'

I waited for Reema auntie to tell Matthew to bring in the tea trays. She turned to me, and said, 'Maya, why don't you go and help Matthew with the tea?'

Surprised, I got up and went to the kitchen. There was another surprise in the kitchen – Matthew had not made tea the way he always did, boiling the milk and water and spices together, pouring the tea back and forth between two steel pots like he was stretching a big piece of taffy, then pouring the steaming froth into tall clear glasses. Today, Matthew had taken Reema auntie's silver tea set from the cupboard, and repolished the pieces so they gleamed. Dainty teacups and saucers were on the tray, and they were unfilled.

Matthew gave me a china plate stacked with laddoos,

and another with chili cashews. He stood behind me with his tea tray, and walked behind me back to the drawing room.

I put the plates I was carrying on Reema auntie's new marble centre table, and reclaimed my seat next to my uncle. Matthew put the tea service next to the plates, bowed slightly, and left the room.

Reema auntie said in a casual voice, 'Maya, please serve the tea.'

I knelt on the carpet in front of the table. I took the tea cosy off the teapot, and poured tea into the cups. The tea was translucent, and I realized Matthew had separately provided milk in a small pitcher. There were two sugar pots, one with white sugar, one with brown sugar that was rare here and that I had brought from the States at Reema auntie's request. I poured milk into each teacup.

'How much sugar would you like?' I asked Sanjay uncle, who was seated closest to me.

'Why don't you take care of our guests first, Maya?' Sanjay uncle said.

I felt my face get warm. 'How much sugar would you like, auntie? Which kind of sugar would you like?'

I mixed everyone's tea with the silver spoon Matthew had put on the tray. Because the milk had not been boiled with the tea, it congealed slightly in the teacup, the milk fat leaving a thin film on the top. I stirred again to break the film, but by the time I'd moved to the next cup, the milkfat had surfaced on the first. I gave up, and rising from my knees, walked across the room with a cup teetering on a saucer to give to Suraj's mother, then his father, then Suraj.

When I came to Suraj, he said, 'Why don't you serve your grandmother first, Maya?'

I turned mid-stride and walked over to my grandmother, then saw I was carrying Suraj's one-and-a-half-sugars

cup of tea in my hand, not my grandmother's no-sugar
cup. I went back to the centre table, put Suraj's cup down
on the outer edge of the tea tray, making a mental note of
where I had placed it, and then took my grandmother's tea
to her. Then I went back to the table, trying to decide
between serving Suraj next or my uncle. I looked at Suraj,
and he inclined his head towards my uncle. I headed for
my uncle who I feared would turn me away, but he acced-
ed, then Suraj, then my aunt.

There were exclamations about the fine laddoos, also
about the cut flowers Reema auntie had arranged in earth-
en pots and brass urns and crystal vases around the room.
Reema auntie sent Matthew to tell the gardener to bring a
few stems and root of the crimson orchid that Suraj's
mother especially liked. Sanjay uncle asked about Madras,
and Suraj's parents talked about how the city was getting
more and more congested. In ten years' time it would be
as bad as Bombay, they said. They talked about moving to
Madras from Kerala years ago, they talked about their
ancestral homes in Allepey and who their great-grandpar-
ents were and who their neighbours had been.

My aunt handed me the tray from the centre table and I
went around the room and collected everyone's dishes and
crumpled napkins. My grandmother went to her room to
rest, and we went outside, my uncle and aunt taking Suraj's
parents to the far side of the garden, where there was a
sweeping view of the hills across from us and the valleys
between.

Suraj and I waited for them on the verandah. He said, 'I
think they like you.'

'Do they? That's good.'

'I didn't know how young you were, but I would wait for
a few years. I'm not ready now either, but at least we'd
know what to plan for. And it takes ages to get a visa and

everything.'

What I had feared was happening really was happening. 'Suraj, you hardly know me.'

'I like you, Maya, and I know enough. I know that you're adventuresome and pretty, and the rest I can find out over time. We could have a good life together.'

'I can't believe I'm having this conversation.'

The cluster of adults headed back towards us, meandering through the garden. Suraj said, 'How do you think these things are done, Maya? This is the way your family would want it. In the end, there's only a few right families out there; they know that.'

'How old are you?' I asked.

'Twenty-four. Of course we'd wait four years or so, until you're in college. We could have a nice apartment, so you don't have to live in some miserable hostel and eat bad cafeteria food. Just think about it, OK?'

'OK,' I said. I didn't know what else I could say.

'If my parents say things are working out with your family, I'll write to you. I've never been much of a letter-writer, but I'll try.'

We said our goodbyes, and Suraj's family piled back in the car he had borrowed from the factory. 'See you!' they shouted, waving from the windows, and we shouted 'See you!' into the wind.

'How could you not tell me?' I said. I followed my aunt and uncle into my grandmother's room. The three of us sat on my bed and Ammamma turned over in her bed to face us.

'Not tell you? We specifically asked you before we agreed to meet them,' my uncle said.

'I didn't know what you were asking,' I said.

'I thought you did – I guess there was a misunderstanding. Well, nothing's been decided,' he said. 'Amma, what did you think of them?'

Ammamma said, 'They seem nice, the parents at least. I didn't have much of a sense of the boy.'

'It's easy for me to find out about him; he's worked here for two years. I can ask his supervisors in confidence.'

'Does everyone remember how old I am? I'm fifteen. Ammamma, tell them.'

'Of course we know you're fifteen,' Reema auntie said impatiently. 'We're not trying to make a child bride out of you. We're just trying to look out for your future.'

'Can't we talk about the future in the future?' I said.

My aunt said, 'Maya, we didn't ask to meet them, they asked us. And when your uncle and I talked about it, we thought it might be good to think about these things early in your case.'

'What do you mean, in my case?'

'Some good families won't be interested in girls who live in the States because they won't trust the influences you've been raised with over there. But this family is interested, and they are willing to wait. At least if you make a commitment to someone, then it will help guide your behaviour while you are finishing high school and college.'

'My behaviour? Sanjay uncle, are you worried about my behaviour, too?'

'Maya, you're my baby sister's only daughter. I just want to make sure you have options. You may be fifteen, but the things you do now will have a lasting effect, that will be how people think of you, your reputation. It will reflect on the whole family, and whether or not we've brought you up properly. '

'Why do you talk like I've done something wrong. Unless –' I looked at Ammamma. 'Did you tell them, Ammamma, those things I told you when I was sick?'

'What things?' Reema auntie said.

Ammamma looked at me. 'I'm hurt you are asking that. Of course not.'

'Tell us what?' Reema auntie said. 'Amma, if you know something we should know, you must tell us – we can't go making false representations to our friends. We have told everyone Maya has been brought up under the close eye of her family, and that she has a good and unmarked character. If that's not true, you must tell us now before this goes any further.'

Ammamma sat up in bed, and she was angry which she was so rarely. 'Reema, this is my granddaughter you're talking about. I know perfectly well how much good conduct matters to these society people you know. I would like to rest now and have some quiet.'

Reema auntie looked at Sanjay uncle, and he put his arm around her shoulder, saying to Ammamma, 'Amma, you know we didn't mean harm. We love Maya too.'

Ammamma nodded wearily, closing her eyes. Reema auntie and Sanjay uncle walked out of the room.

I lay on my bed, thinking. Ammamma opened her eyes and looked at me.

'Maya, I went along with this because I thought you understood what it was. You don't have to do anything you don't want to do – you know that, don't you?'

'I don't know how to make everything make sense,' I said. 'I thought when you were telling me I'm allowed to be my own person, it meant I am allowed to make my own mistakes. But then you and Reema auntie and Sanjay uncle want to arrange my whole future for me so I can't make any mistakes. What am I supposed to think?'

Ammamma closed her eyes again for a few minutes. Then she opened them. 'Sometimes when you ask things like that, I feel like I am talking to your mother when she was your age. I don't know what you're supposed to think.

Everything is up to you ultimately. There are a lot of rules here, the way we live, and I think some of them probably should be broken. That might shock your aunt and uncle, but I've seen a lot more than they have. But you have to think hard about which rules to break, and you have to break them because you have a good reason, not because you're reckless. You will lose people, Maya, their understanding and their love, for the choices you make all your life. You have to know that, and you have to make those choices mean something.'

'Ammamma,' I said, beginning uncertainly, afraid to hear her answer, 'Is it true in the Sita story that no one accepts her even though her bad reputation isn't her fault?'

My grandmother nodded slowly. 'Yes, in that story even her husband Rama, an incarnation of our beloved God, he is blinded by the gossip and the rumours. But Mother Earth, she is the mother to all creatures, and she gives Sita refuge. That's what mothers do, Maya. They accept, even when no one else does.'

That night, Ammamma was having difficulty standing up. She said she felt her left leg giving out on her. Reema auntie and Sanjay uncle called a doctor to come the next day. They sent the driver to bring Rupa; it was too late for her to catch a bus. Rupa was to sleep in Ammamma's room, to help her if she had to get up in the night. They asked me if I wanted to move back to Brindha's room so I could sleep undisturbed, but I wanted to stay near Ammamma. Rupa slept on a pallet on the floor between our beds.

I was up most of the night, listening to the moans of Ammamma's troubled sleep. Rupa slept soundly. A couple of times, wondering if Ammamma was having a nightmare I should rouse her from, I called her name, in a loud whisper. But she didn't answer, her sleeping pills had taken her far from me.

I woke early, to a roomful of people. Reema auntie and

Sanjay uncle were stooped over Ammamma's bed.
Matthew, Vasani, and Rupa peered at Ammamma from the
foot of her bed.

Ammamma couldn't feel anything on her left side, not
her leg, or her arm, she said she had no sense of anything
there, not even pain. Her eyes looked dulled, far away.
Reema auntie worked at getting through to a doctor on our
phone, and Sanjay uncle drove to the factory to call people from the phones there, to bring the doctor from the
infirmary, and to try to find a larger car or van in which to
take Ammamma to the hospital. Matthew, Vasani, and
Rupa stayed in position at the end of the bed, not speaking, their eyes big.

I sat on Ammamma's bed on her right side, holding her
good arm with my good arm. I tried to sound normal, saying, 'Ammamma, now you're going to get all the attention
– is that why you're doing this?'

Ammamma smiled at me, her eyes fluttering open, then
closed. 'My daughter, my daughter,' she said.

An electric convulsion ran through me. Was she not able
to recognize me any more? 'I'm not your daughter,
Ammamma, I'm your granddaughter. I'm Maya. Do you
remember?' I pressed her hand.

She squeezed back, opening her eyes. 'I know you're
Maya. Tell your mother, tell my daughter I took good care
of her daughter. I did, didn't I?'

'You did,' I said. I was trying to keep the tears from coming. 'You tell her yourself, Ammamma. We'll bring Mother
from New York, and you can tell her, she'll come right
away, OK?'

'It takes a long time to get here, Maya, you know that.
Don't trouble her.'

'Please wait for her, Ammamma. She'll come, and
we can have Onam together, you can see our dance

performance, and Reema auntie's planning a big feast.'

'That would be nice. Take care of your mother, Maya,' Ammamma said. She closed her eyes. She kept them closed.

'Ammamma.' I called her name again, loud, but she didn't answer. Matthew and Vasani and Rupa looked at me, alarmed. I bent over Ammamma, laid my head on her chest, and listened. I could hear her heart, not loud, but I could hear it. I lay there like that, until Sanjay uncle came back with the doctor and moved me off her bed.

The doctor and Sanjay uncle and Rupa and Matthew carried Ammamma to the verandah. The palloo of her sari floated down like a white flag waving under her. Sanjay uncle had brought a transport jeep from the factory, and Reema auntie and I pushed the fold-up seats against the sides, and spread blankets in the back, and then sheets over the blankets. They had brought a stretcher from the infirmary, so they lifted Ammamma on to the stretcher and laid her diagonally across the floor of the jeep. We tucked sheets around her, and a nurse crouched in the back next to her. The doctor climbed up in the front next to Sanjay uncle, and they took off for Coimbatore.

Ram was woken up to take Reema auntie and me down the mountain. Reema auntie collected clothes for her and Sanjay uncle, and packed some of Ammamma's things also. I packed a small bag and waited for her. I looked over at Ammamma's bed, and there was a valley in the mattress, where she and I had been lying together. I went and huddled there, fitting entirely within the silhouette of her body, breathing her smells – the Vicks, the rosewater, the sweetness of hair oil.

CHAPTER EIGHT

In Hospital

THE RIDE DOWN the mountain was interminable. I kept thinking of Ammamma lying in the back of the jeep, wondering if she felt each bump in the road that I felt. Reema auntie and I held hands in the back seat, neither of us able to think of what to say to cheer the other one up. We concentrated on the road and the forest around us, trying to stay focused on the distracting creatures crossing our path. It was between four and five in the morning, as early as the day we had taken Brindha to school, but I hadn't taken in the outside world that day the way I did today. There were outlines of sleeping bison in the distance, standing clumped together, leaning on each other for balance. We saw two sambar deer, rubbing their three-pointed antlers against a tree, to clear the velvet and sharpen the antlers, Reema auntie said.

Ram rolled down his window and told us to listen for the animals announcing our vehicle's disruption of their morning routines. We heard the howls of wild dogs, the tsk-tsking of bonnet macaques, the protest of the scops owl. We slowed the car to let a fat pangolin trundle across the road, its long narrow ant-eating snout stuck to the ground like a vacuum cleaner.

When we pulled to the side of the road to let the first huge, smoking lorry of the day pass us, Ram pointed at the ditch filled with water on the side of the road. It was an almost perfect circle, a little bigger than a child's inflatable swimming pool. Ram said an elephant had dug the hole out with his forefeet, burrowing deep down until he reached water.

A little while later we saw the elephant, a stony monument under an awning of trees. It was tuskless. Reema auntie said there was a whole breed of tuskless males, called makna. She said with the poachers around, the maknas would eventually be mateless and alone.

The hillside forests were behind us then, followed by a long spell of dodging traffic, and then we pulled up in front of the imposing two-storey hospital. They had just whitewashed the front of the building, and water dripped down the walls into puddles whitened with lime. Reema auntie and I hopscotched around the puddles to reach the entrance. Big banners proclaimed CAMPION HOSPITAL, flanked by slightly smaller banners that said X-RAY, ECG INSIDE, CAT COMING SOON. Reema auntie said Campion was one of the two best private hospitals in Coimbatore. The two hospitals had been founded by rival underworld families, to turn black money into good. Even in philanthropy, they competed with each other. They brought equipment and drugs from as far away as the Philippines, Malaysia, Kuwait, and Egypt. A sign inside over the information desk said THAI KIDNEY MACHINE COMING SOON.

Whirring fans spread the smells of bleach and rubbing alcohol. I stumbled, feeling faint, and Reema auntie tightened her arms around me to prop me up. She passed her handkerchief across my damp forehead, and said, 'Only the sterile rooms, for operating and such, have air conditioning. But there's a nice breeze from that courtyard, isn't there?' She walked me over to a bench facing the rectangular courtyard.

The information desk was in one corner, and around the perimeter were offices, examining rooms, medical wards, and private patient suites. All these destinations were reached by walking down wide cement sidewalks bordering the big open courtyard, filled with lush flowers and even a delicate Japanese bridge. Intruding upon the garden diagonally on one corner was a long narrow ramp connecting the ground floor to the first. As Reema auntie talked to the information desk people, I stared at the orange and black oriole that had just landed in the sprawl of vines in front of me, and saw a team of millipedes crawl out of the garden soil on to the cement path. I watched to see which squad of doctors or which passing trolley would be the first to crush the millipedes, but they calmly crawled along, unharmed. My aunt took my hand and we walked down the hall, looking for Ammamma's room.

When we were still three doors away from her room, we saw Sanjay uncle. He had just left Ammamma's room; he said she was still the same, still unconscious.

'Unconscious? You're sure she's not sleeping?' I said.

Sanjay uncle said he was sure. He told us to go on in, he was going to the billing office and he would be right back. I wasn't ready to see Ammamma. I went with Sanjay uncle. I could hear the door slam shut behind my aunt as we turned and walked away.

The billing office had air conditioning. Sanjay uncle opened his bag – he brought a bag when he wanted to carry more money than would fit in his wallet, usually on business trips or family holidays – and pulled out stapled stacks of hundred-rupee notes. He counted them and handed them over to the billing officer and countersigned the receipt. They told Sanjay uncle that each time Ammamma's doctor prescribed medicines or procedures, he had to sign a receipt and bring it to the billing office and then they debited it from this account, until another deposit was necessary. Sanjay uncle tried to convince them this was completely unnecessary, but, failing that, he got them to agree that I could run the receipts back and forth for him. 'I hear you could use the air-conditioning breaks anyway, Miss Delicate Flower,' he said, elbowing me and smiling for the first time that day.

When we entered Ammamma's room, it was bathed in sunlight, and birds twittered outside the open windows. Reema auntie sat at the side of the bed, her eyes closed, her thumb holding her place in her prayerbook. She opened her eyes, read to herself, her lips moving, then closed her eyes again. Sanjay uncle pulled two more chairs near the bed. I didn't sit right away – it was bothering me the way Ammamma was positioned, her head all the way to the right side, her right shoulder angled upward awkwardly to meet her head. I tried to rearrange the pillows behind her, but Ammamma felt heavy, hard to move. Sanjay uncle helped me cradle her head and shoulder, and he pushed the pillows into place behind her, and then I laid

Ammamma's head squarely in the middle of the pillow. In one jerking movement, her head lolled to the right side again. It made me shiver, the looseness with which her head moved, as if the centripetal force in her body that kept everything in alignment had gone out of her.

I tried to hold her hand but it twisted limply. It received no messages telling it how to respond, how to resist or accept my touch. When, after some hours holding her hand, her fingers closed around mine, I called for Reema auntie to come look. Reema auntie brought a nurse, who showed me how if I removed my hand from Ammamma's grip, her hand still stayed clenched; it had been an accident, a coincidence, she had closed her hand not knowing she embraced mine. To even say 'she' had closed her hand was suggesting too much will on Ammamma's part, the nurse said. The only safe thing to say was that Ammamma's hand had closed itself, or safer yet, her hand was closed, however it had happened.

The doctors came to check on Ammamma and told us to go and eat, to take tea. The youngest one of the three of them, with a sporty checked shirt under his white coat, said, 'You won't necessarily be rewarded for your patience. We don't know if she will come out of this.'

The two older doctors scowled at the young doctor. 'When, not if. We don't know when she will come out of this. Please, Mr Pillai, have something to eat, and take some rest. We are doing everything.'

The young doctor tried to redeem himself with his colleagues, make up for his callousness. He turned to me and touched my bandaged arm. 'What have we here?'

My uncle explained about my fall. The doctor said, 'Now that you are at a real hospital, you really should have that X-rayed. Why don't we set up an exam room for you?'

'I don't think I should leave my grandmother,' I said.

The doctor looked over at my grandmother lying in her white sari on the white bed. Lying peacefully. He said, 'I'm sure your aunt or uncle can come and get you if anything changes in your grandmother's condition.'

My uncle said, 'Yes, yes, Maya, go with the doctor. We should have brought you down to Coimbatore earlier to do an X-ray. You must have one now that we're here.'

I had never had an X-ray before, except for my teeth at the dentist. They would put that heavy lead sheet on me, and then the dentist and the hygienist would leave. It made me wonder, if X-rays were so harmless, then why did everyone else leave the room, and have me face it alone?

'My arm feels fine,' I said, wriggling out of the doctor's grasp. 'The other doctor said the bandage can come off in another week.'

My aunt said, 'Maya, go and have the X-ray done. By the time your mother gets here, at least the doctors can tell her they've looked at you also.'

'My mother? She's coming?' All the argumentativeness drained out of me. The realization of how ill my grandmother must be flooded through me.

My uncle said, 'I called your mother after Ammamma was admitted. She and your father are trying to get on a flight tomorrow. That means they should arrive here two days after that, by Thursday.'

The two other doctors were giving Ammamma's charts and their instructions to the nurse who had come in. More medication, more tests. I couldn't understand much else they said. They started talking to my aunt and uncle and I moved closer to them to listen. My aunt interrupted them to say, 'Maya, go with Dr Kumar now, please.'

'But I want to hear how Ammamma is.'

My aunt looked at my uncle and he shrugged. 'If she

really wants to know, maybe she's ready for these kinds of things.'

They let me stay and listen. The doctors wanted to talk about what the options were if Ammamma did not wake up. The longer she stayed unconscious, the more potential damage there was. It was unclear yet whether she had had one large stroke or several smaller strokes. Right now, she was still breathing on her own, but what if she needed respiratory support – there were a limited number of respiratory machines in the hospital, and the doctors could only put her on one if she had a decent chance of eventual resuscitation and recovery.

I didn't want to hear more. I decided to go with Dr Kumar to get my X-ray. He took me to the first floor to a door marked RADIANT ENERGY LAB. I asked Dr Kumar if sometimes people came out of comas and they were fine. That happened often on the soap operas I used to watch with my babysitter.

'Not usually,' he said. He saw my eyes fill up, and he tried to think of something nice to say. 'We have a new radiologist from Delhi. I think you'll find him as good as anybody in the States.'

The radiologist showed me the X-rays afterwards, and he said we could leave the bandages off. He showed me the faded line in my bone where it had broken, and said it was knitting itself back together nicely. 'Bones are amazingly regenerative at your age,' he said. 'If an old person breaks his hip, sometimes he never recovers. But if a child falls down a flight of stairs, he gets up and cries for a while and forgets it all if you give him a toffee.'

He asked me if someone had accompanied me to the hospital, and I explained where my aunt and uncle were. He put his hand over his heart, shaking his head sadly, saying, 'Very sorry, so sorry,' when I told him about my grandmother. He said, 'Don't worry, it is a very good hospital here, even the Tigers know to come here.' He moved aside a box of rubber gloves and a glass jar of gauze on the counter to reveal a small altar, with incense sticks and a small unlit diya ('just for show, the smoke would contaminate the machines') and some marigold petals. A small figure of Jesus on the cross leaned against the back of the counter. 'I am a believer in His miracles, so I will say a prayer to Him for you.'

I went back to my grandmother's room, where nothing had changed. My grandmother lay still, my aunt meditated, and my uncle wrestled with the leg of a chair, trying to get it to screw in more tightly so that the four legs would balance evenly. The room hardly looked like a hospital room – there were no machines or medical instruments around, the bed had no support rails, the walls were bright blue and adorned with a framed picture of a seashore. Steady sunshine poured in through the windows, and occasionally the winds would toss a few petals or leaves into the room. The scent of sickness and chemicals had been so overpowering at the hospital entrance or when I passed by the large patient wards. In here, in these nice private patient rooms, you started with a clean slate – if there was anything unpleasant, anything that reeked of decay and deterioration, you had no one to blame but yourself. I thought of what the driver had been telling Reema auntie and me in the car, about how animals, especially animals in distress, leave scents along their path, more enduring than footprints. When Ram went hunting with his brothers (the sanctuary was open for shooting for a couple of weeks a year to control the population of deer and goat and boar) he said they would try to conserve their ammunition, so often they would only shoot one or two bullets, only enough to wound their target. Then, for the next few days, they would walk through the hills, following only the scent through dark, fireless nights, the smell of death growing stronger and stronger. They could tell by the scent that the day had come that the animal would give itself up and kneel meekly before them in some grassy corner. Ammamma lay in full view of us, under soft natural light. If the end was coming, would we know it by scent or sight first? Would we have a sign? I willed Ammamma's body to keep doing its work, cleaning its house.

Two men rolled a trolley into the room and lined it up next to Ammamma's bed. The man at the head of the bed took the pillows out from under Ammamma, and her head thudded flatly against the sheet-covered mattress. They untucked the corners of the sheet, and then, in one coordinated heave, picked up the sheet with Ammamma on it and moved her to the trolley. The ends of the sheet puckered underneath the trolley's metal tabletop.

'What's going on?' my uncle asked.

'For tests,' one of them said.

'Which tests now?' my uncle said.

'I don't know,' the same one said. The other one stayed silent.

We stood and followed the trolley. We walked single file because there were a lot of people in the halls now, and I was last behind my aunt and uncle. The trolley started up the ramp to the first floor. I was far enough behind to catch a sudden full-length view of my grandmother lying prone on the trolley on the incline that suddenly seemed so steep, her body tilted almost vertically. My heart lurched as I saw her left leg slip off the trolley table and hang limply in the air. Her leg was exposed from the knee down, pure white skin from knee to ankle that had never seen the sun, and dark blue veins latticed across it. I wriggled past some people to catch up to Ammamma. I picked up her leg – it was heavy, I started with one hand, then added the other for a better grip – and lifted it back into place, smoothed her sari over it, and kept my hand on her firmly, walking all the way up in step with the trolley's stops and stutters.

There were smaller, everyday tests that occurred in Ammamma's room, right in front of us. Doctors and nurses would casually come in, prick her palms with needles, pries open her eyes, put a stethoscope down her blouse, hammer on her knees and elbows, and then leave. Reema auntie had brought a stack of Ammamma's white saris, not knowing when we left home that Ammamma would stay unconscious and lying down the whole time. It would be very hard, impossible really, to wrap a sari around someone who was lying down. Reema auntie tried, with a nurse helping, but it wasn't working. So they took off the old sari and put a new petticoat and blouse on Ammamma, and no sari. When Sanjay uncle and I were let back in the room, it was the first time I'd ever seen Ammamma without a sari. Reema auntie touched the hem of the long starched petticoat skirt, saying, 'See here, this is one of Ammamma's best petticoats. See this pretty embroidery that her sister did for her.' She looked perfectly modest and neat in her blouse and skirt, but just not like my grandmother.

My mother did not look like my mother, either, when she arrived. Her hair was pulled tight off her face, secured with bobby pins she usually bothered to hide. Her face was pale and taut, and small. It had closed in upon itself. Her lips were unlipsticked but unnaturally dark, as if they were grape-juice stained. She wore sweatpants and a T-shirt, which I hardly saw her wear at home, and never before on a plane trip, or in India. She had no makeup on, no earrings, no rings. Also, she carried nothing. A porter

carried the three pieces of luggage. My father had my
mother's office briefcase in one hand and her stuffed
handbag slung across his chest like a baby in a Snugli.

And she didn't speak. She dropped her head on to her
brother's chest and sat next to Ammamma's bed for over
an hour before she found words to say anything. Even
then, when she asked about Ammamma's stages and what
had the doctors said, and what medications, it was not in
the normal authoritative way my mother asked most
things. She spoke listlessly and did not challenge the
answers she was given; she watched from the sidelines as
if she knew what was going to happen and couldn't hope
to change it.

People came. Ammamma's two sisters, my grandfather's
sister, nieces and nephews in the Middle East and their
children. Madhu's parents came from England, and
Madhu heard through them and left her trekking to come.
She had little braids, cornrows, all over her head that some
backpacker in Goa had done for her. Madhu's parents had
been very attached to my grandmother because Madhu
and her mother stayed with Ammamma for some months
when they were waiting for a visa to go and join Madhu's
father in England.

Reema auntie's parents came, the sister with the new
baby, my father's family. Friends of Sanjay uncle and
Reema auntie came down from the hills early in the day,
so they had time to go back up before dark. Friends of
theirs who lived in town came after work – some of them
came several days in a row. Childhood friends of my
mother and her brother came who could barely recognize
each other now. Old friends and their children, now old
and even grey themselves, came from the northern city my
grandmother lived in when she was first married. These
friends had the longest trip – two overnight trains and a

bus, and they made me the most worried. The more people who came, and the farther away they came from, the more it meant everyone thought this was the end. I felt like they were betting against my grandmother.

Though I saw that they cared enough to make the journey they were on the edges of this grief, just like Madhu, with whom I had wanted to be so chummy just a few weeks ago, and the other second cousins and third cousins and neighbours. I would walk out in the hall, and two children of my uncle's college room mate would be playing card tricks, and their father would take the cards and everyone would fall silent as I came by. That was the difference between friends and distant relatives, and our close family. We were the ones who could not play cards, or trade addresses with people we had not seen in a long time, or go back to the office afterwards to receive a late night package delivery. Everyone there would probably never forget my grandmother, but we were the ones who would never forget losing her. Even in our close family their were divisions of grief and I felt cut off from my mother and her brother, who were losing their mother, and there was nothing else, no one else, who could match that.

My father and I spent a lot of time together, especially in the evening when the hospital did not allow more than two visitors to stay in patient rooms. We were all staying at a small hotel near the hospital, where most of the other families we saw in the hospital also stayed. The hotel was clean and well-kept but gloomy all the same, full of tearstained guests in the lobby, and a staff that knew better than to attempt levity. The poorer families were accommodated in the hotel restaurant adjacent to the lobby, which at night was cleared of all its tables and chairs and refilled with charpoys, bedding down in conditions no more overcrowded or uncomfortable than the public wards their relatives were in at the hospital.

Even in their rush to the airport, Dad had thought to bring me some things: a recent newspaper article that profiled my high school's swim coach, a package of Snickers bars, and some cinnamon Big Red gum. He was also the one who noticed right away that my hair was pinned in an odd way – I couldn't do the ponytail with the hairpiece without Ammamma's help. He made me tell him the whole story. He wanted to see for himself, and so I took out the hair grips. I showed him the smooth flat scar just below what had been my natural parting when I parted my hair on the side.

I begged him not to tell Mother – I didn't want her to have to think about me right now. Whatever tension there'd been between them at the beginning of the summer had disappeared, and I was relieved to see them close again. Dad was hesitant – keeping a secret from Mother seemed like breaking ranks to him. Whenever I had sworn him to secrecy in the past, it meant he would tell no one else but my mother. Finally he agreed to wait a day or two, until we had a better understanding of what Ammamma's condition was, and until Mother had had some sleep and was more herself. To agree even to wait at all meant he was very worried about Mother.

When my mother did find out, she was very worked up. She took the hair grips out of my hair and found the scar and asked my father to call my doctor at home and put him on the phone with the doctor I saw at the hospital and also to call the neurologist at the medical college who had come up to the house. And set up appointments for me back at home with all the necessary people.

'The doctors were good here, Mother. I'm not worried any more,' I said.

'You're not worried? Well, that's good that *you're* not worried,' my mother said, sarcasm so immediately at her disposal.

My father said to me later, 'You have to know how hard on her it is, with your grandmother so ill right now. I'm sure she's overreacting about your situation, but it's probably because she can do something about that at least. With your grandmother, there's nothing to do.'

My father and I took care of the mundane things so that Sanjay uncle and Mother didn't have to leave Ammamma at all. We brought food to them, we sent their clothes out to be washed, we went to the bank to exchange money, we went out in the street to hail rickshaws to take everyone back and forth between the hotel and the hospital. Every evening we laid out an outfit for the next day for Mother, matching sari, petticoat, and blouse, on the chair next to the bed, so when she woke up, she could dress in the same numb daze she did everything else in. I had moved from my uncle and aunt's room to my parents' room. I was on a bed that had rolling wheels on the bottom (it resembled my grandmother's trolley) and was positioned at the foot of the double bed my parents were sleeping in. In the early mornings, I could hear Mother moving around and I tried to lie still so she did not know I was awake. I didn't want to be alone with her; I didn't know how to do that. It was easier when there was a roomful of people and when I was doing things – helping one of Ammamma's brothers find his walking stick or corralling the second and third cousins together and monitoring them as they did their homework hunched over on benches in the hallway, peering into thick textbooks. One morning Mother was crying, for the first time I'd ever known of. She cried quietly so as not to wake my father. I lay still with my face turned into the pillow, slowing my breathing the way we did at swim practice.

Ammamma's blood pressure was worse that day, and the doctors said her heart was getting tired. I had stopped wondering whether a person could be in a coma and come out of it and be all right. I had started wondering whether a person, and everyone in that person's life, could be in a coma and stay in it forever. This change in Ammamma, it was not a good change, but it signalled the passage of time – that events still happened in a sequence, that stories had a beginning and an end.

Brindha was coming that day. She was brought by Reema auntie's sister's husband, who was her favourite uncle. Suhash uncle took his portable radio with him so they could spend the whole ride from St Helena's talking and listening to other people on the air waves and there'd be no opportunity for her to ask questions. Reema auntie had called ahead to arrange things with Miss Granville, and even with Old Granny, tragedy parted the seas. Brindha could come, and stay, for as long as we thought she should. In some ways, this was not what Reema auntie wanted to hear. She wanted someone else to take charge and say, ten years old is too young to come home for death. Let her stay in school and do sums and play jacks. And then Reema auntie would not have to decide for herself whether ten years old was too young, and what the right and compassionate and sensible thing was.

Brindha was the only one among us to be really loud in grief. It had been a typically quiet morning, the five of us sitting in Ammamma's room. Sanjay uncle, who had offered to help me on my summer homework, was speed-reading through *The Adventures of Huckleberry Finn* and suggesting more passages to analyse in my term paper. Suddenly, we heard screams of 'Amma! Amma!' Reema auntie's face went pale and tight, and she joined me in the hall, closing the door to Ammamma's room behind her.

Brindha ran towards us, a blur of white shirt and blue tie and pleated skirt, with Suhash running behind her, dodging staring people.

'Amma!' Brindha tackled her mother, almost knocking her down. Reema auntie backed against a wall, Brindha pressing into her stomach, Brindha's tight fists full of folds of sari. 'Amma, are you ill?'

'What? Oh, no, darling, I'm fine,' Reema auntie said. 'Suhash uncle could have told you that.'

Suhash uncle said, 'She was teaching me movie songs the whole way in the car, only when we drove up to the hospital, she started screaming . . .'

Reema auntie said, 'I meant to meet you both at the front lobby, so we could go for a little walk and have a talk. Shall we go for a little walk, Brindha?'

Brindha looked mournfully at Suhash uncle, at me, at some aunts who were murmuring a prayer together, at people passing by in white coats. 'Just me and you, OK, Amma?' she said in a quiet voice.

'Yes, darling, of course, just us, we'll have a walk now. Let go for a second so Amma can arrange her sari, OK?' Reema auntie said, nodding her thanks at Suhash uncle over Brindha's head. She disentangled herself from Brindha's grasp and straightened her sari.

'Is Brindha all right?' Sanjay uncle asked when I went back into Ammamma's room. He sat next to my mother on one side of her bed, I took one of the two empty seats on the other side. The seat was warm from the sun.

I said, 'Reema auntie took her on a walk to explain everything. They'll be back soon.'

My mother looked up, her face brightening, thinking about the seven-year-old version she had last seen, spindly legs, two pigtails that stuck out at funny angles. She would be surprised when she saw Brindha in her starched pleats, crisp and serious.

Brindha came in the room, Reema auntie behind her. Everyone reflexively stood up. Sanjay uncle went over to her to hug her, but she slipped through his grasp. 'Come sit by me,' my mother said, patting Sanjay uncle's vacated chair.

Brindha said nothing to any of us. She went up to the bed and looked. She looked for a long time, then she put her head down close near Ammamma's mouth, as if she thought something might be whispered she alone could hear.

Brindha turned around and looked at us. 'This isn't my grandmother,' she announced. She said this matter-of-factly, with the assurance of a coroner, so that for a second, we looked again at the bed.

I was sitting at the side of the bed near the window, and Brindha was standing on the other side of the bed, and she walked around the foot of the bed and came towards me.

'Do you see this?' she said, grabbing my arm, pulling me towards the bed. Her fingernails dug into my arm, and I tried to shift away a little.

'I know, Brindha, I've seen her,' I said gently. I didn't know what else to say. I backed away from her and found my chair again.

It was very sudden. She sprang at me, hitting me with curled fists on my upper arm and shoulders and stomach, opening her palms to draw quick pictures in my skin with sharp nails. 'It's your fault! Do you see what you've done?'

I tried to stand up from under her, half-carrying her, her head ramming against me, almost pushing me back down. The chair fell over as we struggled.

'Brindha!' Sanjay uncle came to pull her off of me, but before he reached us, hardly thinking about it, I threw her to the floor. She landed, hard, and she curled into a little ball, rubbing her hand over where her thigh had bruised. Sanjay uncle stood towering over both of us, unsure who to go to. Brindha saw him coming to pick her up off the floor, and she moved herself, still in a ball, farther out of his reach, lying in a patch of sunshine right under the window.

My aunt and my mother did not move from the other side of the bed. It was like they did not know us. They looked at us like they were looking at wild creatures out the window of the car, and they were afraid to move or attract our attention.

Brindha was crying, and yelling, but out of breath from the crying. 'I told you to watch her while I was away. I told you. Instead you get yourself hurt and she has to take care of you. How could you let her? Don't you know she isn't strong?'

All the orderly paths inside my head, all the thoughts I kept in separate walled-off spaces, collapsed. For the last few days, I had been feeling something infiltrating, weeds cropping up in orderly gardens and hedgerows of thought. Now I knew it was guilt. I had pushed it out of my way into the dark corners, and now here was Brindha shining a light on it so everybody could see, and agree. It was my fault Ammamma was dying. I didn't know how I let Ammamma take care of me. I didn't know she wasn't strong. I did know she begged me to let her do everything. I did know Ammamma had taken to her bed to keep me company and then I had got better and she had not.

Still sitting in the chair, I bent over my knees, trying to make the nausea go away, the blood rushing to my head. I cried, covering my face with my hands.

My aunt unfroze. She came around the bed. My uncle had scooped Brindha off the floor and carried her out.

Reema auntie came over to me and stroked my back. 'Maya, don't think about it, please. Brindha's just upset. None of us think of it like that; you mustn't either.'

I couldn't look at her. I didn't believe her. 'That is how this happened,' I whispered from between my hands. 'She was tired and she was staying up with me at all hours and she was missing her pills.'

'Maya,' my aunt said, 'we found out she was missing her pills even before. The doctor told us that when he came to the house. We don't know why she wasn't taking them – maybe she was already becoming forgetful or depressed. We don't know. We were going to have a girl come and stay with her full-time and watch her. We were making arrangements. We weren't fast enough; we didn't do enough. I keep thinking that.'

'If Amma was depressed, it was my fault, too,' my mother said softly. 'I have held myself apart from her for so long. We come for our scheduled visits, yes, but I've never asked her to come visit us in New York, or come to live with us. She must have seen so many of her friends go live with their children abroad, and notice that she's never even been asked.'

'Don't.' My aunt went over to my mother and put her arms around her. 'Amma couldn't have gone to live with you, she knew that. Her health was too fragile, and she hates cold weather. We all knew it was simply not an option.'

We could hear Brindha's howling in the hall and my uncle's voice, getting more frantic the more he tried to calm her. Reema auntie went out to try to help.

My mother and I were left in the room, the two of us alone with Ammamma. My mother was crying. I didn't know what to do.

'It's true, you know, Mother. Ammamma showed me old

photos she had kept of our house covered in snow. She said she imagined it must be like living inside the refrigerator. She didn't want to come to New York. '

My mother put a handkerchief to her face, and tried to blot the tears. 'The awful thing is, Maya, I was secretly glad she couldn't handle the cold, because it meant we never had to be open about the real reason she couldn't come stay with us. Which is that I didn't want her. And I know she knew that. Nothing could be more unforgivable.' The tears streamed down her face, and she gave up on the handkerchief, crumpling it up and putting it in her bag and looking for another one.

I tried to think of all the things my grandmother had said all summer, and what she would have said right now if she could have, and what my mother needed to hear. Jennifer had read to us at her last slumber party from a book about channelling spirits, and I wished I could remember what she had taught us.

I looked at my mother, her shoulders limp, strands of hair stuck damply to her face. I said, 'Mother, Ammamma forgives you. She wasn't angry. She told me to tell you that.'

My mother, turning the words over in her head, eyed me hungrily, seeking more. 'What else did she say? What else did she tell you?'

'She told me everything.'

'Everything?' my mother enunciated the word.

'About when I was born. And Shivani dying. And how no one knew how to comfort you.'

'Why is it when something terrible happens, you need it to be someone's fault? It mattered to me so much then to shut her out and make her feel guilty. Now it seems pathetic,' my mother said in a low voice, raspy from crying.

'When I had my accident this summer, she wanted to prove to you that you could trust her. She said returning me healthy to you was the most important thing she could do for you. She wanted you to know that she took good care of me. That was the last thing she told me,' I said. My mother was ambushed by fresh tears. She came over to me and knelt next to my chair and I moved towards the edge of the chair so she could put her hands all the way around my waist. We hadn't touched each other in more than a perfunctory way in a very long time. She lowered her head on to my lap and awkwardly, we held each other.

I didn't tell her that the real last thing Ammamma had told me was to take care of my mother. I couldn't take care of my mother, in general, but I could try to do that right now. It was like all the generations had been mixed up, and I understood what Ammamma meant, but I didn't want my mother to take it the wrong way. The time you probably needed your mother the most was when your mother was dying. And because Ammamma could not be there for her daughter through that, I think Ammamma wanted me to be her surrogate. So I tried to help my mother, but eventually, I wanted my rightful role back. My mother had to be a mother, I didn't want her thinking there was any way around that. Because I needed her. And I wasn't going to take as long as she had taken to realize that.

CHAPTER NINE

Karma

BRINDHA AND I weren't speaking after our brawl. That is, she wasn't speaking to me, so I wasn't speaking to her. In an odd way, I felt like she and I alone knew the truth – I felt, with a deep-seated grimness, that I had worn Ammamma out, made her weak and receptive to further illness. No one would admit to believing me, my aunt and uncle and my parents consumed with their own guilt, their own failures – except Brindha. But she despised me for it, and in a way, her not talking to me was a fraction of the punishment I felt I deserved.

Brindha was unwilling to talk to our other relatives either. She wanted only to be with her parents, but at the same time could not bear to be at Ammamma's bedside, which was where her parents wanted to be. I would sit next to Mother holding her hand, my father sitting on the other side, holding her other hand, while Brindha clambered on to her parents' laps, tried to cajole one of them into taking her on a walk or buying her candy or going back to the hotel to watch television.

Sanjay uncle had Rupa brought to the hospital to keep Brindha busy. He gave them money to buy snacks in the cafeteria and trinkets in the gift shop. And he told them he had a 'very important job' for them. 'But then again,' he paused, as if undecided, 'I don't know if a young girl like you is up to such a very important job.'

Brindha, eager and solemn, her eyes big, begged, 'Achan, yes, yes, I can do very important jobs.'

Then he turned over my duties of running receipts back and forth to the billing office to Brindha. 'Except of course,' he said, 'Brindha and Rupa will instruct you, Maya, to get the receipts if they are otherwise occupied. But Brindha will be in charge of deciding that, won't you Brindha?' Brindha nodded proudly. Sanjay uncle winked apologetically at me, and I winked back, pleased to be invited to be among the adults in indulging a child.

A few times each day, Brindha would be too engrossed in a card game with Rupa or in spying on a family of turtles in the courtyard and she would brusquely order me to get the receipts. The more rude she was to me, the more I could play the patient older cousin, above quarrelling or cattiness at such a painful time. Rupa was oddly mute around me, we had lost the ease of our companionship. I think this was because the more I claimed my place among the adults, the more securely a part of this family I became, the less possible it seemed that we could have considered ourselves friends. Remembering the long, simple days with her and Ammamma, the loss seemed doubled.

Mother and I were trying to be sensitive to each other, trying to be our best selves. I felt like a better person, not just the way I was behaving, but the way I could tell she was thinking of me. I had become more visible and intelligible to her, I had come into focus. I was one of the people she made eye contact with while telling a story; sharing grief, she reached for my hand as often as my father's. A closeness blossomed in these moments as she was losing her mother and I was finding mine.

I felt conscious of trying to be my mother's daughter when Suraj and his parents came to visit at the hospital. They said they had come to say how sorry they were to find my grandmother in ill health, although Reema auntie said later that they had also heard my parents had made an unexpected visit and they wanted to take the opportunity to meet and advance their suit. They said nothing explicit about the marriage proposal that had been extended – it would have been too unseemly. This time, I answered no questions and raised none either, just sat next to my mother and smiled when it was expected. His mother stared at me in her openly appraising way, noticing approvingly that my cast had come off, commenting that I was looking less gaunt than last time. I did not even make eye contact with Suraj, and he gave up trying to catch my gaze after a while. He spoke politely to my mother, he was more discreet than his mother, more conscious of the strangeness of their presence in this hospital room. I found myself warming to his deep-voiced soft-spoken expressions of empathy to my mother. I couldn't imagine any of the boys I knew knowing what to say in a situation like this, not to me and certainly not to my mother. I watched Mother to see how she was reacting; we had never been in this situation before. She didn't like Steve, I knew that, but I didn't know if that applied to only Steve or all boyfriends. I had never thought to find out whether she wanted me to get married in this traditional way, or whether she assumed I would marry of my own choosing in the American way. I did not know what she wanted partly because I had not cared, up till now.

Mother was polite, but very noncommittal. She refused to be distracted by Suraj's mother's chatter or led on to topics that were too far from our present situation to be appropriately discussed. Mother only glancingly talked about where we lived and what she did, but mostly she trained her eyes on Ammamma and resisted being drawn into further conversation. Suraj picked up this cue, and eventually got his parents to acknowledge his quiet but persistent nudging, and leave. Reema auntie walked them out.

'She's really something,' Mother smiled cryptically at Reema auntie when she returned.

Reema auntie said, 'She wants a horoscope, Kamala. I told her I would get back to her after talking to you.'

Mother looked at me. 'Do you want a horoscope, Maya?'

I did not know how to take her question. I finally knew something about my past, and I wanted to know something about my future. I didn't want to be protected from knowledge, however lucky or unlucky. But if a horoscope was being prepared now for the sake of determining my compatibility in marriage, then was Mother asking if I was conceding to an arranged marriage in general and considering this marriage to Suraj specifically? What I wanted to ask Mother was, what did she want the answer to her question to be?

A knock at the door interrupted the silence between question and answer. My father stood to answer the door, saying wearily, 'More visitors.'

My mother said in a thick whisper, 'We don't want more visitors right now. Send them away.'

But there was no sending these visitors away. Involuntarily I stood up, my chair falling back and clattering on the floor. Reema auntie, Sanjay uncle, my father, and my mother turned to look at me. Then they turned to look at the visitors.

The visitors were three men wearing black pants and black shirts, and the shiny black belts with gun holsters. I recognized them as colleagues of the James Bond people from the airport. I also recognized, before anyone else in the room did, that one of them was carrying my suitcase.

A fourth man entered, steering Brindha and Rupa into our room, holding them each by the shoulder. Then it was Sanjay uncle and Reema auntie's turn to rise up suddenly from their seats, startled, their mouths agape.

Sanjay uncle was the first to regain speech. He went over to stand by Brindha, putting his hand on her free shoulder, implicitly claiming her back. He said tersely, 'What is the meaning of this?'

'Crimes have been committed,' said one of the men.

They were from the Central Bureau of Intelligence, with the Special Investigation Team that had been assembled to track down the Tamil Tigers involved in Rajiv Gandhi's assassination. There were several Tigers convalescing in this hospital, and some of them had medical receipts that had been paid by a Mr Sanjay Pillai.

'That's not possible,' Sanjay uncle said. 'There's been some mix-up.'

No mix-up, said the intelligence agent gripping Brindha and Rupa. These two girls had been seen going into and out of the patient wards where the Tiger patients were. They had been seen carrying receipts. The other girl, Maya Krishnan, she had been seen carrying receipts too, although she had not been spotted making contact with a Tiger patient herself.

'All three are part of ongoing activity. We have investigated thoroughly and found this out,' the agent said, with a leer of self-congratulation. He said that he had gone to St Helena's yesterday and interrogated Brindha's friends. He pulled an envelope out of his pocket and on the tray next to Ammamma's bed, spilled its contents: there was the cyanide capsule, and there were my silver star earrings.

They had also gone up to our tea hills and scoured the Pillai house and its environs. They said they had found evidence of illicit behaviour in 'the room that the three conspirators had at various points resided in'. The agent carrying my suitcase looked for a large flat surface on which to lay it down, and, noticing that there was empty space at the foot of the bed my grandmother was lying in, he moved towards it. Mother stood up to block him from coming near the bed.

He backed away a few steps uncertainly, then knelt awkwardly and opened the suitcase on the floor. In the big black cavity of the suitcase the items seemed meagre, but successfully lurid: the Tamil Tiger pamphlets and the pictures of Subha and Sivarasan, the movie magazine centrefolds, my medical records, the syringes my mother had sent with me, letters from Jennifer and my parents from throughout the summer, the birth control pills and hairbrush from Madhu's room, the fluorescently yellow-and-black cover of the Cliffs Notes for Huck Finn.

'We need answers,' the agent said, standing up, brushing off dust from the knees of his fitted black trousers.

I waited for my uncle to say, 'We won't speak till we have our lawyers,' the way that everyone did on the police dramas. I thought about all the ways I could explain, how we could defend ourselves.

'They're only children,' Sanjay uncle said.

That was not one of them. I felt like Alice in Wonderland, like I was being pushed back through the mirror and into a world on the other side where I was forced to be a child again. I wanted to protest. 'But Sanjay uncle, we – '

'Not now, Maya,' Sanjay uncle said sharply, cutting me off. 'Not now' did not just mean me, it meant Reema auntie and my parents – we were not to say anything, we were to leave it in his hands. He turned to the agents again. 'Please, sir, they're only children.'

The agent looked at Sanjay uncle doubtfully. 'The Tigers have death squads now that are only women and children. Everyone is capable of crime these days.'

'Not these children,' Sanjay uncle said. 'They didn't know what they were doing. Isn't that right, Brindha?' He knew he could count on his daughter.

Brindha looked at her father uncertainly. 'Achan, I was helping Rupa's friends. Ammamma had medicine and they didn't. You always say we're supposed to help people . . .'

'That's right, Brindha, I know, but sometimes it's more complicated than that,' Sanjay uncle said, extending his arm around her shoulders, nearly touching the agent's hand still clamped there. 'She doesn't know better, you see, officer? She and Maya, our niece Maya, they're just children.'

Something curdled inside of me as I realized Sanjay uncle was not mentioning Rupa. They were not going to try to help Rupa. They were isolating her as the trouble-maker, winnowing out Brindha and me as innocents. There was a lot more talking – but it all amounted to that. Rupa didn't have anything to do with the assassination herself – Sanjay uncle and Reema auntie wrote out and signed the agents' reports saying that Rupa had slept in their house every night since their daughter had been home on holiday from boarding school, from March through June. They had to initial the sentence in the report that said specifically that Rupa had slept in their house the night of Rajiv Gandhi's murder, which had in any case taken place a whole night's train ride away from our tea hills. The agents interrogated Rupa, who had been silent the whole time, and when she refused to answer, they switched from English to Tamil to Hindi. She still refused to speak. They couldn't prove that Rupa had done anything worse than what Brindha and I had done – not turned in people she knew to be Tamil Tigers. The agents were letting us go because Sanjay uncle had convinced them we were different from Rupa, that we didn't have the same motivations, but that wasn't necessarily true. They weren't accounting for our fascination with danger, Brindha's and mine, with the forbidden and the unknown. They weren't accounting for the thrill of rebelliousness, the power we felt for having secrets, for knowing more than the people – family, journalists, employers, the bureau of intelligence – who were supposed to know everything.

They weren't accounting for the loyalty and love we could have for someone, even when she might have done something wrong, that could keep us from turning on her. That was not something we shared only with Rupa – it was something we shared with our parents, who would have signed anything or said or paid or sold anything to keep us out of trouble. But the agents were taking Rupa, the four of them surrounding her in our grandmother's hospital room, and they were leaving us. Brindha, who the agent had released into her father's embrace, wriggled free. She pushed two agents aside and flung herself at Rupa. For a second, I imagined it to be a repeat of her earlier attack on me. But Brindha clung to Rupa, and Rupa smoothed Brindha's hair, patted her back soothingly. 'Come back to us soon,' Brindha said, in a muffled voice. I was frozen, not child enough to throw myself on Rupa. Not child enough to stand up for her, and not adult enough either.

AMMAMMA DIED THE next day. We emerged from two weeks in the hospital into the middle of the Onam holidays. Many people came to the funeral in their festival clothes, straight from boat races and elephant parades and flower shows. People were already waiting for us at the house when Reema auntie, my father, and I got back. Sanjay uncle and Mother would come after taking care of final arrangements at the hospital. Brindha had wanted to stay and wait with her father. In all her waking hours and some of her sleeping ones, she refused to let go of his hand. Ammamma was brought back to Sanjay uncle's house in the same jeep she had come down in, wrapped in blankets, dressed in white.

Reema auntie sent me into the garden to collect flowers for Ammamma. I could hear the chatter and arguing of factory workers and tea workers as they built a pyre on the side of the house beyond the garden. They brought their own bullock-carts from hillside farms, full of wood fuel. Some walked in sets of two, one on each end, carrying long branches of stripped mango wood, roped together around the middle. The branches were cut to even lengths and tied together to form a narrow bed.

I sat on the bed in her room where my mosquito nets still hung, their sides raised up and draped over the top to form an opaque canopy. Three of my mother's cousins, all sisters, washed Ammamma and dressed her in a new white sari. She lay on a bedspread on the newly swept floor next to our beds, where she often took her afternoon naps.

They trimmed her fingernails and brushed out her hair. They put sandalwood paste on her forehead and on her throat. When they were finished, three workers came with the mangowood stretcher, lifted Ammamma on to it, and carried her to the drawing room.

The carpets had been rolled up, and the furniture moved to the guest rooms. Ammamma was laid out in the centre of the drawing room, and the priest brought a tall temple velakku with him which had five wicks on each tier, six tiers high. He started chanting and lighting incense sticks and camphor, and blue smoke rose up around him and my grandmother.

Outside behind the kitchen, Madhu's mother directed the other ladies and Matthew and his wife and Sunil in cooking for the guests. No food could be cooked in the house until after the ceremony, so Matthew had built a big open fire. They made rice in big urns and boiled milk for yogurt. They soaked lentils and stirred red chillies and black pepper with tomatoes for rasam. Tea brewed in big pots, releasing vapours of clove and nutmeg.

Vasani and the gardener were outside the house near the well, where they had opened one of the pipes that carried cold clear water into the house. Vasani kept her fingers over the end of the pipe to direct the burbling flow into buckets that the gardener lined up around them. The buckets said FIRE on them, they were the big red ones usually filled with sand at the tea factory. Everyone had to bathe before the last rites. Madhu and Reema auntie were distributing clothes to anyone who was ready. White mundus for men, white saris for women. As the workers finished building the pyre, they came to the well, to accept a bucket and a tin cup to pour water over themselves. They took a sari or mundu and slipped behind the kitchen or into the servant's quarters to change. Mother and many of the ladies bathed inside the house, simple, fast, cold baths, everyone emerging into bright sun with soft white cotton sticking to their wet skin, wet hair streaming down their backs. Reema auntie and Madhu and I bathed outside, each of us in four or five quick, deft motions, baptized in cold water from deep in the earth, blanketed in hot noon sun. Mother took me into Brindha's room to help me with my sari, folding and pleating and draping. I looked for hairclips on the dresser to cover the cutaway spot in my hair. Brindha came into her room just as we were finishing, and started tugging clothes out of her dresser and cupboards. She was wearing her school uniform.

'Brindha, do you want some help?'my mother said.

Brindha looked at us, sadly. 'I want to wear my uniform but some aunties out there said I have to change. And I'm too young to wear a sari. I don't know what to do.'

My mother said, 'I'm sure Ammamma won't mind if you want to wear your uniform. That's the only person you have to think about today, really.'

Brindha's face fell. 'I can't think about Ammamma. It's too sad.'

'I know it's hard for you,' my mother took Brindha into her arms. 'Both of you should do whatever you feel up for. If you want to be in the procession and see the pyre, come, but if you don't want to, don't.' I finished clipping my hair in the mirror. We could hear my father calling for my mother to come out, so she kissed each of our cheeks, and left.

I turned to follow her, but Brindha tugged on my arm. 'Maya . . . do you want a chocolate?'

She produced from her schoolbag the shiny package of Snickers bars that my father had given her at the hospital.

'They're going to begin the hymns,' I said. 'Don't you want to come?'

Brindha punctured the plastic with her thumbnail and

started unraveling the packaging. She wiped away tears from her eyes. 'Can't we just wait a little while?'

I sat with her on the bed and we shared a chocolate bar. I could feel the caramel slithering through my teeth, settling into gaps and crevices. We could hear the chanting get louder as more people joined the priest.

'Let's go, Brindha,' I said. 'Or you can stay in here and I'm going to go.' I wanted to be part of things. It didn't seem right to hide out in a back room like I was a kid and be excused for it. I didn't want to be excused, I wanted people to see me sitting with my mother, my uncle, and know that I knew my place.

Brindha didn't want to go but she didn't want to stay in her bedroom by herself. She held my hand but dragged her feet to try to slow my pace. We crossed through the dining room, and I could see and hear all the people sitting cross-legged around Ammamma and the priest. We would have to walk in front of them all to enter. On the dining table, there was a small pile of flowers left on a banana leaf, all that remained of the baskets I'd collected from the garden. I gave some flowers to Brindha in her outstretched palms, and I gathered flowers in my own hands cupped tightly together. We walked in together, the chants coursing over us. I tried not to look at anyone, and to walk slowly and primly, like a bridesmaid.

Brindha and I squeezed in between my mother and Reema auntie, near Ammamma's head. There were flowers heaped on her, except for her face. I tried to let the chants enter me and make me think about God and how he would look out for Ammamma. But I couldn't stop looking at Ammamma, who looked more now like she used to look, better than she'd looked in the hospital, like a snake who reemerges young from a crackly old skin. Her hair was shiny and perfectly in place, and she no longer looked uncomfortable, her shoulders relaxed, her hands resting at her side. I could see the scar from the long-ago monkey bite on her upturned wrist. A fat buzzing fly landed on Ammamma's face and I waited for her (expected her) to swat it away. I could hear the fly buzzing under the chanting, buzzing in a tonal scale all its own and then quietly landing for an investigation of Ammamma's chin, the corner of her mouth, then buzzing again. I looked at my mother, whose eyes were closed in prayer, at my father, who was looking at the ground. I rapped my knuckles against the ground in front of the mat we were sitting on, hoping to distract the fly. It was undistracted, too devoted to Ammamma to notice me. I felt angry, and disgusted, seeing it perched on her chin. I got on my knees and crawled the small distance into the middle of the circle of people, and I raised my hand and swept it across Ammamma's face.

The fly jumped up and buzzed away, and people looked up. I felt hot and embarrassed, realizing they had not seen the fly but had seen me reach out to touch Ammamma. I kept making grand flapping motions over her face so that gradually people would understand that there must have been an insect or something. But I couldn't look at her face as I bent over her, because touching her had established something that looking hadn't yet but might soon confirm: she was cold, smooth and rubbery and cold, and there was no life in her.

I crawled backward receding into my place near Brindha. She took the hand that had touched Ammamma and held it up, inspecting it closely like there was some residue she thought might be there, something that might make touching me be like touching Ammamma herself.

The priest moved on from chanting to call-and-response prayers. He called, in deep, assured tones, and we responded, some uncertain, some heartfelt, some in tears, some in meditation. I knew the words to some of the prayers, Ammamma had taught me long ago, so I spoke some of them, and others I just lip-synched. At certain points in the prayer, the priest showered Ammamma with more flower petals, and nodded for us to do the same. I stripped petals off the flower stems and tossed them, with a timid, underhand swing.

Brindha threw all of her flowers, stems and all, and didn't save any for the next interval. She used her now free hands to cover her eyes. After a few minutes of sitting like that, she tugged at me, and whispered, 'Do you think we might have another chocolate bar now?'

I shook my head no, not wanting to move. I hoped no one had heard her, sounding so frivolous and unfeeling even though she wasn't. I knew she didn't want to watch, but I did; I was repelled but also transfixed, and it mattered to me to be strong like everybody else.

There was a lot of whispering and rustling among my mother and father and Sanjay uncle and the priest. A piece of gold – we needed a piece of gold for Ammamma. Reema auntie and Mother had taken all their bangles and rings off, all they were wearing were their wedding necklaces that they never removed. Brindha was wearing no jewelry at all. I took off my necklace, and gave it to Mother. She looked at me gratefully, recognizing it to be Steve's necklace. She yanked hard and the clasp came off in her hand and she gave me the remnants of the necklace back. She moved in towards Ammamma and the priest took the gold clasp, blessed it, and gave it back to Mother with directions. She said a low, halting prayer, and then put the gold in Ammamma's mouth.

Mother started to cry as we all stood up and men scur-

ried around us to join Sanjay uncle and my father in carrying Ammamma on the bier. For a second, I imagined
Ammamma still on the trolley at the hospital, just getting
more tests. Some flowers tumbled off the bier and clung to
our saris. We fell into a procession around the men.

Ammamma was laid on top of the pyre, her feet facing
south, and the priest recited more hymns. Brindha asked
Madhu's mother what these hymns were that she had
never heard before. Madhu's mother said they were por-
tions of the sacred Veda text only recited for the dead. We
were asking Yama, Lord of the Underworld, to prepare a
good place for Ammamma among the ancestors. We were
asking Agni, God of Fire, to carry the departed soul safely
to the next realm. We were asking Mother Earth to be kind
in accepting the body.

We stood there around the pyre, dressed in white and
bathed and cleansed and praying and still guilty for the
various ways in which we feared we had failed
Ammamma. We wore guilt invisibly – no one else saw or
knew. Was that how it was for everybody, did it come in all
sizes? There was no discovery process for personal crimes
the way there was for political ones: while you were never
proven guilty, you never felt innocent again.

Sanjay uncle walked around the pyre pouring coconut
oil. The priest poured water into a big earthen pot and
Sanjay uncle picked it up and made another full circle
around the pyre. The pot had holes in it so the water
dripped on to the ground, making a line in the red dust.
Then Sanjay uncle stood facing away from Ammamma
and threw the pot backwards, and it fell nearby and
cracked open. He set the pyre alight. Sandalwood and
incense and curls of blue woodsmoke ascended upwards.
The flames blazed higher around Ammamma. Some more
flowers fell off the bier and landed on the ground near us,

crumpled roses and lilies, their faces blackened by flame. The flames lapped at Ammamma's sari, and the white cloth shrivelled and darkened, cauterized.

'How much longer do we stay out here?' I asked Madhu's mother.

'It usually takes about an hour for the skull to crack,' she said. 'When we hear it, then we can say the final prayers for today and bathe. The fire will burn itself out after about a day – we don't have to watch the whole time.'

I couldn't stay. Ammamma's sari was getting blacker and blacker.

I whispered in Brindha's ear. 'Do you still want some chocolate?'

Brindha nodded yes immediately, her whole face thanking me, relieved. She grabbed my hand and this time I dragged my feet, so it made it clear to everyone that she was the one initiating this flight, I was leaving only to help her, accompany her. We stepped on plants and vines crossing through the garden, but we didn't care, choosing the shortest diagonal. And then there was the quiet of the house, and the meticulous unravelling of the candy wrapper and the stickiness on our hands and teeth and lips. We ate candy bar after candy bar until the sun went down and everyone came back inside.

THERE WAS, OF course, a lot of talk at the funeral rites and afterward, a lot of whispering and gossiping about Brindha's and my entanglement in Tiger activities. But no one blamed us in the least. The aunties would say to each other, 'The Pillais had a Tiger sneak into their house and try to convert their poor young girls! Can you imagine?' They would shudder, and shake their heads, and bolt the doors at night between their rooms and the rooms where their servants slept. And count the silver because terrorists probably wanted the silver as well as the fealty of young girls.

Brindha and I coaxed our servants to bring us any news of Rupa, in case they knew people who knew her brothers or her parents. But they could not, or would not, tell us anything. Sanjay uncle found us in the kitchen trying to bribe Sunil with sweets for information. He noticed our anxiousness, and thinking that I was angry with him, said, 'There wasn't anything more we could have done.' I didn't believe that. I couldn't argue with him now, not when I had just seen him so full of love and grief at his mother's funeral. I didn't respond. Sanjay uncle cleared his throat in the silence.

'I finished reading your Huck Finn,' he said. 'Do you know, in the introduction in your book, it says that the story of Huck and Jim is based on a boy the author knew who befriended an escaped slave hiding on an island in the Mississippi. But in real life, the black man died on the island. It is just like an American to try to have a friendship like that and think it can make a difference.' He did not wait for me to speak, but turned and exited the kitchen.

Usually when Sanjay uncle said something was American, it was something I didn't want to be. This time I wasn't sure. Even if trying to have that kind of friendship – the kind that made you see the other person's humanity as equal and sacred – wasn't very realistic, it surely was better than not trying.

Our names, Brindha's and mine, were entirely vindicated when, three days after my grandmother's death, there was fresh news that the police ended their manhunt in a village hundreds of miles away from us. Moments before the paramilitary commandos stormed the Tiger hideout, Subha and Sivarasan, as well as five other allies, had chewed their cyanide capsules. Sivarasan had also shot himself in the head for good measure. The government was frustrated – they had wanted live quarry to prosecute and execute themselves, but they pretended it was a victory. Police allowed reporters into the house to see the heap of bodies, and finally there were fresh photo stills for the television news and the morning papers. Brindha and I read every edition of the newspapers, simultaneously searching for Rupa's name and hoping not to find it. The most gossip surrounded the fact that Subha was found with a newlywed's silver rings on her toes. It had mattered even to the nation's biggest outlaws to legitimize their union before death's reckoning.

People moved on to these new titbits and stopped whispering about Brindha and me and the Tigers. But I was acquitted of some crimes more easily than others. Everyone had heard about the birth control pills in my suitcase. Madhu spoke up and said they were hers, and when she saw how distressed everyone was by her confession, she was furious. She said this was the last time she was coming to India anyway and she didn't really care what they all thought of her. As in Sita's story, the truth didn't make anything better for me. Reema auntie reported that Suraj's parents had written to rescind both their request for my horoscope and their related marriage proposal.

'We can hardly blame them,' Reema auntie said to my mother, bringing the newly delivered letter to the lunch table. Sanjay uncle and my father had already excused themselves from the table and retired for afternoon rest.

'They can hardly blame Maya – those were Madhu's pills,' my mother said archly. 'They didn't bother to find out the details.'

Reema auntie looked up from reading their letter, surprised. 'Kamala, you've been away too long. Don't you see that Maya should know better than to even give the appearance of impropriety? Haven't you taught her how important these things are?'

My mother looked over at me. I was looking down at my plate, pushing the potatoes and the coconut chutney around. They were talking as if I wasn't even there, so I was concentrating on pretending I wasn't.

My mother sighed. 'Reema, I spent years feeling like India had taken a daughter from me, and that was probably not fair. But I don't want India to take my only living daughter from me now. If I try to make Maya live in America the way we would have lived here, I'll lose her. I can't bear that, after everything that's happened.'

It mattered to hear my mother say those things. She wanted to be a mother, my mother – if she hadn't always, then at least from now on. It didn't mean we were going to be close or happy or understanding all the time, but it meant we had new aspirations.

We were leaving for New York at the end of the week. I'd received a letter from Jennifer telling me what she was wearing to the first day of class. New York – it was the other side of the planet – seemed so far away. I hadn't expected it to be so hard to leave, to feel so confused about what I was going back to, to remember startlingly that we called that place home. That place was home even though here was where I had gained and lost a grandmother, gained and lost a friendship, a sister, a marriage proposal. Here I had gained (however tenuously) a mother, a conscience, and the awareness that compassion often mattered as much or more than justice.

Reema auntie agreed to let Brindha stay until we left, but I couldn't just run around with her in the hills. First there was finishing my summer reading and reports, and there was packing to do. There wasn't much to put in my suitcases. The gifts that had weighed my luggage down had been given away, usually replaced by a collection of pickles and preserves and banana chips and dried chilli and tamarind candy that had not been cooked this time, out of respect for our mourning. As I was packing my few things, Sunil crept into my room. He brought his hands out from behind his back, holding the notebooks Ammamma had written in for me during my convalescence. When the intelligence agents had come and turned the house upside down, Sunil had squirrelled the notebooks away. He gave them to me now, and I flipped through them. In the pages after Ammamma had stopped writing down my memories, she had started writing down her own. Her own stories about my first steps, my first words, which neighbours I liked the most. And she had written out my birth chart, and asked an astrologer to read my stars, and pasted my horoscope into the notebook.

Not just in these notebooks, but all summer, Ammamma had given me maps of my past and future to navigate by. Sanjay uncle had said there weren't maps for where we lived, but that wasn't true. There weren't maps of our roads and our homes, but there were maps for the inside, maps of the heart, and they could only be drawn by those who loved you. Maps of the physical world were changed all the time because history and memory ultimately trumped geography. With what Ammamma had given me, I had a suspicion that I, too, could surpass geography. I could live anywhere, be grafted and take root anywhere, and anywhere could become home.